THE TWIN FLAMES, THE MASTER, AND THE GAME

A Journey to Enlightenment

RICHARD LANOIX, MD

BALBOA
PRESS

A DIVISION OF HAY HOUSE

Balboa Press books may be ordered through booksellers or by contacting:

Balboa Press
A Division of Hay House
1663 Liberty Drive
Bloomington, IN 47403
www.balboapress.com
1 (877) 407-4847

Print information available on the last page.

ISBN: 978-1-5043-8435-3 (sc)
ISBN: 978-1-5043-8437-7 (hc)
ISBN: 978-1-5043-8436-0 (e)

Library of Congress Control Number: 2017910844

Balboa Press rev. date: 09/19/2017

Acknowledgements:

Jed, Abigail, Mother Vine, and Don Diego

PROLOGUE

Consciousness

Floating … dismembered … fragments of thoughts … just Being … just Consciousness. There is no sensation of a discrete self … there is only Consciousness. There is no discrete body … there is only Consciousness. There is no ego in this infinite space … there is only Consciousness. Words such as *peace, tranquility,* and *love,* cannot approximate the experience of being in Pure Consciousness. You cannot find peace, because in Consciousness, you are peace. You cannot find tranquility, because in Consciousness, you are tranquility. You cannot find love, because in Consciousness, you are love. No thing can be found looking outside of yourself, because there is no self.

Just floating … dismembered … fragments of thoughts contained in no thing … just Being … just Consciousness. Floating in an infinite ocean of love, without any concept of an "I"—a body, a mind, a structure—that separates the object and subject. Just "Isness," Being.

In Consciousness, you are the infinite. It is the very act of a "you" that results in a contraction from the infinity of Consciousness to the illusion of you, from the infinity of "Isness" to the limited you that is constructing a local experience. There is only Consciousness.

It was not always like this. Eternities ago, although still an illusion, there were thoughts, desires and all the peripheral emotions related to that other state—fear, desire, jealousy, pain, things to do, and things to accomplish. Illusions. All illusions.

What a journey! What an adventure! The memories of that former existence are like wisps floating in the wind. These memories arise like a movie you've seen many times. You can recite the lines simultaneously, like *The Rocky Horror Picture Show* audiences that showed up every Friday night at the New Yorker Cinema at Eighty-Eighth Street and Broadway in New York City. They dressed up as the film characters and played out the roles as they were occurring on screen to the accompaniment of an old upright piano. Memories … illusions.

So many illusions of past lives to arrive here, or rather, to realize that one has never left or could never leave. Even with this knowledge, even if off by light years in its magnitude and scope, why was it so difficult to grasp its ultimate simplicity? Why the repetitive structure of sunglasses upon sunglasses, ad infinitum, preventing one from seeing the simplest truth?

A perfect metaphor is human existence in the earth-realm, where the vast majority of humans are not even aware that they have a consciousness, much less that they are, in actuality, Consciousness. They simply exist and live out their illusory *"metro, boulot, dodo"* lives until their illusory deaths. At this level, there is a thought, which leads to another thought, which leads to another, creating an endless pattern that is called "a life."

In the state of Consciousness, there are thoughts,

but they are recognized for what they are: passing distractions, a radio playing in the distance. They don't have substance, and therefore, one who has achieved this state makes no attempt to grasp them. Occasionally, however, a particular thought catches such a person's attention. Such a thought, too trivial even to be memorable enough to recite, serves as a catalyst. Once engaged, the catalyst is the hand that toggles the lever of the toilet of Consciousness, instantaneously flushing one from the realm of Being, out into the earth-realm, with barely the faintest memory of whence one came. It is here that our story begins.

CHAPTER 1

Lost Lives

Opium Haze

Floating … dismembered … fragments of thoughts contained in no thing … just Being. Orfeo was lying down on a comfortable bed, propped up with cushions in which the scent and stench of many others had settled, maintaining a balance with the fragrant plumes of incense-like smoke that lingered in the air. There was no time here, and here, there was no place, only an oblivion that comforted him, that recalled a distant memory of a similar no-thing where there was no here, no place, and no thought. Any feeble attempt toward a coherent thought dissolved into the no-thingness of this no place that was not here and not there, just oblivion.

An olive-hued hand lovingly caressed his head, attempting to arouse him back to this other place that seemed even less real than nowhere. The hand held a pipe to his mouth, as a mother would lovingly offer the nipple of her engorged breast to her infant, offering the elixir of oblivion. He envisioned a large, luscious breast pressed onto his face, and the nipple teasingly rubbed on his lips. Like the infant, there was no thought or contemplation of whether to imbibe. There was only the stimulus of a mother's love offering life and a reflex that only knew yes. Orfeo's lips surrounded the nipple and forcefully sucked in that fragrant nourishment. The aroma of sweet flowers with hints of burning maple syrup filled his body with the love that he had been seeking since time immemorial. Oblivion—it was so comforting; he was like a baby wrapped in its mother's arms with so much love and warmth. He recalled having felt this feeling before but didn't remember the circumstances. There was only oblivion.

Orfeo felt his body being jostled more and more violently. This was certainly not the loving caresses he had grown accustomed to as intermezzos to the grand symphony that was composing itself in the nothingness of nowhere. He could not cogitate but was aware that there was a struggle taking place between the two dimensions of his oblivion and that lesser reality that others unwittingly called reality. His consciousness was the rope in a tug-o-war, and like the rope, he was disengaged and dispassionate. There was an understanding below the level of rationalization that it was all indeed contained within the oblivion. There was the vague image, almost dreamlike, of being hauled from the depths of a dark ocean like an oil tanker that had sunk to the bottom. There were vague thoughts arising and sinking back to the depths, momentary images that urgently seemed to be asking for recognition, breaths taken that seemed to be arising from elsewhere. Oblivion was such a powerful ally. There was no struggle on her part. She was not pushing or pulling. Rather, there were gentle caresses beckoning Orfeo to dive deeper into her womb, where he was coddled and bathed in a warm, fragrant elixir that was life itself. He settled into her, and everything again fell away.

Just before he entered into her loving embrace, he had a vision. It was a vision he knew very well, one that often came to him in his sleep. He was walking in a vast desert. The sun was sweltering, and the sand was red and hot like molten lava. He was weary, and for some reason, he was crying. Each tear boiled as it rolled down his cheek and scalded him. The pain was insufferable, yet he endured and continued.

The pain of the desert began to fade as he descended into the sweet, warm darkness of oblivion's all-encompassing arms. He returned to floating in her warm womb until he again felt a counterforce drawing him out. Out of the no-thingness there were incoherent sounds, fragments of his name, a sensation of icy liquid pouring over his body that was completely dissociated from the chills and shaking that seemed to be taking place elsewhere. He began to hear his deep breathing and echoes of his name, and he became aware that there was a body that was being drawn and held in a seated position. The gentle caress of oblivion seemed further away, beckoning him to return to her, but the outside forces were too great. The images coalesced into faces that seemed familiar, and he recognized that the voices calling the name Orfeo were in fact calling him, trying to get his attention. He was now back among the dream-walkers.

He recognized Mark, his friend, and Judy, his lover. She was standing behind Mark against the wall, crying. He began to understand the theatrical piece being enacted, but he had forgotten his lines. He felt that he had lines to read at this juncture in the performance but was paralyzed. The spectacle went on, as was mandated. He wondered if his colleagues were improvising until he regained his composure and got back on track with his lines.

He finally uttered, in the hoarse voice of one who had been brought back from the dead, "Where am I?" There was a long pause punctuated by Judy's sobbing. Were those his lines, or had he inadvertently awakened within another play? His body was too weak to move, but his gaze wandered the room searching for clues.

He saw Ai on her knees, her radiantly nude, olive-hued body gracefully picking up everything that had been knocked over onto the worn tapestry near the bed. She was a lovely, exotic Asian woman who had the capacity to transform into a goddess. She had been his steadfast, loyal, and reliable companion who accompanied him, as Beatrice accompanied Dante, to the gates of oblivion. Ai was also crying but for an altogether different reason than Judy. She was saddened that Orfeo's journey into the void had been so explosively interrupted. She could not comprehend why anyone would assault Orfeo so violently. For Ai, this was as much of a crime as taking a baby from her mother.

Ai understood her role and was a master. Some would call her a prostitute, but anyone who really cared to understand would know that would be the equivalent of calling a nursing mother a pumping station. There was much more than met the eye. Her pear-shaped, almost black eyes, seductive touch, perky breasts, and luxurious vagina were merely in service of higher purpose. Ai, whose name meant "love and affection" in Japanese, was merely a portal, and the true masters, as she clearly was, were humble, because they had the awareness that they were simply the vessels that facilitated the voyage to and from other realms. This was a sacred calling that came to very few.

Orfeo slowly began to recognize the theatrical piece he was in and the role to which he had been assigned. He desired to comfort Ai for a brief moment but knew that that was not part of the play, and such improvisation would be quite disruptive. Orfeo's eyes fleetingly made contact with Ai's, and everything was understood. He could now fully engage in his character and only hope that his role was favorably mentioned in the reviews.

A day later, after sleeping for what appeared to be an entire day, he did not actually feel thirst but simply could not stop drinking. Judy was in the kitchen and offered him some tea and breakfast. He had not eaten for three to four days. He was starving, but he knew that he had to introduce food back into his system very slowly in order to avoid any subsequent nausea, vomiting, and cramps. He accepted the tea, thanked her, and sat.

He felt that he should hug her and apologize again for what happened, but he knew that it was pointless at this juncture. Judy was no longer crying and appeared strong and resolute. She looked deeply into his eyes as though she had arrived at some profound knowledge that made everything clear to her. He met her eyes with his but could not sustain the direct eye contact. He again had that disconcerting feeling that he was in a play and had forgotten his lines. Orfeo wondered if he was really cut out for this role, in light of the fact that he was always forgetting his lines. Nonetheless, he surmised that the show had to go on, and he simply had to improvise as best he could.

Judy's voice was soft when she said, "Orfeo, I love you so much, but I just can't do this anymore." Silence. There was a long, uncomfortable pause.

"Whenever you disappear like that, I feel myself dying. Even worse, it starts every time you even step out to buy cigarettes, because I fear that you'll disappear again."

"Cigarettes." He hadn't thought of it yet, but he desperately needed one now. He was about to get up for a smoke but had the sense to know that this was not the right time. He focused and gave his full attention to this woman, who he loved so much in his own seemingly pathetic way and whose love for him, he knew from cold, hard fact, was unfathomable. He didn't recall ever having loved like that and was totally impressed that she could do it, at least up until this act of the play, so faithfully and unconditionally.

"I love you so much," she said again, "but I just can't continue giving and giving without getting anything back."

He started to interject to say that this was not true, but she gave him an icy stare, which instantly conveyed, "Stop bullshitting me, and stop bullshitting yourself! Just stop!" That look stopped him, mouth open, dead in his tracks.

"Also," she continued, "I can't just sit back and watch you destroy yourself with the drugs that you do. I just can't anymore." Orfeo knew that the fact that she had not brought up Ai meant that this was much more serious than he had considered. He now knew for certain that this was the end of the line for their relationship. Yes, he did love her, but despite this, he felt that all the words at this point were superfluous.

Her speech was more pressured and agitated now. "Orfeo, you were gone for a week! Each time you disappear for longer and longer periods. What are you looking for? What are you running away from?" At this point, her words just faded away. He wanted to get up, thank her for her indulgence, take a bow, and gracefully walk out. It wasn't because he didn't care. In fact, he cared for her more than he could ever express, and even if he were able to express it, she could never believe it. However, he did not have the answers for her, or for himself.

Yes, Orfeo was looking for something that he knew was all-important, but he didn't know what it was or where to begin. He also knew that it would never go over very well to say to her, "Listen, babe, I love you so much, but there's something else that is much more important than you. You could never match up to it. Moreover, this is not something that you can help me with, so please be understanding and give me some space." How would that sound? he wondered.

Despite his urge to bolt, he sat patiently and tried to appear as contrite, compassionate, and understanding as possible. She had given so much of herself to him over the years, and in his own way, he loved her dearly. Allowing her to get everything off her chest was the least he could do, no matter how painful it was. He considered for a moment how considerate the character he was playing could be during moments like this and how an audience would be able to sympathize with him.

"Are you listening to a word I'm saying?" she pleaded.

"Yes, love," he replied, "I'm hearing every word and am so sorry I put you through all of this. It was never my intention to hurt you, and I definitely don't want to hurt you anymore. I agree that I should leave, give you peace, and really try to get my shit together." Wow, he thought, those were really great lines.

Re-entry Issues

Orfeo definitely felt the change. This had been the thirteenth or fourteenth time he had entered the earth-realm, and each time was more difficult. First, there was the issue of time in the earth-realm. He had to endure a human lifetime before being able to return to Consciousness and then, based on clues he had pieced together, select another time-space to enter where he would hopefully find Carina.

The trouble was time. In the state of Consciousness, his domain for so many eternities, time did not exist. It was only a mental construct. He had forgotten that in the earth-realm, time took form and was palpable, measurable; moreover, it had to be navigated, endured.

Second was the issue of engagement. He was born into a family and had to play the game until he was old enough to venture on his own or run away in order to embark on his mission to find his love. At first, Orfeo was cold and calculated in his purpose, but slowly, he encountered hurdles that had to be overcome. He experienced the love of his earth mother, father, and siblings. They had no clue that they were simply spending a brief moment in this earth-realm for an experience before returning to Consciousness and then, for as long as it was necessary, repeating this process until they had learned the required lessons from their earthly voyages. For them, this was it—reality, life—and their "family" was limited to what they called mother, father, sister, and brother. Hence, they clung with dear life to these illusory attachments. Although this earthly love was less than a shadow of the love he shared with Carina, he still was able to feel these emotions of familial love and, more and more, found it difficult to tear himself away so cold-heartedly.

The third complication that Orfeo had not accounted for, and that he recognized to be the greatest hurdle, was that each time he entered, he had this foggy feeling and could not precisely recall his mission, his only purpose for entering the earth-realm and what he, in fact, believed to be the only purpose of his existence. At first, he would have absolutely no recollection that he had "entered" from elsewhere into the earth-realm. He would then have flashes of memory, sometimes in the form of dreams or feelings of déja vu, which would alert him that there was something else at play. Little by little, although it had been taking longer and longer, he would remember. This was quite disconcerting.

In the first few entries, there was total recall even while in utero. After a few more, recall began taking place at later and later ages. During his last attempt, it was not until his thirties that he woke up to his purpose. This distressed Orfeo tremendously. Thirty years wasted! He began to deduce that he was developing a form of dementia that worsened, not so much with age, as was the case with Alzheimer's dementia, but rather with every "entry" into the earth-realm, each departure from Consciousness. He now began to understand why earthbound humans seemed so clueless about the truth of their Being, that they were infinite and were, in fact, Consciousness. They were suffering from a devastating affliction that took their precious memories of who they really were and from whence they came. It now made sense. They were likely returning for their quota of human experiences and, unsuspectingly, were developing progressive dementia until there was total amnesia about anything other than the human experience. The horror!

This led to another major complication. During the time that it would take Orfeo to wake up and realize his purpose for being in this earthbound form, he started to form relationships and fall into a career. In one recent incarnation, he awakened to find himself married with children. It would then take him years to find the courage to leave this family behind and again resume his mission to find Carina.

These departures from loved ones, careers, and attachments began to take their toll and would lead to bouts of major depression. He could never forget the look in the tearful eyes of his children, asking in their innocent way why he was abandoning them and where he was going. How could he explain to his wife, with whom he had shared most of his adult human life, that he loved her immensely but that there was someone else for whom he had a greater love that overshadowed her—a higher mission that he had to complete? Their faces would come to him and haunt him in his sleep. He began to feel schizophrenic, torn, and more and more, a failure in two significant respects: as a partner, father, friend, child, and his mission to find Carina.

Now, in addition to his drive to find Carina, he was further driven by the idea that he was working against time. It became increasingly clear that he could not, ad infinitum and with impunity, come and go to continue his search for his beloved. He recognized that with every departure from Consciousness, the affliction of amnesia would inexorably and insidiously take its hold until the lifetime when he would succumb and remain a prisoner of the earth-realm for all eternity. In moments of utter despair, he would occasionally wonder which was worse, a life condemned to the earth-realm, without any memory that he was there solely to have a human existence, or an existence without Carina. It was the thought of either of these possibilities that provided Orfeo with the impetus to push on against all odds.

Psychosis

In one particular lifetime, Orfeo could no longer contain himself. He became more and more despondent, withdrew from his present family and friends, his career, and basically cracked. Everything became jumbled in his mind: Pure Consciousness, having been in a state of union and merged with Carina, losing her, his lost past lives, his mission to find her, his great desire to return to Consciousness with her. He started speaking aloud, babbling incoherently about his thoughts, plans, who he was, and why he was on earth. As one can imagine, this caused great consternation and concern in his family, friends, colleagues, and love ones. When confronted, even in the most loving way, he became severely agitated and at times violent.

Orfeo was becoming more and more paranoid. He framed his situation as a battle in which he was on this great, heroic mission to save his loved one, Carina, and everyone, including his family, was trying, in very subtle ways, to prevent him from reuniting with her. He felt that he was able to see through their cunning ways and manipulations. At times, he would find devious ways to circumvent their imagined thwarting, and at other times, which were now occurring with increasing frequency, he would become overtly aggressive in his resistance.

His present wife, Margot, was becoming more and more concerned, especially as Orfeo would babble to himself continuously and was now rarely bathing or eating. Orfeo had always been a stickler for his grooming, but now, his hair was always disheveled. He'd grown a beard that he never trimmed and that contained traces of whatever little he had nibbled on days before. He never changed his clothes or showered and consequently stank to high heaven. Days would pass without any sleep, and he would be up and about with increasingly manic vigor, spending his days and nights ranting on about Consciousness, conspiracies, Carina, and the inevitable war that was coming. He would pace back and forth for days and then crash, sleeping for increasingly prolonged periods. Whenever Margot would approach him with food or try to cajole him into bathing or going out for a walk, he would dismiss her violently, saying she couldn't possible understand the importance of his mission and that he was too busy to concern himself with such banalities.

Orfeo had not gone to work for almost two weeks, and Margot was at her wits end. It was clear to her that Orfeo was losing all connection with reality. He was barely eating at this point and was physically fragile and gaunt, looking more and more like an AIDS victim. She could no longer bear it, and with the support of their friends, Margot consulted with a recommended psychiatrist, expressing the urgency of this matter. The psychiatrist, Dr. Sackler, made a house call to assess the situation, but Orfeo would not open the door. Margot pleaded with him, but he wouldn't listen. Orfeo accused her of being a traitor, for which he would kill her a thousand times. Dr. Sackler obtained consent from Margot to involuntarily admit him to the psychiatric ward based on his assessment that Orfeo clearly did not have capacity, was of danger to himself, and was possibly dangerous to others.

The police and EMS arrived shortly thereafter and, after a lengthy, unsuccessful negotiation period and with the permission of Margot, knocked the door down and forcefully restrained him. He kicked, cursed, spit, and screamed, expressing every expletive under the sun. He cursed Margot, stating that this was all her fault and that she would pay dearly. Margot sat in the corner crying uncontrollably. She could not bear seeing him like this, held down like a wild animal, frothing at the lips, eyes bulging from his head, sweating profusely as they strapped him into the gurney and placed him in the ambulance. Nonetheless, within the weeping, there was a clear sense of relief, for she knew deep in her heart that this was best.

Orfeo continued to struggle violently throughout the ride to the ER, screaming over the wailing of the sirens. His wrists, which were handcuffed behind and under his body, were abraded and bleeding, and his forehead was bruised from repeatedly banging it against the gurney railing. Even with restraints, it required both policemen and the emergency medical technician to prevent him from jerking his torso violently and turning the gurney over. He was cursing at them and incoherently spewing every expletive that he could come up with, calling the black police officer "Jewish scum," the white officer a "nigger," and the white EMT a "Chinese checker head." He was trying to spit at them, but his mouth was so dry from all the yelling that there was nothing to project. The police officer tried to cover his mouth, and Orfeo almost bit his finger off, at which point they lost all patience with him and used a hospital gown to gag him, which caused him to become even more violent and diaphoretic. His eyeballs appeared as if they were going to pop from their sockets.

When he arrived in the ER, a doctor was called immediately to assess Orfeo for sedation while still in triage. The doctor removed the gag from Orfeo's mouth and started explaining, with consternation, to the EMT and police officers that placing a gag over a patient's mouth was inappropriate because of possible airway compromise. As he was doing so, Orfeo managed to draw up whatever residual moisture had accumulated in his mouth since the gag was placed and landed a blob of spit directly in the doctor's face. He then resumed the incessant flow of expletives, now directed at the "Nazi" doctor who was not qualified to treat a stray dog and the "bitch" nurse who would suffer the wrath of Allah for her sins. The doctor rushed to the sink to wash his face while the "bitch" nurse, who when making eye contact with the EMT could barely contain her laughter at what had just happened, threw the sheet over Orfeo's head.

When the doctor returned, he made no comment regarding the sheet covering Orfeo's head and, and as though nothing had happened, ordered sedative medications to be administered intramuscularly. The doctor politely asked the police officers and EMTs if they could stay to help restrain him until he received the medications and was sedated. Orfeo was becoming increasingly agitated, hitting his head against the gurney, bucking the gurney, and whenever he was able to wrestle his legs loose, kicking in every direction. His outbursts were abruptly interrupted by the sharp, stabbing sensation of a needle entering his shoulder, followed by a deep, burning sensation. At first, he ignored what he had just felt and continued his vitriolic string of expletives and demands to be released, explaining that he answered to a higher power and was on a mission of the utmost urgency. Then, within a few minutes, his vision became blurry, and a fog descended upon him. He envisioned himself a powerful, wild animal who had just been tranquilized. He understood the conspiracy before him and resisted the sedation that crept over his body. He saw their faces and imagined them mocking him as he drifted to sleep. His last thought was of Carina and the state of union with her that he so longed for.

Is this Hell?

Orfeo awakened in a small, bare room, containing only a cot and a plastic pitcher of water. He felt calm. There was silence. He asked himself, expecting an answer, "Where am I? How did I get here?" Then, like a small wave that becomes bigger and bigger, the voices crept in and started again to fill his head. Images of past lives, the state of union, and Carina, each with its own voice, filled his mind and expressed themselves simultaneously. He felt an urgency to get out of there, to get back to his mission. Time was passing too quickly, and the longer he delayed, the further away Carina would be.

He pounded on the door until his hands were bruised and bleeding. Outside, the orderlies waited patiently for this wave of agitation, which they had witnessed in other patients so many times before, to subside. After almost two hours, it became clear to them that Orfeo was not like the others. His energy was boundless, and he would not desist until his hands or the door were destroyed. They had to intervene.

The door opened, and many large men in white

attire entered into the room. Orfeo was surrounded. For a second, seeing all these men dressed in white, he wondered if he had not already died and was in heaven. This thought faded because, in his mind, he was already intimate with heaven, and there definitely were not any large, muscular men in white attire. Another thought immediately made its way through all the competing voices and somehow got every other voice's attention; he asked himself, "Is this hell?"

Before he could receive an answer, he felt the familiar sharp, stabbing sensation of a needle entering his thigh, while the very large men held him down on the cot. He somehow knew that any struggle was futile, but at a deeper level, it seemed more futile not to struggle. Shortly afterward, the fog crept over him, and he felt a drowsiness gently cajole its way into his head, silencing one by one the rebellious voices driving his resistance. This was followed by glimpses of the oblivion he knew so well.

Bruce Lee

Orfeo awakened again in the same room. He thought to himself that perhaps this was, in fact, hell. The voices heatedly argued the validity of this assertion but quickly returned to how he would make his way from hell to find Carina. Despite the madness, there was clarity, and he was as precise as a laser in his intent.

Some of the voices urged him to resume his efforts to break the door down, but the other voices pointed out the folly in this tack. He paced back and forth in his small prison, contemplating all the offered suggestions. Finally, there was one voice that gained prominence and brought to mind two movie clips. The first was the scene in *Enter the Dragon* where Bruce Lee was trapped in Dr. Hahn's lair and, rather than panicking, sat in half-lotus and meditated to conserve his energy and allow himself to regroup. The second was from the fourth *Star Wars* installment, *The Phantom Menace*, where Qui-Gon Jinn and his young padawan, Obi-Wan Kenobi, are fighting Darth Maul and are briefly separated from him by an energy field. In what surely must have been a tribute to

Bruce Lee, the voice pointed out, Darth Maul is seen pacing frantically back and forth, waiting for the energy field to lift while Qui-Gon quietly sits in half-lotus to conserve his energy. As soon as the gates open, they both immediately spring into action. The voices huddled and concluded that both Bruce Lee and Qui-Gon must have been onto something profound.

Orfeo immediately sat in half-lotus and began to meditate. For at least an hour, and for what appeared to be many hours to Orfeo, there was silence. There was tranquility. He recalled basking in Carina's energy. He could have sat there for hours if he had not been distracted by the door opening and Dr. Sackler entering behind the very large men. They were clearly impressed by his calm, meditative posture and felt it was an opportune time to intervene. The voices rapidly deduced that if they were in hell, then this man behind the large men must be the Devil. Orfeo again closed his eyes and maintained the outward appearance of tranquility, but the voices were dancing in his head again, doing their fire dance.

As soon as Dr. Sackler started to introduce himself, Orfeo sprung up from his half-lotus and was on top of Dr. Sackler, punching him mercilessly like a seasoned mixed martial arts fighter. The Devil's aides, the attendants in their white outfits, forcefully restrained him, almost wresting his shoulder out of its socket, causing him to scream in pain. But it was not enough to curtail his resistance. He would fight these Devil's soldiers with the very last breath in his body. Amid the screaming and yelling, he heard someone yelling "B-52, B-52, B-52!" which he would later learn was a combination of Benadryl (an antihistamine), Haldol (an antipsychotic), and Valium (a sedative).

Again, there was the sharp, stabbing sensation in his thigh, followed by a lingering, burning sensation at the site. Then, the fog came, and despite all of Orfeo's resistance, an overwhelming sleepiness ensued, ushering him into the void. There were fragments of images floating in his head, slowly taking the place of the voices: large men holding his limbs; someone in a bloodied suit and tie holding his face to capture the blood, perhaps as an offering; the serenity of the bare, white ceiling with long, fluorescent lights and their surrounding halos. Despite the madness, there was a fond, momentary recollection of that state of Consciousness, pure awareness. This lasted for just a few seconds after the sedative and before the void, when there was a perfect balance between the quieting of the voices, alertness, and complete awareness. As he drifted deeper into the void, he wondered what Bruce Lee or Qui-Gon would do in his situation? No answer was offered. He wondered if the voices had abandoned him. Regardless, he thought to himself, the fight must go on.

Highfalutin Hierarchies

While in the void, an image of someone walking in the desert appeared in Orfeo's mind. The face was covered, and under a bright, blinding sun, there was only red, molten sand for as far as the eye could see. When he awakened this time, Orfeo found himself on his back, all four limbs restrained by thick, leather belts. He pulled and jerked as hard as he could, but they wouldn't budge. Orfeo wondered if he would be tortured or perhaps dismembered and eaten alive. Even this would not deter him from his mission. Among the random thoughts flying through his mind, he saw the Black Knight in battle with King Arthur in *Monty Python and the Holy Grail*. After chopping off the Black Knight's arm, King Arthur says, "Sorry, old chap. I didn't mean to do that, but the fight is over now. I'll be on my way." The Black Knight looks at his shoulder stub and says, "It's just a flesh wound," and continues to attack. King Arthur then cuts off the Black Knight's legs and other arm, and the Black knight, upright on his pelvis, continues ranting. "Don't you dare walk away, you coward. I'll bite your legs off." Orfeo started laughing out loud but suspected that this may be his very predicament. He would continue to fight for his true love in the same manner.

The voices were back but were subdued. He thought that perhaps they too were restrained. He was very much aware of the sleeping medicine coursing through his body, pulsating in his head. His thoughts were interrupted by the sound of the door opening and the bodies of the very large men, the Devil's assistants, towering over him around what would soon be their instrument of torture. He braced himself and wondered if he would finally get to look the Devil directly in the eye. Orfeo asked politely, "Where is your master? I would like to speak to him."

With impeccable timing, the man in the suit and tie, which were no longer bloody, walked into his line of vision, now with a white bandage across his nose. Orfeo quickly surmised that this certainly could not be the Devil.

"Hello, Orfeo."

Silence.

"My name is Dr. Sackler. I'm here to help you."

Silence. Orfeo's eyes wandered, studying the faces of each of the Devil's henchman and the spaces between them, as though contemplating an escape route.

"Orfeo, would you mind if I asked you some silly questions?"

Silence.

"Do you know what year it is? The month?"

Orfeo smiled. The voices again huddled and concluded that these were trick questions, as everyone knew that there was no such thing as "time," and hence there were no measures of time, such as months, years, days, and hours, especially in hell. There was only eternity. He knew this for a fact, based on his own experience. For this he was willing to die, as he had already done many times before. This thought comforted him. He had never considered this before, but Death was in fact his ally, his old trusted friend. Orfeo wondered how he could find him here in hell. This was the second comforting thought he'd had while in this predicament: he was not alone and had a trusted friend he knew he could rely on. He swore to himself, regardless of the method of torture and the excruciating suffering he would have to endure, he would never rat out his friend.

The man with the bandage on his nose who wore the suit and tie that were no longer bloody and who certainly was not the Devil then asked, "Would you like me to remove the restraints? Would that make you feel better? We are here to help you."

Orfeo nodded yes.

"Do you promise to stay calm?"

Orfeo again nodded yes.

Dr. Sackler told the orderlies to remove the restraints and reassuringly told them, as though trying to convince them, that Orfeo was calm now and that everything would be okay. They all looked at the doctor and then at each other, acknowledging that this was not a good idea. They knew it was their place to follow the doctor's orders, that they did not have years of education, a medical diploma, the title of psychiatrist, or the authority of the doctor, but they did have their years of experience and collective wisdom. And their alarm bells were sounding, indicating that this was a terrible idea. Moreover, their collective experience and wisdom saw in Orfeo's eyes the glare of one who is fighting for a higher cause and, as the saying goes, marching to the beat of another drummer.

They didn't need a highfalutin diploma glued on their foreheads to know that the odds were always in the favor of those fighting for causes, beliefs, their country, or God, because they were fighting for something outside of their puny, petty selves. These orderlies, who clearly knew their place in the pecking order of this noble establishment of healing, also knew that there was another kind of fight. It wasn't a fight to the death but rather beyond death. This was the fight they saw in Orfeo's eyes. It was a fight that welcomed death because it knew that this was where the true battle was fought. To die and to take as many perceived enemies with you were merely the basic requirements to enter the battle that mattered. They looked into Orfeo's eyes and saw Rocky Balboa (*Rocky*), Tony Montana (*Scarface*), and Beatrix Kiddo/The Bride, codename Black Mamba (*Kill*

Bill), all rolled up into one and then pumped up with a Brobdingnagian dose of crystal meth and crack cocaine.

This was why they hesitated to remove the restraints, and in the few moments that had passed since Dr. Sackler's order to remove the restraints, they had arrived at a telepathic consensus among themselves and delegated one of them to demurely state their case.

"Dr. Sackler, with all due respect, sir ..." He paused when Dr. Sackler stared at him with furrowed brows and squinted eyes, which in combination with the dressing across his nose gave him an ominous, strange, and comic air."

"Yes, Leroy. You were saying," Dr. Sackler said impatiently.

Leroy, now even less sure of himself but remembering the CUSS-TeamSTEPPS methodology training they all received in order to improve staff communication and patient safety, which at the time they had all thought was a waste of time, continued. "With all due respect, sir, we're really *concerned* about removing his restraints."

Dr. Sackler, oblivious to the fact that he was being "CUSSed," responded, "I don't think there's any need to be concerned. The patient—look at him—is calm now, and I'm concerned that the restraints will limit the therapeutic relationship we're trying to forge."

The orderlies looked back and forth at each other, and their eyes urged Leroy to press on. Leroy, nervously said, "Dr. Sackler, this patient has already attacked you twice. We are *uncomfortable* with this." He laid particular emphasis on the word *uncomfortable*."

Dr. Sackler was now visibly annoyed. He looked at each of the orderlies in turn and responded, "Gentlemen, can you please remove the restraints?" His tone clearly indicated that this was more of a command than a request.

Leroy, himself now somewhat irritated by Dr. Sackler's total disregard for their concerns, their input, and finally, this "CUSS-TeamSTEPPS" methodology that they were assured physicians would acknowledge and honor, asserted, "With all due respect, Dr. Sackler, in accordance with TeamSTEPPS, please *stop*. This is a patient *safety* issue."

Dr. Sackler had a disconcerted look on his face, which again, in combination with the Band-Aid across his nose, gave him a bizarre look. It had suddenly struck him that he was being CUSSed and that the orderlies were in fact following a specific protocol used for conflict resolution and to promote patient safety. He stood in silence, looking at the floor and shaking his head incredulously, not because he now understood that he was in the middle of a conflict relating to a patient safety issue of which he himself was the root cause, but rather because his authority was being questioned. His arrogance would not allow him to see, despite having already been attacked twice by Orfeo, that the orderlies were making a very astute observation that deserved, at the very least, to be respectfully acknowledged and discussed. In addition, his arrogance would certainly not allow him to acquiesce to the demands of orderlies who did not have highfalutin diplomas pasted to their foreheads to match his own.

Dr. Sackler took a deep breath, raised his head as though to show clearly his highfalutin diploma to those without them, and completely ignoring what had transpired, asked in the most condescending manner, "Can you please remove the patient's restraints so that I may proceed to establish the patient-doctor relationship?"

Dr. Sackler, while smiling assuringly to Orfeo, gave a look of insistence to the orderlies that belied the politeness of his request to "please" release the restraints. The orderlies, with their collective experience and wisdom, immediately recognized the demons Orfeo was battling. Beyond a shadow of a doubt, they knew that this was a terrible idea, but the doctor had spoken.

As they released the restraints, Dr. Sackler smiled in a soothing, nurturing, yet rehearsed manner while repeating that everything would be okay. He assured Orfeo that they were all here to help him get through this temporary crisis and that soon enough, he would be reunited with his wife and family and get on with his life.

Yes, Orfeo thought to himself, *find Carina and get back to my life.* The tears flowed from his eyes, and he sobbed. Dr. Sackler continued to utter comforting words.

Orfeo relaxed into a cooperative demeanor as the orderlies reluctantly removed the restraints. Just before doing so, without any words, they looked at Dr. Sackler as if to ask *Are you sure about this?* and without any words, Dr. Sackler responded, *Yes, of course I'm sure. I am the doctor here.* The underlying message, which even Orfeo picked up on, was "how dare you question me?" The restraints were off. Orfeo remained motionless on his back. The doctor expressed an air of "see, I told you so."

The orderlies knowingly took a step back, almost as choreographed as a synchronized swimming team, their body language becoming defensive, expressing that this was definitely a stupid-ass, cockamamie idea and that it was not going to end well.

"Would you like to sit up?" the doctor asked, exercising the technique of empowering the patient by having them meet the therapist and the ensuing therapeutic manipulation eye to eye.

Orfeo's eyes expressed a feigned gratitude for the doctor's graciousness, and he slowly sat up, scanning the room. His eyes were on a reconnaissance mission, assessing his options. He still felt the previous medications coursing through his veins. The battle was already taking place within him for full control of his mind and body.

"Would you like to talk a little, Orfeo? I'd really like to help you, but I need to know what's going on with you? Can you articulate what's going on inside you head?"

Orfeo looked at the doctor as though considering the doctor's request, and then he looked at the orderlies. The doctor understood immediately and asked the orderlies to leave in order to give Orfeo some privacy. They looked at each other as though he were battier than Orfeo and told the doctor that they would be right outside if he needed them, which they knew would be the case as surely as the crackhead needed his pipe.

Orfeo rationally knew that resistance was futile at this point. He reasoned that his best option was to cooperate and attempt to finagle his way out of this Kafkaesque predicament. The voices in his head, however, were telling him otherwise. He heard keys jingling in the doctor's right jacket pocket. He had a plan and thought it best to think it through, but the voices insisted otherwise.

He remained calm outwardly, but as soon as the doctor looked away, he leapt upon him like a leopard would a wildebeest. Unlike Orfeo's first assault on the good doctor, in which he rendered a flurry of blows in the ground-and-pound manner of a mixed martial arts fighter, this time he grappled him into a choke hold and whispered in his ear to have the orderlies open the door, adding that if he did exactly as Orfeo commanded, he would not get hurt.

"Curtis, Leroy, Jenkins ... open the door! Help!" The orderlies rushed in and immediately assessed the situation, then they looked at each other, acknowledging that this wasn't at all a surprise.

"Now tell them that they must lie on the ground in the corner over there. Tell them to do as I say; otherwise, I will break your neck. Tell them now!"

They started to move as though they would comply, but then, like a well-oiled football team executing a play they had rehearsed hundreds of times, they rushed Orfeo and the doctor with such force that Orfeo was caught completely by surprise. He didn't have a moment to react, and both he and the doctor were knocked to the ground. The doctor was winded but not hurt. He yelled out: "B-52! B-52! Stat!"

This time Orfeo did not struggle and simply waited for that now familiar sensation of the needle, the burn, the fog, and finally the void. While in the void, Orfeo woke up in a dream, and a stream of thoughts ran through his head:

I look up, weary, deflated,
and see the endless desert before me.
I have been on this path for so long.

The heat is insufferable.
The air stifling.
Every breath sets my lungs on fire.
Every movement is excruciating.

Yet, I am compelled to press on.
But to where? Why continue?
How did I end up here? When?

Upon awakening, his eyes were filled with tears. He was on his back, again in restraints. He didn't attempt to move. He suddenly had clarity of mind. The nature of his mission was clear, and he didn't have a minute to spare. He realized at that moment that the voices were gone for good.

When Dr. Sackler entered the room hours later with his entourage. Orfeo looked intently into his eyes and said, in a very soft and commanding voice, "I am ready to talk now, Dr. Sackler."

Therapeutic Manipulation

The first sessions were held in that same room where Orfeo had been restrained. At first, he remained restrained during each session, and the orderlies were always present. During these early sessions, Orfeo remained very calm and cooperative and answered all of Dr. Sackler's questions. After a while, he gained the trust of Dr. Sackler, and the restraints were removed. Shortly after this, to the dismay of the orderlies, Orfeo was left alone with Dr. Sackler, and then the meetings were moved to his office.

"How are you today, Orfeo?" asked Dr. Sackler.

"Doing really well, thanks. And you?"

"Just fine. Have you been hearing any voices lately?"

"No. As I told you before, I have not had any voices since that last time in the cell."

There was a pause. Dr. Sackler wanted to see if there was anything else that Orfeo would offer. When he didn't continue, Dr. Sackler replied, "That's great! It is rather unusual to have a clean break like this from such a profound level of psychosis, but I am seeing it for myself. That's really great! Where were we last time?"

"I was trying to explain my purpose, what I have been trying to accomplish for so long."

"Yes," Dr. Sackler responded, "I remember. You were explaining that after many incarnations, you entered into a permanent state of pure Consciousness without any further bodily incarnations. Is that correct?"

"Yes, it is a pure state of Consciousness where there are no thoughts, there is no physical body, and there is no concept of time. There is only Being."

"What do you do there?"

"Do? There is nothing to 'do.' This concept of doing is a function of being in the earth-realm. However, even in this realm, there is the possibility of evolving to a point, as many sages have done, where one has the understanding that there is nothing to 'do.' This has been called wu wei, the art of nondoing.

"But what is the point of being human if there is nothing to do? Wouldn't you get bored?"

"From a limited perspective. I really don't mean to insult you, but this line of reasoning is a reflection of your level of evolution. As you evolve, you will understand that there is a current of energy that flows through every aspect of the Universe, and all that is required is to be one with it, allowing yourself to be like a leaf that his carried by a stream. Just as the leaf surrenders to the stream, one realizes that all one has to do is surrender, that one will be guided to wherever one needs to go. Consequently, there is nothing to do."

"I am somewhat familiar with Eastern philosophy, but this seems very farfetched. Why are you here, then? If this state of pure Consciousness that you describe was so great, why did you return? Why return to this hellhole?"

Orfeo paused for a very long time before answering. He did not know where to begin without appearing unhinged. After all, his goal was to be released from this "hellhole" psychiatric facility to continue his search.

He began very slowly and thoughtfully. "I was blessed many eternities ago to meet what you, in the earth-realm, would call my 'twin flame.' We bonded in Consciousness and merged in that state. There were no longer two of us, but one. Then she suddenly disappeared."

"Disappeared? How so? I thought you had merged?"

"You see, in order to remain in the state of Consciousness, concentration is required. Something must have distracted her ... I don't know ... but suddenly she was gone." Orfeo looked down at the ground, his head bowed into his hands as though crying.

"You must have really loved her."

Orfeo looked at Dr. Sackler, almost annoyed by the comment. "Yes, I loved her dearly and still do. But it is not the kind of love that you experience in earthly terms. When you have been one with someone for eternities, it is not a love for other; it is just love. I guess the term that comes closest is *agape*. Love is merely a shadow of agape.

"What's her name?"

"She is called Carina."

"Then what happened?" Dr. Sackler asked with genuine interest.

"At first, I waited. I presumed that she had been pulled back into the human realm, but after waiting so long, I started to worry."

"What were you worried about?"

"At the time, I didn't know, really. Even if she had been sucked back into human form, even for a multitude of lifetimes, she should have returned. When she didn't, I worried. Now, having taken human form many times since then, I have a better understanding of what happened."

"Are you able to share?"

"Yes, of course. I returned voluntarily to find her. So, the first few times I—"

"First few times?" Dr. Sackler interrupted in an incredulous tone.

"Yes, I have chosen to reincarnate in human form many times."

"You can do that? You simply choose to return to human form ... It's that easy?"

"At a certain level of evolution, yes, Dr. Sackler, it's that easy. However, what is difficult is to retain Consciousness."

"What do you mean by that, to retain Consciousness?"

"The first few times, I regained my memory shortly after adolescence and knew my life's purpose. I discovered the hard way that with every incarnation, it took longer and longer to remember. There were some reincarnations where entire lifetimes were spent without any recollection of my mission to find my love Carina. So you see, Dr. Sackler, returning is quite simple, but the rest is quite challenging."

"This is quite interesting," Dr. Sackler replied. One could see the wheels spinning in his head.

"I came to the conclusion that this was what happened to Carina. She is lost, and I must find her." Again, Orfeo buried his head in his hands. "Do you mind if I stand up while we talk?" Orfeo asked politely. "This session has been particularly difficult for me."

Dr. Sackler was lost in his thoughts, trying to understand the implications if what Orfeo was saying were true. But then he caught himself and thought that, of course, Orfeo's story could not be true at all. It was simply the ravings of a schizophrenic. But what if …? Dr. Sackler was looking at his notepad and rhythmically tapping on it with his pen.

"Dr. Sackler," Orfeo repeated louder, "would you mind if I stood up while we talked? I really need to stretch."

"Sure," Dr. Sackler responded. "Sorry, I was distracted."

Orfeo wandered about the room, perusing Dr. Sackler's bookshelf. After a while, he said, "I understand that this must be very difficult for you to grasp, and I'm sure you're wondering if this isn't just part of my delusion."

"Well ..." Dr. Sackler was about to start, but Orfeo continued to speak in the same soft tone of voice that he had so meticulously practiced.

"Dr. Sackler ... what is your purpose in this life? Do you have any idea?" Orfeo paused to give him a chance to catch up. "Do you understand that, as many sages and enlightened beings have suggested throughout the ages, you are presently living in a state of amnesia, here to have an earthly experience, and are also attempting to 'return' to a higher state of Consciousness?" Orfeo slowly made his way to the window and looked out as he spoke.

"I understand what you are saying, but I'm of the Jewish faith and personally do not subscribe to such beliefs."

"Then what do you think of those who do subscribe, not to such beliefs but to this way of being?" Orfeo remained at the window with his back to Dr. Sackler. He paused while counting the fourteen stories below the same level of the building facing Dr. Sackler's office.

Dr. Sackler stuttered, "I ... I ... of course, I have a great deal of respect for everyone's beliefs."

"Then if you respect the Christians who believe that Christ was crucified, buried, and rose again on the third day, then why is what I am telling you so incredulous?" *Check,* Orfeo thought to himself.

"It's not that I don't believe you," Dr. Sackler responded nervously. He was clearly not the confident, cocky physician Orfeo had met in the hellhole.

Orfeo now faced Dr. Sackler and walked directly to him. He put his hands on the desk and, looking directly into Dr. Sackler's eyes, asked, "Then why am I still here?" *Checkmate.* They looked deeply into each other's eyes. There was nothing left to say. "Dr. Sackler, I want to express my gratitude for the work that you do and for your kindness. But in the same way that you have a job to do, I have mine, and I cannot postpone it any longer. Thank you."

Dr. Sackler had no idea why Orfeo would say that at this moment. It seemed completely incongruous with their conversation. He was just about to ask Orfeo a question about his incarnations and what happened in between them when Orfeo suddenly turned and ran at full speed toward the window, hurling himself headfirst through the glass.

Dr. Sackler was paralyzed. He couldn't comprehend what had just happened. He couldn't believe it. He walked over to the window, stepping on the pieces of shattered glass, and looked out to see Orfeo's body on the pavement, twisted like that of a contortionist, surrounded by a curious crowd.

CHAPTER 2

The Master

The Room

At first glance, they seemed like metal ceiling fans. One of the fans was oriented horizontally just a few inches from the floor, and the other was perpendicular to the floor, forming a L-shaped configuration. Both were rotating very slowly. All the parts were chrome and had a clinical air about them. There were many pairs of these "fans" adjacent to each other in a line and then rows running parallel to each other. On the ground below each row, running the length of the floor, there were trenches that were about two feet deep and two feet wide. On the ceiling, there were metal bars, also in chrome, running the length of each row. Other than the metal structures, everything in the large room was in white tile. Upon closer scrutiny, however, one could perceive that the fans were actually sharp blades, like the meat slicers found at the local deli. *Such a strange configuration,* one would think while attempting to figure out its purpose.

Dolton sharpened the blades meticulously as he hummed a long-forgotten song from times past.

"Is everything ready," the Master asked.

"Yes, Master," Dolton responded like an excited child with a new toy.

"The instrument is better than ever … the materials available now are far superior than before … so precise … I can't wait to try it … When can we start, Master? When? Can we—"

"Dolton!" the Master chided, "focus!"

Dolton fell silent and looked down like a child being reprimanded.

"Is the instrument ready?" the Master asked again.

Dolton nodded, still looking at the ground.

"Then let us begin."

"Yes, Master, yes. I will prepare."

Self-Sacrifice

There were men and women hanging from the supporting ceiling bars by metal harnesses. They were naked. Many of them were crying quietly, as though it were a private affair. They all stared at the floor below them, tears and snot flowing down their cheeks. They were intensely concentrated, preparing themselves for what they knew they would endure.

The Master walked in front of them and stopped before each one, as though he were a drill sergeant inspecting their uniforms. He asked them, "Are you ready?"

There were no words uttered, but there were nods of affirmation accompanied by an increase of whimpering and sobbing.

"What is the sobbing about?" the Master asked. "Are you not here of your own volition?" There was more sobbing and, again, nods of affirmation. "Then let's get on with it. We are happy to serve you."

The Master looked over to Dolton, which he understood to be the signal to begin. He flipped the switch, and the room was filled with the sound of engines that set the blades into motion. The sobbing ceased immediately, and the men and women closed their eyes in preparation. If one could only see their faces, it would appear that they were meditating.

Both the horizontally and vertically oriented blades rotated and moved, almost imperceptibly, closer to the men and women. Other than the sound of the engines and the occasional drops of tears and snot hitting the ground, there was concentrated silence. After a long while, the razor-sharp blades made their first contact. The vertical blades sliced barely a layer of skin from the shoulder and knuckles. The horizontally oriented blades close to the floor and under them, because the people were lifting their toes in apprehension of the pain that would ensue, sliced a thin layer of skin from their heels. The whimpering now completely subsided. There were only grimaces of pain and concentration.

The blades continued to turn, at first at the same longitude and latitude that claimed the first layer of flesh, their subtle breeze creating an unbearable burning sensation at the site of the open wounds and an even more unbearable anticipation of what each of them knew would follow.

After a moment that must have seemed like an interminable amount of time, each of the blades again, almost imperceptibly, moved in and up, slicing deeper, longer pieces of flesh from the shoulder, arm, forearm, back of the hand, and bottom of the foot. Incredibly, there were no screams, cries, or pleas for mercy. There were simply isolated gasps, grunts, and deep breathing. Muscles and tendons were now exposed as trickles of blood dripped into the trenches.

Again, the blades continued to spin in the same location as their last point of contact. One of the men threw his head back and emoted a harsh, long, "Aarrgh!"

"Silence," the Master admonished. "You must focus your mind. Do not disturb the work of the others."

Time passed like molasses here. A long period passed before the blades were again set in motion and exacted their duty, separating another layer of flesh, another layer of earthly baggage. The sighs now grew deeper and, at moments, appeared to be in unison. Bone was now visible on the arms, and the feet were now gone. Blood was now flowing in the white-tiled trenches. Dolton hurried to every individual that was bleeding too profusely and, with an electrocautery, stopped the bleeding. The air filled with the stench of burnt flesh and coagulated blood. They barely flinched, and one could see a slight movement of their heads and eyes signifying gratitude for stopping the bleeding. In the old days, Dolton reminisced, he used fire, which was not as effective and caused unnecessary pain. He always looked forward to exploring for new and exciting gadgets.

The next cycle began, and the sound of the blades cutting through bone was piercing. Then the next cycles continued at their same slow, deliberate pace. The Master observed and was obviously pleased by the level of concentration these men and women maintained. There was barely a whimper now. Every now and then, there was a gasp, a deep exhalation, and there was the occasional vomiting that occurred under such circumstances. Dolton lovingly wiped the sweat, tears, and vomit from the individuals' faces and bodies and offered sips of water for sustenance.

When the participants were able to maintain such concentration individually, it elevated the entire group to unprecedented states. Aeons ago, the Master used to work with one individual at a time, separating the participants into different areas. Sometimes, with exceptional individuals, the experience was glorious. But more often than not, it was disappointing, because the participants would lose their concentration. Still tethered to their physical reigns, their bodies, they would begin to wallow in their pain, scream in horror, and pathetically plead for mercy. The Master and Dolton would then have to terminate the process prematurely without any dignity for what they had or could have endured or experienced. The Master had learned that it was similar to the meager strength required to break one pencil, as opposed to the incredible force required to break a bundle of pencils.

The Master luxuriated in the humming sound of the blades exacting their precise due and no more, in the sight of useless flesh and strips of bone piling up in the white-tiled trenches, washed with blood, and in the intermittent, sweet smell of scorched flesh and blood. He relished the power of the grace and concentration exhibited by these noble men and women who understood the power of sacrifice. They understood that the body was temporary and that its only truly value was the energy it relinquished in its destruction.

Tattoo artists, on a more superficial level, could certainly understand this. They comprehended that the body was transient and insignificant. Consequently, it could be utilized as a canvas to express, albeit temporarily, a perhaps more significant meaning or purpose in the form of an image, a color, words, or a collage. For some, the tattoos reflected art and beauty, while for others they reflected a statement or simply a map of the psycho-spiritual territories their bodies had traversed in their earthly journeys.

This was a beautiful concept, completely missed by mainstream society and even most of those tattooed with images bereft of significance even to themselves. These latter simply wanted to identify with a particular group of people, who in this case painted or pierced their skin. What was missing in this paradigm was the creation and release of energy.

Similar to the chemistry of the energy released when burning calories, the sole inherent value of the physical body was akin to the kindle and wood used to start a bonfire: fuel. Yet, human beings placed such value on it rather than on that which was permanent, immortal: their Consciousness. These men and women, offering their bodies in sacrifice, understood that they were spiritual beings having a human experience. They understood that the highest form of energy was derived from the return to spirit.

If someone were to stumble into this scenario and fully took in what was transpiring, the natural conclusion he or she would arrive at, after first being shocked and horrified and then likely vomiting at the sight of dismembered bodies and the overwhelming stench of burnt flesh and blood, was that this was a "splatter" film in the making. From the participant's perspective, they were subscribing to a higher cause and would consider the rest of the world "vanilla." They knew deeply what the "vanilla" world could never grasp—that everyone was in the process of returning and that the time spent in the earth-realm was simply a passage that was bereft of meaning unless one was ascribed. For everyone, there was pain that was so deep that it often defied being acknowledged as such. Hence Henry David Thoreau's statement, "Men lead lives of quiet desperation." These men and women, on the other hand, embraced that pain and elevated it to an offering, a sacrifice. Moreover, by enduring such intense physical pain with dignity and concentration, they believed that they would save themselves from suffering in their next incarnations and perhaps save their loved ones from such pain as well. For them, their path of suffering was far superior because it was embraced with respect rather than feared and shunned.

CHAPTER 3

Mother Ayahuasca

Journey to Pucallpa

Orfeo was sitting in a slender, motorized canoe, barely wide enough for two people but long enough for twenty and tons of baggage in the middle. He was feeling very anxious about this trip. Here he was, moving slowly through a river in the middle of the Peruvian Amazon at dawn, and despite the grandeur and beauty of the plush, dense jungle, with trees leaning over the edge of the river as if to wash their leaves or take a sip of water—or even better, reenacting the role of Narcissus gazing at his own beauty and majesty in the reflection of the water—he was filled with a fear that was so deep that he couldn't rationalize it. Everything that he had been told about this excursion, this *dieta*—sleeping in open-air huts, mosquitos, and wild animals such as jaguars, tarantulas, and snakes—didn't seem, at least on the surface, to concern him at all. His was a fear that transformed all those other fears, which the group discussed with feigned laughter, into the list of attractions one would find at a destination resort for retirees.

The water was deep green and brown. It was crystalline

and still as ice, serving as a perfect mirror for the sky and Narcissus-like vegetation, until the canoe cut through it like a knife. There was the beautiful sound of birds and occasionally a sighting of a colorful one who would briefly venture alongside the canoe, flying just inches above the water before saying goodbye.

Every now and then, you could see tiny wooden shacks along the shoreline with tin, corrugated roofs. The windows were basically areas where the wood was cut out. There were kids playing in the dirt or kicking balls around. They wore Western clothing that appeared tattered and dirty. The indigenous people were obviously very poor, yet when they waved and smiled as the canoe passed, they seemed radiantly happy. Orfeo reconsidered this thought, realizing for the first time that the word *happy* represented a Western, contrived sentiment that was often used to mask the underlying misery of a bankrupt Western existence. Orfeo thought that, rather than happy, the people toiling at the riverbed seemed simply to accept their reality as it was dealt to them. There were no artificial demarcations, like the man-made borders between the African countries that at times divided kinsmen and sometimes brought together mortal enemies, between themselves as people and their condition. There was simply reality. This resulted in a sense of contentment with their lives, a satisfaction with their condition that could not be apprehended through the Western lens.

Orfeo was clearly making shit up in his head at this point, but he idealized the notion that they had learned, through centuries of being, that there was something beyond the superficiality of their existence, and it was at this level that true joy was found. At that moment, Orfeo was bitten by several mosquitos, which jolted him from his line of reasoning, and he again reconsidered that perhaps he was completely full of shit and that it was his Western eyes that allowed him to imagine that such people in dire poverty could possibly be "content" with their lot.

The jungle was full of sounds emanating from every direction, blending into a symphony. Occasionally, there would be a solo, a single voice rising above the rest. Orfeo looked about as though looking for the teleprompter situated in the seat in front of the spectator of an opera that tells the viewer what the opera singer is actually saying. What a bizarre notion, Orfeo thought to himself, to require a gizmo to tell you what was going on. What was the point? Orfeo, despite considering himself open to all kinds of music and art in that blasé, cosmopolitan, looking-down-your-nose sort of way, had always hated the opera. People in ridiculous costumes screaming at the top of their lungs in a way that, he was convinced, could not be understood even by those who spoke the language. He was sure that it had been started as a hoax by some drunken street performers seeking coins for their next drink without any pretension that what they were doing was anything else other than making total asses of themselves. Yet somehow, this had caught on as an art form that attempted to convey the deepest emotions. Even so, at least at its origins, Orfeo could appreciate that it had been intended as a pastime for the downtrodden and presented in their own language. But now, in this day and age, he could not rationalize the adoption of this art form by the upper classes who couldn't even understand a word of what was being uttered. They first had to read the libretto beforehand, which recounted the story that would be told, and then had the benefit of a teleprompter in front of their seats. Why not have simultaneous translation, Orfeo mused, or a sign language interpreter in full costume signing her lines, or better, a mime miming as the music played? Life itself should have such a gizmo, he thought, as no one seemed to know what the hell was going on.

At that moment, there was a particularly loud and pleading solo from a bird, or perhaps a monkey, that really seemed to be trying to communicate something. Orfeo sensed that it was remarkably similar to when someone was trying to communicate something urgently to someone else who spoke another language. He always found it interesting that even though you know they don't understand a word of what you are saying, you end up speaking louder and louder, as though they were hard of hearing, somehow believing that screaming will penetrate the communication barrier. Orfeo felt that the soloist had a message for him, perhaps telling him that this was a big mistake and that he should get out of there while he still had a chance.

Fear. It filled every pore of his body; like the cool breeze, it covered his body. It was injected into him by every mosquito; it entered his ears with the cacophony of sounds emanating from the trees and his body with every breath of the humid, damp air. Fear. He looked at the others in the adjacent canoe, studying their faces. He could see a similar fear oozing from their skin, like the cloud of cigarette smoke that Lauren Bacall blew from her lips in one of those old black-and-white classics, the one that lingers in the air as she says some witty line to Humphrey Bogart that Orfeo can't seem to recall; or rather, like the heavy stench of a homeless man that is so dense that you can see it like an aura surrounding his body. There was a fleeting moment of comfort accompanying the realization that everyone was carrying fear on their elevator ride to the gallows, but this notion was squished like the mosquito on his arm that he'd just terminated as he realized that there were many levels of hell and that he somehow had the feeling that he was going really deep. Where's that damn teleprompter now? Orfeo thought, all the while laughing to himself at his hypocrisy.

Orfeo's butt was aching from sitting on the hard, wooden plank for such a long time, and the idle chatter wasn't enough to distract him from the pain. After about an hour and a half, they pulled over to the shoreline, where some men greeted them with warm smiles and helped them off the canoes. He wondered if he should just stay on the boat and return home, but he felt a calling to get on with it.

He picked up his backpack, drank some water, and then walked with the group for about a mile over narrow paths that cut through the jungle. As they walked inland, the jungle grew more and more dense. Orfeo had hiked in many of the national parks in the United States, but the Amazonian jungle was nature on steroids. There were trees of so many varieties, all growing literally on top of, adjacent to, and twisted around one another, forming bizarre configurations yet existing symbiotically. There wasn't a square inch of earth that was not inhabited by such trees and plants, and reportedly because the land was not very deep, their roots coursed like anacondas just above ground.

The humidity was stifling, and with the strain of the weight of his backpack, Orfeo was drenched. They arrived at a central clearing with a large, open hut in the center, in which there was a large table. A heavy-set woman with a warm, welcoming smile greeted them and, with the minimal English she could muster, beckoned them to sit and eat. The morning's journey had started at 5:00 a.m. with an exhausting, perilous, two-hour car ride over bumpy dirt roads. It seemed as though the drivers of the cars that transported the twenty-three of them had made a bet about who would arrive first. This was followed by the ninety-minute canoe trip and then the mile hike with all the belongings they would need for the next ten days on their backs. They were exhausted, and the smell of chicken soup was like a call from heaven, especially since those who had already made the journey had warned them that they would only be fed plain rice and plantains, once on certain days and twice on others. They were told this had something to do with breaking the body down in order to allow the spirit to emerge. Many discussed their concerns about being hungry in the jungle, but Orfeo somehow knew that this would be the least of his concerns.

The fellow seekers had prepared them well thus far, but there was a gross omission regarding what would happen next. They were directed to their individual huts, called *tambos*, and told to rest for the initial ceremony that evening. Each tambo was separated from the others by about two hundred meters, and because of the thickness of the jungle, they were in complete isolation. Amid the drone of the crickets, monkeys, birds, and other unidentifiable creatures that made strange noises, one could hear the sound of someone chanting a mantra in the distance.

The Dream

Each tambo was about ten feet by six feet in size and was made of wood cut from the jungle. The floor was supported on short blocks to make it level and, presumably, to make it a tiny bit difficult for the small insects and animals to climb aboard. The roof was made of leaves, and it was completely open on all sides. In each tambo, there was only a single bed covered by a mosquito net, a small desk and stool, a hammock, and a five-gallon water dispenser. About seven feet from the tambo, there was a latrine, which was basically a hole in the ground covered by a two-foot-high wooden box with a hole cut out from the top. They were instructed to kick it a few times so that the spiders, scorpions, and other bugs would not be surprised and reflexively attack. Orfeo considered how pathetic it would be, of all the glorious ways to die in the jungle, to die from an anaphylactic reaction or from being poisoned by a scorpion bite to one's testicles.

Orfeo settled in and lay down under the cover of the mosquito net, resolving to surrender himself to the experience. He pondered how crystal clear it seemed to him at that moment that everything that had occurred to him in his life had conspired to bring him to this place to have this experience. With this in mind, and while listening to the hypnotic drone of the crickets, which now seemed to form a solid, undulating wave of sound, punctuated by the isolated calls of the monkeys, birds, and jungle entities, he dozed off into a deep sleep.

He awakened in the dream he knew so well. He was in the desert.

I look up, weary, deflated,
and see the endless desert before me.
I have been on this path for so long.

The heat is insufferable.
The air stifling.
Every breath sets my lungs on fire.
Every movement is excruciating.

Yet, I am compelled to press on.
But to where? Why continue?
How did I end up here? When?

I see someone in the distance.
Another mirage?
Another figment of my imagination?

He was lulled out of his reverie by the sound of a man's voice approaching his tambo, calling out, *"Ceremonia, ceremonia."* The man, who would later introduce himself as Serafin, was carrying a thurible with burning incense, swinging it around the tambo as though trying to bathe it in the incense. He then gestured that Orfeo should step out of the tambo and extend his arms. Serafin proceeded to swing the thurible all around Orfeo while chanting some sort of incantation. Serafin then indicated that Orfeo should proceed to the maloca, where the *ceremonia* would take place.

The experienced seekers had prepared them well for what was to come, except for this part. It was somehow perceived as a rite of passage for which there could be no preparation. It was simply understood that this should not be relayed to the uninitiated.

They all arrived in the maloca in silence. It was circular, had a high-pitched, tepee-like thatched roof, and was completely open on its sides, surrounded by the dense jungle. There were cushions placed at the perimeter of the maloca, and at the center, there were twenty-three large buckets of what appeared to be dirty water and twenty-three smaller buckets and cups that were empty.

Don Carlos, the shaman who would conduct the ceremonies, arrived unceremoniously and briefly explained the importance of the work they would be doing, adding that solitude and respect for each of their inner processes were of the utmost importance. He then put some black powder in a cup, added water, stirred it, and recited some incantations while blowing air, which Orfeo would later learn were called *soplos*, into the cup. He called them up one by one to drink a cupful of the concoction. Judging by the grimaces everyone was making, Orfeo assumed the drink was bitter, but when his turn came, he didn't think it was that bad. Afterward, he returned to his cushion.

It was not until after everyone had drunk that Don Carlos briefed them on what they had imbibed. It was called the "Dragon's Herb" and was used to cleanse the system before starting the *dieta*. It was an emetic that caused one to vomit. Don Carlos described the cleanse not so much as a physical one but as an energetic one to prepare them for the *dieta*. He then instructed everyone to take both a large and a small bucket and a cup. After getting the buckets and returning to their seats, they sat in silence for about half an hour, during which time Don Carlos very quietly and nonchalantly hummed and whistled tunes, which he later explained were "*icarros*." The word *icarro* is translated as "song," but in the shamanic tradition, it means much more. Don Carlos explained to them that *icarros* had been passed down from master shaman to apprentice over millennia, and what was transmitted were not so much the words or even the melodies but rather energy. This energy was utilized during ceremonies to facilitate and guide the seekers in their journeys. After this period, he told them that the water was from the river and instructed them to start drinking. After a while, the Dragon's Herb would cause a rhythmic contraction of the stomach that would cause them to vomit. He emphasized the importance of maintaining a rhythm in order to keep their stomachs full of water, because the spasms with an empty stomach could result in severe pain and vomiting blood.

No problema, Orfeo thought to himself as he stared into the four gallons of sediment filled, murky river water and started to drink. After about five cups, he felt a rumbling in his stomach, and with a burp, he purged all the water he had drunk. He felt no pain or discomfort with the first four or five cycles. He drank until he felt full, and without any drama, the water came back up. There was a helper who walked around emptying everyone's buckets. After that, however, Orfeo noticed that some of the others were having a harder and harder time drinking. As he decreased the amount that he was drinking, the vomiting became more violent and painful. He felt horrible and started to sweat profusely and tremble. He forced himself to drink. Many of the seekers started to moan and groan. He looked into his bucket of misery and saw that he had barely drank one third. Don Carlos's instructions were to drink the entire bucket. He could barely take another sip of water and was now sweating profusely. The next wave of stomach spasms caused him to double over in excruciating pain, and without enough water in his stomach, he regurgitated bile and mucous.

There was no feigned laughter at this point. Orfeo thought that someone passing by the maloca in the distance, without being able to see, would surely believe that there was major torture going on. The moans and groans had now escalated to cries of anger and pain, shouted pleas to a god who was likely cut off from this forsaken part of the jungle without internet or cellphone reception to stop the pain. He drank another five cups of the murky river water, which he calculated would be enough to prevent the excruciating pain, and then lay down on his side to gather his energy, wondering what the hell he was doing in this place. What was he looking for? Regardless, Orfeo knew that he had crossed the point of no return.

After he had managed to drink about two-thirds of the river water, the spasms were not as strong, and there were longer periods of respite from the vomiting. Don Carlos had already told a few of the seekers that they could return to their tambos. Orfeo was praying for Don Carlos to release him but was also fearful that he would continue to purge without anything in his stomach. Would he start to vomit blood and die of a massive gastrointestinal hemorrhage deep in the Peruvian Amazon, at least five hours from the nearest medical facility? He chuckled at the thought that this would at least be categorized as a glorious death.

When Don Carlos finally told him to return to his tambo, Orfeo could barely make it back. One of the helpers saw him struggling and put Orfeo's arm over his shoulder, supporting him at the waist for most of the way down those narrow paths. It was already dark out, and the symphony of jungle sounds had become more intense. Orfeo realized that even if he had had the strength to walk, he would never have made it back to his tambo alone in the dark without getting lost.

When he arrived, he plopped himself onto his bed and wondered for how long he would feel so miserable. He could hear some of the other seekers still moaning and vomiting in their tambos. After he had squirmed in his bed for a while, the spasms returned with a vengeance, and Orfeo started to dry heave uncontrollably. The pain was unbearable. Finally, some thick, white froth came up. The pain subsided, but Orfeo was covered with sweat, and he had shaking chills that persisted. He fell asleep to the rhythmic cries of suffering from the distant tambos.

In his dream, he found himself again in the desert.

I look up, weary, deflated,
and see the endless desert of Consciousness before me.
I have been on this path for so long, forgotten eternities.
I have established a pace, a routine.

The heat is insufferable.
The air stifling.

Every breath sets my lungs on fire.
Every movement is excruciating.
I chuckle, which scorches my lips, with a rare thought:
In comparison, hell is merely a Bikram yoga class

Yet, I am compelled to press on.
But to where? Why continue?
How did I end up here? When?

I know that this sea of red, molten sand is a construct.
I know that the sense of moving forward is an illusion.
Yet, I am compelled to press on.
But to where? Why continue?
After all, there is no destination.

At first, before I understood, I thought the destination
was God.
How ludicrous that thought has become.
This desert—the red sand, the blinding glare, the
interminable heat—is all God!

I see someone in the distance.
Another mirage?
Another figment of my imagination?

Las Ceremonías

Orfeo awakened to the sound of Serafin, who waited patiently for him to get out of bed and handed him some leaves and a cup of dark-colored something. Orfeo hesitated, fearing that it was the Dragon's Herb, but Serafin, in his broken English, insisted that he drink it. Don Carlos later explained that they would receive the plant-based tea every morning and that it would create a foundation for the work that would follow. Serafin mimed that Orfeo should fill the large bucket at the side of his tambo with river water and allow the leaves to soak in it and that this water should be used to bathe. Don Carlos had reminded them that nothing with a scent, such as soap, toothpaste, or mosquito repellent, could be used during the *dieta*. None of this disturbed Orfeo, except for the mosquito repellent. At least half of his body was already covered with mosquito bites, and this was only the start of the second of ten days.

Orfeo spent a few hours organizing his stuff, took another nap, and made an entry in his journal describing what had happened the day before, underlining, capitalizing, and putting in quotes his statement just before he started drinking the river water: "NO PROBLEMA!!!!!" He then wrote in parentheses, "Haha!!!" Afterward, he bathed in the river, which was just about knee high. He was about to sit and meditate when Serafin passed by, ringing a bell, saying, "*Ceremonia, ceremonia.*" Orfeo stood up, got dressed all in white as instructed, and made his way to the maloca, thinking to himself, *Game's on!* He had no idea what he was in for, but he knew that everything in his life had brought him to this moment, and he was ready.

Almost everyone else was already seated when Orfeo arrived at the maloca. There was a lot of nervous laughter and chitchatting, as though the Dragon's Herb ordeal was a distant memory, a half-forgotten nightmare. Some were just seated, meditating, and others were preparing their "altars," laying their crystals, trinkets, and other so-called power objects in front of their cushions. Orfeo simply sat and attempted to relax and stave off the anxiety that was building in his chest.

Orfeo closed his eyes, meditated on his breath, and prayed to Mother Ayahuasca for guidance. He'd always known that there was more to life than was apparent and that he had another purpose for his existence. From his readings on Eastern philosophy, religion, and shamanism, he understood that this was a central theme for humanity: the search for meaning. Yet he was convinced, to the point where he questioned his sanity, that he was different and not like the others. He believed that he had been brought here to Mother Ayahuasca for answers to the questions he had been carrying for most of his life.

What had transpired during that first ceremony was a blur in Orfeo's mind. He remembered drinking the "medicine," visualizing undulating colorful patterns, feeling nauseous, and purging a few times. He remembered hearing Don Carlos sing in a beautiful voice, and then all was blank. He'd really expected something dramatic to occur, and while making his way back to his tambo, felt disappointed, feeling that this was another dead end on his quest for an answer for which he did not have a question.

Don Carlos explained that when the mind was experiencing something so profound, it sometimes short-circuited, and there would be no memory of what happened. This did not provide Orfeo any reassurance. After the same thing occurred in the second and third ceremonies, he resolved himself to simply surrendering to the moment and utilizing the *dieta* to catch up on much-needed sleep. Orfeo essentially checked out mentally and was ready to go back home.

During the fourth ceremony, something interesting happened. Orfeo started purging violently, and after a bout of dry heaving, he seemingly awakened in another realm. He was conscious of the sounds of the jungle, the purging noises emanating from within the maloca, and

Don Carlos's *icarros*, but they were all taking place in what he perceived to be a bubble of immense proportions. Interestingly, he was not an observer of this bubble but rather was part of the bubble. His thoughts arose in the same way that sounds emanated from parts of the bubble. He was aware of his breath, which Don Carlos suggested was a means of staying centered and focused, but rather than breathing, he had the sensation that he was being breathed. Somewhat disconcerted, Orfeo attempted to analyze the situation, but the thoughts seemed outside of himself. He could not identify "himself."

Once he relaxed in that state of Being, he felt an overwhelming sense of peace that seemed so familiar, so natural. It was almost as though he had arrived home. Every worry, concern, objective, and purpose that Orfeo had ever experienced vanished into the bubble. He could see them but could no longer attach any relevance to them. It was similar to the descriptions of near-death experiences, in which people universally said they had crossed a threshold and, in no uncertain terms, did not wish to return. He understood now, not intellectually but experientially, what they were describing.

The following integration day was filled with so many questions. Orfeo could simply not grasp what had transpired, but he knew without a shadow of a doubt that it had not simply been a drug-induced hallucination. It was too real, and he sensed that this was where the answer lay. He slept most of the day and the following night.

Orfeo entered the final ceremony with a newfound confidence. The fear was gone. It was as though a key had been turned, granting him access through a portal into not another dimension but rather a larger dimension that encompassed his present one. Almost immediately after drinking the medicine, he walked into this dimension. It felt even more familiar now, as though he had been there many times.

Orfeo experienced the eternal. He understood that the perception of outside reality was an illusion. There was only Consciousness. Everything else was an illusion. He recognized that even the notion of peace was an illusion, because there is only peace and tranquility, from which all else arises. There were no thoughts in this state, no desires. There was simply Being.

Orfeo began to remember. The memories of a former existence, like wisps floating in the wind, began to coalesce into recognizable forms. He felt as though he were awakening from a dream that seemed so real, so tangible. For a moment, on the precipice, he did not know where the dream ended and reality began. Images of the desert, well known to him, entered his mind. This time, however, it felt more real than ever.

How did I end up here? When? It seems an eternity ago. Long ago, there seemed to be many others.

They provided good company on this arduous path.

The conversations, at first enticing, were later recognized for what they in fact were:

Pedestrian pleasantries between those on death row.

Mere distractions.

As when a child learns how the magician's trick is performed, the magic disappeared.

With this understanding, the others began to fade away.

I could no longer maintain the illusion.

They were all mirages, creations of my imagination to ease the drudgery of this journey.

But after eternities, I learned that even the journey is an illusion.

Then why continue?

I seemed condemned to follow this path

Like Sisyphus, condemned to push his rock up the hill, only to have it roll down the other side.

The futility of it all.

At least he had a motive: to defy the gods!

What is my motivation?

Every century or so, I ask myself this equally futile question.

It seems that with every eternity, there is the gift of a precious morsel of understanding, a pinch of clarity.

I recall from long ago, as though it were a dream,
vague images of cities, people, great oceans, hopes,
grandiose ambitions, relationships.
Then one day, it all vanished.
All that was left was this desert.

At first it was unbearable.
I developed all sorts of techniques to cope with the desert:
traveling during the evenings—there were periods of
cool nights and hellish days back then—loose clothing,
turbans, and so on.
Techniques were shared with imagined travelers—what
comedy!

Then I was graced with the insight of total, radical
surrender.
What a blessing!
Surrender to what is, as it is.

This journey has been one of stripping away everything,
a sharp razor peeling away one's skin.
Eternities ago, this was a struggle, seemingly painful.
Now, there is nothing left except the desert.

Orfeo felt a rumbling in his stomach followed by an irrepressible urge to vomit. He brought the bucket to his face, but there were only dry heaves. The nausea persisted. The call of the bucket was very strong, but again, only dry heaves. He got on his hands and knees and released a deep burp that sounded as though it originated in the depths of hell. This was followed by a series of dry heaves that at last brought forth what must have been a teaspoon of bile. Orfeo considered the idea of perspectives, how in this circumstance a mere teaspoon of bile could provide such satisfaction.

The nausea abated, and he pondered the desert. This image, limited to fragments, had always been with him, usually in his dreams. What did it mean? Orfeo thought to himself as he wiped his mouth and contemplated a sip of water. Fearing that it would trigger another round of nausea and vomiting, he decided to simply rinse his mouth and spit the water into the bucket.

Orfeo settled into his cushion and scanned the maloca. There were sounds of crying, pleas for mercy, and purging. He noticed the concentration of some of the seekers, who were doing their work quietly. Don Carlos stood in front of someone who had passed out and was performing a *bendiatta*, which one of the other seekers explained was a sort of healing. He then recalled Don Carlos's insistence that everyone concentrate and focus on their own inner process. He closed his eyes and almost immediately found himself back in the desert.

On this journey to nowhere, I see you in the distance.
Another mirage?
Another figment of my imagination?

Over eternities, I have encountered so many mirages.
Lonely, I welcomed the distraction.
Long ago, I believed the engagement to be worthwhile,
even pleasurable at times—
exchanging pleasantries, thoughts, feelings, and bodily
fluids.
With experience, I now ignore them.

Like sand mandalas, markings imprinted on the desert
of Consciousness are immediately swept away by the wind.
All that is left is the red, molten sand.
Not even a trace of a shadow is perceived.

Yet, when our paths cross,
your eyes radiate the waves of the ocean.
Your full, luscious lips are an expansive lake in which
to luxuriate.
I am captivated, compelled.
You are an oasis for my weary soul.

I want to reach out and touch you
but dare not for fear that you will disappear.
I gaze into your eyes for sustenance.
I become light, a feather in a long-forgotten breeze.
I become cool, like a rainforest nourishing Mother Earth.
I become the water that rejuvenates the dry, parched
plains of the Serengeti.

In your gaze, I am transformed.
What is it that you see bowing before you?
  It has been an eternity since I saw myself as an incarnate
being apart from the desert,
  an eternity since the last vestige of the emotion I recall
as love.
  May I rest my soul in the oasis of your bosom?

Orfeo was deeply immersed in the effects of the "medicine," and he was luxuriating in the images of this strange desert encounter with a love so deep and all-encompassing, until a single thought emerged that would bitch-slap him into a state of wakefulness: *Carina!*

The thought of Carina struck Orfeo like a bolt of lightning, short-circuiting his system and catapulting him into a catatonic state. Although his eyes were open, he did not speak, move, or eat for days. Don Carlos performed daily *bendiattas*, bathed Orfeo in a variety of plants, and in a special ceremony, instilled a concoction deep in his nose that typically caused one to react violently and cry profusely as it entered into one's sinuses. Orfeo did not blink.

The *dieta* had ended, and except for Orfeo, everyone had left the jungle. He had no awareness of the outside world or of what was going on with or being done to his body. There were daily *bendiattas* and baths, and various plant medicines and pureed sustenance were placed in his mouth. In his mind, he felt as though he were at the periphery of a tornado, whirling around and around in a soup of thoughts, dizzy with fragments of memories of an existence that took place eternities ago and feelings of being so close to someone that there were no boundaries between them. In those thought fragments, he perceived that it wasn't merely the physical boundaries that were effaced but all boundaries. They were one.

As the days passed, he felt himself making his way to the eye of the tornado. Here, there was clarity developing in the chaos. He slowly began to remember his purpose, which was to find Carina. He thought of the lives, lost lives, and felt as though he had betrayed his love for her in taking so long to arrive at the starting line. He believed deeply that his love for her should have been sufficient to recall his purpose, but instead, all he had were the lost lives, which were too numerous to account for, to show for his so-called love for Carina.

Slowly, the catatonia subsided. He was full of self-doubt but nonetheless felt grateful to Mother Ayahuasca for lifting the fog that had clouded his mind during those lost lives, for revealing his purpose. He had no idea where or how to start, but he was comforted by the thought that he now had a goal in hand that had evaded him for so long. He recalled the saying by Lao Tzu: "A journey of a thousand miles begins with one step."

Just as suddenly as he had entered his catatonic state, he awakened with a clarity of mind and purpose. Orfeo put on his detective hat and ran over in his mind, again and again, what precious morsels he knew for sure, what he had to go on. He knew for sure that if they had in fact been one, in a state of union that was beyond time, then the compass to find her would be his heart. It was an inner journey as much as one across the Earth's continents that he was prepared to embark on. He thanked Don Carlos and everyone who had so diligently cared for him and left the jungle.

CHAPTER 4

The Reunion

First Date

Orfeo had been following her for months, all the while thinking about how he could connect with her, "meet" her again, as though for the very first time. His mind was frantic, and the same questions popped up again and again: What should he say? Would he scare her away? Knowing that she was now aware that he was staring at her, he had no choice. The die had been cast.

Feeling very awkward, he finally mustered the courage to approach her and awkwardly blurted out, "Hi … I don't want to invade your space, but would you mind if I chatted with you?"

She smiled graciously and replied, "Not at all. You look familiar. Do I know you?"

He bit his tongue, his heart torn apart thinking of the eternities they had spent not together but as one. Now, she had no recollection at all of their profound connection, except for an energetic, visceral alarm that there was something happening beyond their superficial encounter, similar to a fragment one recalls from a dream but about which one can't quite remember enough to make it coherent.

Orfeo replied, "Perhaps. You look familiar as well"—Orfeo forced a smile—"but I can't quite make the connection."

There seemed to be interminable pauses between their utterances. He felt anxious, like a schoolboy asking a girl out on a date for the first time. This was the anxiety of the first meeting, the first seduction. However, this was not a seduction. For Orfeo, it was much more important. It was regaining a part of himself that had been lost. The drive was to become whole again. The risk of losing her again was too great.

Orfeo thought of the many lifetimes that had passed and his Herculean efforts to find her. He remembered a particular life of eighty-seven years that had ended in a nursing home, where he was confined to a bed by the ravages of age, a Foley catheter inserted in his penis that not only drained his urine but his very life force. He remembered being callously turned over by uncaring nursing aides to halt the progression of fetid bedsores that had already eroded to the bone. The only thoughts that consumed his then-feeble mind while waiting patiently for death to allow him to renew his search were of Carina and of how, yet again, he had failed. Nonetheless, despite so many failures, which were too numerous to count, his resolve to find her had never waned. He knew that it was only a matter of time, and he also knew that time was nothing more than an illusion. Now, finally in the presence of his great love, the only emotion that Orfeo had was bliss. Pure bliss.

"What are you doing right now?" he asked shyly. "Would you like to have some coffee or tea with me? There's a really great café not too far from here."

"Sure," she replied, "but I only have about an hour before I have to get to class."

"Great!" He then suddenly remembered that he did not know her name in this incarnation and asked, "What's your name? I'm Orfeo."

"Orfeo. That's an odd name. Are you from Brazil?" she asked with a smile.

"Brazil? No. What made you think of Brazil?

"The way you pronounced it made me think of the Brazilian movie *Black Orpheus.*

"That was a great movie. Maybe my mom saw the movie and named me after the main character. Interestingly, I was in Brazil not too long ago and fell in love with the country and the people. If I could, I would spend the rest of my life there."

"Don't tell me ... let me guess. It's because the women are outrageously beautiful and exotic."

"They are almost as outrageously beautiful as you are," he said, immediately wondering if he had overstepped his boundaries. She didn't seem to mind, so he continued. "But that's not the reason."

"Then why?" She was obviously really interested to know.

"Well, I've traveled quite a bit, and it is one of the few places where, almost to a fault, the people are not afraid to embrace you."

"What does that even mean?" she blurted out.

"Haven't you noticed that here in the States and in most of Europe, people can be really nice, but there's always a wall, a protective layer, as though they fear that you are going to steal something from them. It's similar to the way some indigenous tribes refuse to have their pictures taken because they believe that the picture takes a piece of their soul. These people are the same. The thing is that this is almost imperceptible because everyone does it ... see? It's only when you've spent time in a place like Brazil where, even though you've never considered yourself to be closed or shut-off, you are caught off guard by their openness and you ask yourself if they're trying to take something from you. That's a real eye-opener ... a game changer."

"I absolutely get it! I've often felt this way and wondered why I had this feeling that there was something terribly wrong with people, but I just couldn't put my finger on it."

Orfeo thought to himself, *If she only knew how charming she was. Of course she gets it. She's been there and done that. Although she doesn't remember, she knows this terrain like the back of her hand.*

She continued like an excited child who had just opened a present. "I've often wanted to make funny faces, pull people's ears, jump on them like a kid, or just tickle them until they are on the verge of peeing in their pants just to get them to open up a tiny bit." There was a long silence as she contemplated this with a huge sense of pleasure, as though she had just figured out the secrets of the universe. She then asked, half-jokingly, "Will you take me to Brazil?"

"I know of an even better place," he responded, almost in tears from the joy bursting from his very core, "but I'll take you wherever your heart desires. Your wish is my command." Orfeo paused and then continued. "I only ask for one thing in return."

"And what could that possibly be in return for all that?"

Orfeo stopped walking, became very serious, and asked, "What's your name?" They both burst into laughter.

"Carina, my name is Carina."

"Okay, then, let's get on with it. Where should we begin?"

As they walked, his heart was singing at again being in her presence. For a moment, it did not bother him at all that she did not know who he was or what they had previously shared. He wondered if the feelings he was having were at all similar to those of a person whose partner of fifty years developed Alzheimer's dementia and no longer remembered him or her. The affected person is ostensibly the same person by every outward appearance, but something quite important is missing, as though he or she were cored. For them, every day is the first day of the relationship, except for a tinge of familiarity that suggests that the other is not a total stranger. Orfeo concluded that no one's heart was singing in that situation because there was only loss. In his case, there was renewal, hope, and the possibility of return.

This thought of Alzheimer's dementia reminded Orfeo of Kostos, who had emphasized the importance of memory. In a previous lifetime, when Orfeo was in his early twenties, he had had an affair with a slightly older and infinitely more mature Greek woman. That particular relationship had been inconsequential, but as he would learn later, there were no coincidences in the universe. What was significant was that she introduced him to her former boyfriend, Kostos, who was ten to fifteen years older than her. She had told him about Kostos and mentioned that it had been a long and significant relationship. At that point, Orfeo had not yet had a significant relationship, but he understood enough to realize his insignificance in comparison. This caused him to feel awkward when meeting Kostos, because at that stage of that particular incarnation, his sense of self had been largely derived from comparisons with others, and Kostos was quite a formidable character.

In his forties, Kostos had the deep facial creases of

one who had lived an expressive life. Aside from the fact that he was Greek, he had the air, knowledge, and wisdom of a Greek philosopher. Orfeo had a particular quality that would serve as a double-edged sword in that lifetime. On the one hand, at least for most of his early life, he had searched for greatness in others, and very much like a child who sees wonder in the simplest of things and is quite impressionable, he would revel whenever he encountered someone who stood out. Unfortunately, Orfeo would often discover that he was mistaken, and in fact, the so-called individual would turn out to be much like everyone else, which to him was not very interesting.

Kostos, in fact, was truly an individual, and Orfeo reveled when in his presence. He felt as though every word Kostos uttered was a pearl. Even as an adult in that lifetime, many years after their acquaintance had ended, Orfeo had wondered if something Kostos related was true or was simply a confabulation to serve his ends. At the time, Kostos had been selling a futon mattress. Orfeo had never considered sleeping on a futon mattress, and his own bed at home was perfectly adequate. However, being the impressionable young man he was, the fact that someone he so revered slept on a futon convinced him that he, too, should sleep on a futon. What was curious was the fact that Kostos was selling his used futon mattress for double the price of a new one. When Orfeo, who did not consider himself to be a dupe, protested and stated that he would rather buy a new one, Kostos calmly explained that Orfeo was missing a key element in the proposed exchange.

Kostos explained that with this futon, Orfeo would not simply be purchasing an inert mattress on which to rejuvenate his body but a mattress infused with many years of profound memories and dreams that would feed his soul. Kostos related that the mattress contained his dreams, thoughts, and struggles, his adventures during his travels to other dimensions, and the years of energy exchange and creation during passionate lovemaking. Kostos pointed out the similarity to reading a book written by a wise old person. The reader, if he or she truly knew how to read—read not simply the words and meaning but rather the energy contained within the pages, something which Kostos felt was a lost art—could extract the collected wisdom of the writer and add that to their own life experience. After all, Kostos would say, was there not a collective consciousness? Yes, he would reply before anyone could attempt to utter a syllable. He believed that we have all lost our conscious connection to this fountain of wisdom, which had in this sad epoch of human existence been relegated to the subconscious mind and dreamscapes. What he was selling, Kostos stated, was a connection to this fountain of wisdom. Kostos was clear that this fountain certainly did not originate from within himself, nor did he create it. He, like the futon, was merely a conduit. This all made sense to Orfeo, but what created confusion in Orfeo's mind was the fact that Kostos had presented this in the tone of a used car salesman. Orfeo would often ask himself, was this a sage or hustler?

Kostos was clear that he was not invested in selling the futon. He stated that he could easily just throw it out in the hope that some homeless person, or even a rat, would benefit from the memories imbuing the futon, which would perhaps allow that hapless being to transcend his, her, or its reality into another, more auspicious one. Kostos often spoke of other dimensions. Although Orfeo had had no idea at that time what Kostos was talking about, he was nonetheless impressed.

Orfeo recalled that on another occasion, over drinks one evening while they were all somewhat intoxicated, Kostos had emphatically pointed out that, from his perspective, there were five important things in this life. This was to be one of the pearls that Orfeo would carry like a precious gift for most of his life. Kostos, in rapid fire, listed them.

"First, there is love. Love of life, of others, of everything or anything that is beyond oneself, which then allows for the true love of self. Second is passion—to permit oneself to be truly excited and overwhelmed by life. What is love without passion? Third is adventure, the thrill of stepping into the unknown, of tasting fear and making it your friend and ally. Fourth is risk, willfully stepping out of one's comfort zone." Then he quoted someone who

Orfeo could never remember. "'A life never ventured is one never gained.' Last is memory, without which all is rendered irrelevant."

Kostos had added that for anyone else, he would have sold the futon for three or four times its value, and it would still be a bargain. He'd stated that, in fact, because he had an affection for Orfeo's enthusiasm for life, he had already reduced the price. Needless to say, Orfeo had gladly purchased the futon.

Orfeo would often return to these five most important things that Kostos shared, and for most of his life, he subscribed to them and would often share them with others. Later, however, he came to understand that these things were of the earth-realm and were not translatable to higher realms. He learned, after much pain and suffering, about surrender. He learned that surrender was not the least important thing or the most important thing but rather the only thing. Orfeo thought that if he were now in Kostos's position, considering mentoring a bright-eyed enthusiast, he would only have one thing to teach: surrender. But how does one convey this concept, which is so all-encompassing, like water to a fish, that it doesn't allow one to ever perceive it. It cannot be apprehended, and the conscious decision that one makes to surrender is futile when confronted with that which one has to surrender to. This sacred teaching, which Orfeo now understood to be the most important of teachings, could only be apprehended through the experience of surrendering, and the opportunities for rehearsal are abundantly provided in what one calls life in the earth-realm. Like the water in which the fish swims, breathes, and lives and which it cannot live without, life in the earth-realm provides all that is necessary to learn. The lesson and the learning are one and cannot be separated. Hence, there is nothing to teach. Many sages have passed on the wisdom that "when the student is ready, the teacher appears." Consequently, Orfeo's greatest wisdom at his later stages of evolution was that he had no true wisdom to share. But when pressed, he would offer these five most important things. Orfeo often wondered if Kostos "knew," but he would never find out.

This led Orfeo to think about what life would be like, at least an earthbound life, without memory. He thought of the village in Gabriel Garcia Marquez's *One Hundred Years of Solitude*, where the people lost their memories and relied on labels to remember objects but then forgot what the labels stood for. The horror! It was upsetting not only because of the idea that one person or an entire village could lose all the memories that, like a symphony, a grand oeuvre, literally composed their lives, but more so because Gabriel Garcia Marquez, perhaps unwittingly, was describing the human condition. Earthbound humans had all acquired a form of dementia whereby they had lost the memory of whence they came, of why they were here, and of where they were going. Fortunately, however, the human condition was more like a state of sleepwalking. One might get punched in the face attempting to wake a sleepwalker from his or her delusional state, but after a while, perhaps after innumerable lifetimes, there is the hope, the possibility, no matter how remote, that the sleepwalker will awaken to the truth. However, the demented patient without memory or the capacity to create memories is eternally lost. This person no longer has the capacity and is eternally tethered to the earth-realm.

This idea brought to Orfeo's mind an even more disturbing thought he'd had when walking through the Museum of Modern Art (MoMA) in New York City. It had been a rainy, lonely day. He had been walking by the MoMA and decided to wander inside for no particular reason except to pass the time. He'd wandered aimlessly into various galleries and was pleasantry surprised that, after so many lifetimes spent reckoning with the bitterness of his utter and complete failure to find his true love, he could still be inspired by art. He then realized that after all, this was the purpose of art, if one allowed—to inspire and move us. Art was simply one tool, one vehicle that tapped us on the shoulder, whispered in our ear, and reminded us to look, open our eyes, feel.

As he continued his peregrination through the MoMA, he coincidentally walked through an exhibit where there were a variety of beautiful frames of varying sizes, some as large as doors and others in various geometric shapes. The frames were standing or hanging in scattered positions in the very large space. Portals came to Orfeo's mind. Orfeo contemplated how art was simply one of an infinite number of portals available to humankind to leave behind the quotidian of human existence—not to escape, but to transcend. These portals were everywhere. Art, music, and literature were merely the obvious ones. The earth-realm was resplendent with such portals, imploring us to look beyond our noses to the glorious dimensions just beyond. Whether a child laughing in play, or the dirty, stinky, belligerent, homeless person who appears to be extending his or her hand for charity, or the children dying of starvation in Africa and other atrocities that perpetually assault us, Orfeo believed that they were actually angels or muses who beseeched us to allow ourselves to be moved, to open our hearts in order to experience an emotion deeply and be inspired.

Orfeo continued thinking about this. He believed that the all-too-well-developed rational mind, which was often quite irrational and detrimental to us, would ask, "Inspired to do what? What am I supposed to do? Is it my responsibility to do something?" Orfeo answered in his mind, *Game, match, point. You lose, buddy. Try again in the next lifetime.*

For Orfeo, the purpose of portals was simply to perceive. One had windows at home to be able to open them, look out, and breathe, not to jump out, unless there was a blazing fire of course. Orfeo was amused by this thought, and the gravity of his predicament was momentarily lifted as the melody and lyric of Antonio Carlos Jobim's song "Corcovado" came to mind: "Quiet nights and quiet stars. Quiet chords on my guitar floating in the silence that surrounds us. Quiet thoughts and quiet dreams. Quiet walks by quiet streams. Looking out the window at the mountains and the sea, how lovely."

He'd continued to move through the museum aimlessly, from one gallery to the next, before finding himself in an exhibit of René Magritte. For the most part, he had been absorbed in his thoughts and had barely noticed the paintings on the wall, but there was one painting that caught his eye. It was the one where objects were labeled with their names. This had disturbed Orfeo tremendously, because he wondered if God himself had not developed an advanced stage of Alzheimer's dementia and needed to label his creations, like Gabriel Garcia Marquez's characters, as reminders. But then, God too would forget the meaning of the labels and ultimately, their function. This would certainly account for the chaos that humankind was experiencing. Disturbing indeed!

The Dinner Party

Orfeo and Carina had been together for a little over six months, and everyone who met them remarked on how it seemed as though they had been together for much longer. In such a short time, they were already deeply in love. It was a textbook romance. Orfeo was happier than he had been in, literally, so many lifetimes. In a way, he felt as though he were cheating, because he already knew so much about her, but at the same time, it was as though every day he were meeting her for the first time. It was also uncanny to him how easily she was able to see so deeply into him and read him like a book.

He often thought of the return to Consciousness with her, but there was less and less pressure to get there in any hurry. After so many lifetimes of searching, he was content to simply be with her, and he found his bliss in the small, day-to-day events with her. He luxuriated in watching her sleep and wake up in the morning, brush her teeth, comb her hair, or just read a book. He looked forward to their long walks, hand in hand, along the Hudson River in Riverside Park in New York City.

He loved lyrics and would often sing her beautiful songs. She would laugh, because he was really a terrible singer, but she loved the passion in his voice. It was as though he had written the song just for her. Her favorites were "I Didn't Know What Time It Was," "That's All," "Corcovado," and "Live for Life." There were beautiful moments with friends when he would play a song over and over again, insisting they pay attention to the lyrics. His passion for the beautiful words was contagious.

Their apartment was always filled with the music of Sarah Vaughan, Mark Murphy, Abbey Lincoln, Johnny Hartman, and Jobim. Carina always felt that he should have been a poet, because he always seemed more impressed with the lyrics than the music. But what melted her heart was the fact that it was evident to everyone that for Orfeo, those beautiful lyrics, such as those of Ivan Lins's "How I envy the glass that knows your lips," were written for her and only her.

A song that Orfeo loved more than any other was "Live for Life," sung by the legendary Abby Lincoln and written by Jack Jones, who, as Orfeo would always point out, also wrote "All the Things You Are," another song Orfeo loved. At home, there were times when this song would come up in one of his playlists randomly, and he would start to cry. Of course, the songs Orfeo loved, in some way or another, always had to do with Carina. In the most unlikely circumstances, like when they were waiting in line for something or were in a restaurant with friends, Orfeo would sing those beautiful lyrics.

There were fleeting moments when the desire would come over him to tell her the truth, but just as fleetingly, he could not find a reason to do so. Their lives together were so simple yet so profound and happy. It became increasingly rare for him to think about their past together, and he found himself more and more blissfully living in the moment. Orfeo was now developing another kind of amnesia about the state of Consciousness, a willful one resulting from the fear of losing his present earthly life with Carina.

Orfeo was still cooking when the first group of guests arrived. He stopped at intervals to meet them, the vast majority of whom were Carina's friends. By the time he was sautéing the portobello mushrooms for the salad, the kitchen was filled with guests. They commented on the rich aroma emanating from the oven, which he had just opened to add the soaked apricots and prunes to his chicken-tagine–coq-au-vin mélange, peppered with large quantities of sea salt, fresh thyme, rosemary, and onions. For Orfeo, it was not so much the cooking itself he enjoyed as the gesture of cooking, of sharing the performance of cooking with his guests, an offering to their souls of friendship. He often lamented that the art of being a host, opening one's home by inviting friends over for a meal, was lost to New York City society, which in his experience mostly preferred to meet at restaurants.

The meals at a great restaurant were undoubtedly superior to the fare one's palate would encounter at a friend's home, but what was lost was the generosity and love shared by the act of being invited to someone's home.

Orfeo felt that everyone who supped with them was reminded of the grand pleasure of someone taking the time and effort, especially in light of the hectic pace of New York City life, to prepare something expressly for him or her. It was a gift to bask in the luxury of taking one's sweet time between courses without the vacuous and disingenuous interruptions and smiles of a server asking, sometimes even before one has had the opportunity to taste the food, if the meal is to one's liking. It was also quite special to have your ears feted with music that, even if not thoughtfully selected for the evening to enhance the mood and conversation, at the very least reflected the host's taste. Most of all, it was good to be able to take one's time and settle into a natural pace established by the alchemy of the wine, music, food, guests, and conversation, rather than into the conglomeration of varied external sources that bombard the senses in a restaurant. It's not that Orfeo didn't love going out for a great meal in a restaurant, because he did. What he tried to revive by setting the example among their friends was the lost art of and great pleasures derived from a simple, home-cooked meal.

Orfeo, Carina, and their nine guests sat at the large table, fitted tightly with their elbows rubbing against each other, on a variety of mismatched chairs, two Cajon drums, and a piano bench. For his first act, Orfeo brought out the appetizer, which he composed in front of the guests. Everyone had in front of him or her a plate with mesclun salad. He made his first round, manually crushing walnuts and gently tossing them onto the salads. His second round consisted of spreading dried cranberries, and the third of symmetrically arranging four slices of portobello mushrooms that were sautéed in olive oil. In the fourth round, he placed a dollop of warm, melted goat cheese in the center of the plate on top of the salad, and finally, he dressed the salad with his own vinaigrette consisting of olive oil, balsamic vinegar, mustard, and seasoning. Aside from the fact that Orfeo enjoyed the performance aspect of serving his guests in such a manner, it was definitely a means of ensuring that everyone's appetite was piqued.

He sat and proposed his first toast, which was of course dedicated to his love, Carina. He raised his glass, looking directly at her, and toasted. "Our love is like two flashlights pointing at each other. The light in the middle shines so bright that it renders irrelevant the question of which one gives and which one takes. I wish that all of you may know such a love in at least one of your lifetimes."

Everyone clinked glasses, and Carina pointed out to one of her friends, as someone always must at a dinner party, that he did not make eye contact when toasting, which she said was of the utmost importance. He, having never heard this, asked why this was so important. She replied that if one didn't make eye contact when toasting, one would be cursed. Now curious, he asked what the curse was. She paused in order to increase the suspense and then said, "Seven years of bad sex!" Everyone laughed, and then they started to clink their glasses again, now exaggerating their eye contact.

Orfeo picked up his fork and knife and opened the meal, saying, "*Aproveita!*"

Of the nine guests, Orfeo only knew one of the couples, and he endured their tedious but unavoidable questions. What did he do for a living? He answered evasively by saying he did freelance work. How did he and Carina meet? "She picked me up in a bar and made me a ridiculous offer I couldn't refuse." How long have you known each other? "Forever." Orfeo had mastered the art of turning questions back to the asker, relying on the fact that the vast majority of people love to talk about themselves, if given the opportunity, which Orfeo did with great zeal and interest. Consequently, Orfeo rarely had to talk about himself and gave the impression to other people that they were really interesting and had so much to say of value. They found him very amusing and gregarious and immediately accepted him in their circle.

They sat and chatted for a while as Orfeo prepared the second course, which was scallops and spinach sautéed in butter, olive oil, garlic, and white wine and served over couscous. Everyone loved the dish. The reality was that Orfeo really only knew how to prepare a handful of dishes that were in his personal cookbook, which was filled with recipes he had collected over many years. His method was quite simple: Whenever he had a great meal at a friend's place, he would first ask for the recipe written in their own hand. He would then set up a date to meet with them and cook the same meal while they explained the recipe and its subtleties, which of course could never be found in the recipe itself. He would add his own notes on the same page that they had written the recipe. He would then cook it for friends a few times, making adjustments to personalize the dish and make it his own.

They had already gone through a few bottles of wine, and the conversation was lively, spanning a wide variety of subjects. It had been a beautiful evening thus far, and although she never had any doubts, Carina was very pleased that Orfeo, who more often than not preferred to stay home alone with her, was such a hit with her friends.

One of Jessica's friends, Yu, was Chinese, and the couple in front of her commented that their child was learning Chinese in school. Before she could comment, Frank commented that pretty soon, everyone would be learning Chinese, as it would become the lingua franca.

Emil, sitting on the other end of the table near Orfeo, asked, "What is the lingua franca?"

Frank responded, "The lingua franca is the language in which business is conducted. For instance, most of the world now speaks English because the United States is presently the world superpower, and it behooves the rest of the world to speak English in order to do business with us."

"So pretty soon, the world will be speaking Spanish!"

"Unlikely, Emil. The lingua franca is not based on population growth. As I said before, in light of their rise as an economic powerhouse, we may all be speaking Chinese at the next dinner party." He raised his glass and toasted China. Everyone followed suit and clinked glasses while making exaggerated eye contact and laughing.

After the laughter had subsided, Emil opined that this didn't seem likely, because despite being vast, China kept to itself. Aimé, who was from Guinea Bissau, in Africa, responded quickly, pointing out that in fact the Chinese had a stronger presence in Africa than the Americans and Europeans combined. He turned to Yu. "Isn't this a fact?" Yu somewhat shyly nodded in the affirmative.

Frank, who was obviously used to dominating conversations and didn't like to be one-upped responded, "Well, that's interesting. It would appear to me that the problem with having China accepted as a widespread superpower is their lack of democracy."

Florent, who was French, piped in sarcastically, "Said like a true American!" There was silence in the room now, except for the music of the Gotan Project in the background that seemed to egg on the discussion.

Frank replied, as though challenged, "What do you mean by that?"

Florent, whose intention was to challenge what he perceived to be the typical, unfettered American babble that was rarely scrutinized or researched before being passed on with so much bravura, immediately replied that, in fact, America had been in decline for years and its biggest export was its culture, represented by the McDonald's franchise, obesity, and its brand of democracy, which had been a failure.

Frank, evidently disturbed by Emil's attack, started to respond when Carina politely interrupted, saying that perhaps a change in conversation would be in order. Orfeo chimed in, asking them who was ready for the third course. Everyone, except for Frank, seemed quite relieved to move on to another subject.

Orfeo returned from the kitchen with the large broiler and placed it in the center of the table. He apologized because this dish required a tagine, a tepee-like clay pot used in Morocco, but the one he owned was not large enough for the quantity of food he was serving. He turned all the lights off in the dining room and asked everyone to close their eyes and focus on the aroma. He opened the lid, and the aroma of the chicken, rosemary, thyme, and onions filled the dining room, allowing everyone to bask in the serenade regaling their sense of smell.

After everyone was served, Emil toasted. "To the one and only enduring lingua franca, love." Everyone cheered and attacked their meal in concentrated silence.

After a few minutes, Orfeo leaned over to Carina and whispered, "This is the greatest compliment to a chef—complete silence."

After a while, Yu, in reference to Frank's comment on China's lack of democracy, quite innocently pointed out that it would be an error to look upon a huge country like China and discuss it in terms of black or white. She added that China's society and government were rapidly evolving and provided many examples to prove her point. Everyone hesitatingly looked at Frank to take up Florent's challenge, but he maintained his focus on his plate and commented to Orfeo that the dish was outstanding.

Jennifer, who was sitting to Orfeo's right, agreed. She stated that it would be like branding America a capitalist society; she admitted that it predominantly was but added that there were numerous examples of socialistic tendencies, notably America's bailout of the banks, the bailout of General Motors, and corporate welfare, just to name a few. The discussion continued around the room, and Sophie, who was sitting next to Frank, added that she did not understand why Americans so often criticized socialist countries, since there were many benefits of socialism, as evidenced by countries such as France and Germany where there was a very high standard of living and people were quite happy. Sure, she added, they paid very high taxes, but they got great, free education, health care, and other benefits and therefore saw where their tax dollars were being spent.

Bill, an African-American, who was sitting at the other end of the table and had been silent up until that point, said, "The issue of capitalism versus socialism brings to mind a quote from Malcolm X. Do you mind if I read it?" Almost everyone nodded. He quickly turned on his iPhone and read, "'It is impossible for capitalism to survive, primarily because the system of capitalism needs some blood to suck. Capitalism used to be like an eagle, but now it's more like a vulture. It used to be strong enough to go and suck anybody's blood whether they were strong or not. But now it has become more cowardly, like the vulture, and it can only suck the blood of the helpless. As the nations of the world free themselves, then capitalism has less victims, less to suck, and it becomes weaker and weaker. It's only a matter of time in my opinion before it will collapse completely.'"

Xavier, Sophie's partner, who was sitting next to her, added, "That's powerful, but what about the issue of human rights? Isn't that a true measure of the progress a society is making? Does it matter whether a country is capitalist or socialist if it represses its people—or for that matter, other people—for its own benefit?"

Finally, Frank was no longer able to suppress himself, blurting out, "Who is suppressing whom? What are you talking about? Where are you getting your information?"

Xavier, ever polite, responded, "Frank, you hit the nail on the head. One of the major problems in this country is that the news media is controlled by relatively few major corporations, and consequently, the population only hears what 'they' want everyone to hear. Everything else is distorted."

"This is so true, Xavier," Florent added. "I happened to be traveling back and forth between France, England, and the United States during the Gulf War, and the discrepancy between what was being broadcast here and in the rest of the world was outrageous." Frank started to say something, but Florent continued. "The sad truth is that the closest approximation to what was being broadcast outside the US was ... what's his name again?" He snapped his fingers, trying to recall. "The comedian ..."

"Jon Stewart on the *Daily Show*," Bill blurted out with a big smile. "Dude, that guy is brilliant, and more and more, he's becoming my main source for the news."

Jennifer chimed in, "Me too. But isn't that pathetic? He's a self-avowed comedian who denies that he is presenting the news, but in fact, he's often more accurate than the main news channels and covers events that they tend to ignore."

Emil added, "Doesn't it make you think of George

Orwell's *1984*, or more recently, *The Hunger Games*, where the news of the rebellion and other issues was withheld from the people. I mean, how can you even form an educated opinion when you can't even get the facts? Do you know what I mean?"

"No, I really don't know what you mean," Frank replied, obviously exasperated. "I take personal offense to the fact that everyone is America-bashing and forgetting that it is America that provides you the freedom to do that. Why not move to China or Russia or Iran and try doing the same? Let's see how long you'd last."

After a period of awkward silence, Bill said, "Frank, it's not a simple black-and-white issue. Yes, America is great in many ways, but there are many problems as well."

Frank smirked as if asking for some proof.

"Would you like me to give you a list?" Bill looked around the table, asking everyone to feel free to chime in, and then continued, holding one finger up. "Let's start with corporate welfare, which accounts for huge expenditures, compared to the public assistance that the right wing perpetually fights to deny the poor and underprivileged." Bill then held up two fingers and said, "How about the prison system that incarcerates black men for long prison terms for being caught with a benign drug like marijuana in order to maintain the profits coming into the prison system? Should I go on?"

Frank was about to jump in, but Carina, noting

that the discussion again was becoming too heated and limited to just a few of the guests, interrupted, saying, "This is obviously a huge issue that we are not going to fix tonight, and if we continue on this tack, there might even be some casualties. So how about looking at this issue from another perspective?" Everyone except Frank seemed really relieved and nodded in the affirmative, thankful that the conversation would take another turn.

"If you'd indulge me, I propose we collectively engage in a thought experiment. Let's look forward to the future when humankind is hypothetically highly evolved. Let's take a moment and form an idea in our minds about what this would look like, ignoring the type of government these evolved human beings would choose. Instead, let's look at what we would likely find in that society." Carina paused while Orfeo opened another bottle of wine and poured it into the empty decanter. She then asked, "Would you find people who abhorred homosexuality and denied gay men and women the right to express their love openly? Would you find Islamic fundamentalists who would kill schoolgirls for the simple act of going to school and being educated? Would you find racism based on one's color? How about ritual female genital mutilation and the ensuing anthropologic discussions worldwide as to whether one should respect another society's right to this practice as a cultural imperative? Would that evolved society contribute to destroying the planet for the purpose of monetary gain when alternatives to fossil fuels have already demonstrated their potential? Would the views found on Fox News be prevalent? Don't you think that future generations will look upon us as barbarians for committing such crimes? I personally believe that they will look upon us with horror, and deservedly so."

Carina paused again, and reminded everyone that this was simply a thought experiment, an exploration of a far-out viewpoint. She continued, "With those questions in mind, I'd like to begin with the premise that, at least to me, the problem is not really a question of capitalism versus socialism or even of government but rather of human evolution."

Yu, who had felt left out of the prior conversation because of its aggressive nature, asked what Carina meant.

"What I mean," Carina responded, "is that the problem is simply due to human ignorance, plain and simple."

"Aiya!" Yu exclaimed jokingly. The others turned to her with puzzled looks, and she informed them that this was the Chinese way of saying "ouch!" Everyone laughed.

"My intent isn't to be insulting, but just think of any prior period in our history … let's take slavery, for instance. Would anyone disagree with the statement that a large proportion of white Americans considered the enslavement of other human beings to be completely natural and just and that it was even supported by major institutions, such as the Catholic Church?" Carina paused to make sure there weren't any objections before continuing. "Looking back at those people from our vantage point today, wouldn't you say that they were ignorant and racist … that they didn't know better?"

Everyone was eagerly waiting for the punch line. There were some skeptical looks across the table, but Carina pressed on.

"Imagine yourself to be part of that future society of evolved human beings. What would you think of our present world, which allows millions of children in Africa to die of hunger when industrial societies have more than enough food to feed them, or to cite the example that Bill used before, what would you think of the insane number of prisons built not so much for the purpose of justice but rather for profit? How would your future, evolved self judge this present iteration of humankind?" Carina paused, letting her words sink in. She continued, "Looking upon today's practices and rationalizations for those practices, our future selves would at worst consider our present selves barbaric and at best look upon our present selves as ignorant. In either case, we would condemn our present selves for our current practices."

Frank, who was calmer at this point, asked, "So what is your point?"

Xavier quickly interjected, before Carina had a

chance to reply, "Are you saying that since our limitation is evolution, there is nothing to do except wait? That we shouldn't even struggle to change things because there isn't any hope until we've evolved? Is that what you're saying?"

"That sounds incredibly defeatist, doesn't it?" Yu asked no one in particular.

Somehow, the point that Carina had made had captured everyone's attention. It was evident that everyone was really thinking about what she had said.

Bill added, "But isn't it our efforts toward change that drive our evolution? Isn't it the results of revolutionaries such as Martin Luther King, Malcolm X, and Gandhi, just to name a few, that drive our evolution?" Everyone at this point nodded in agreement with Bill and looked to Carina for her response.

Carina paused before responding, and when she felt that the concentration in the room was at its peak, she asked in return, "Is it those revolutionaries that drive evolution? This is certainly the contemporary and widely accepted point of view. Or is it rather the evolution of humankind itself that creates the waves that capture capable and talented individuals and bring those individuals and the masses to the historic moments when change is ignited and unavoidable?"

There was deep silence in the room. Orfeo turned to look at Carina and made eye contact, and she responded with a smile and a wink. There was a strong sense of complicity between them, and they both sensed that, somehow, the other understood exactly what was being proposed. While allowing her point to sink in, Orfeo opened another bottle of wine and went around the table again, filling everyone's glasses. He toasted, "To evolution!" and everyone clinked glasses, though more out of formality and, this time, without eye contact.

Carina continued, "Here's a way to think about this. Imagine being in the middle of the ocean with large waves rising and falling. In those waves lie all of history. Using Gandhi's example, there were likely hundreds of Gandhis at times prior to the ascendancy and the revolutionary accomplishments of the historical Gandhi, who was placed by history on the same crest as the repulsive actions of the British and the consciousness of the people, who were now able to actually understand the issues. Without each component aligning perfectly, nothing would have happened. It was the wave that created both the voice and consciousness to hear the message."

"Not only is that complete bullshit, but it's also incredibly insulting," Frank exclaimed with some emotion. "You're condemning humankind as ignorant. I give them ... us ... much more credit than that."

Xavier chimed in, "In your paradigm, there is no hope, no drive to push or demand change. We just wait until change happens."

Jennifer added, "That's a rather bleak viewpoint, but I do see your point."

Yu nodded in agreement and said, "You have to admit that, as Carina started out with, many of the actions and behaviors of our ancestors, from our perspective today, seem ignorant. It's not condemnation Frank but just an observed fact. I'm really beginning to get what Carina's saying. When children do stupid things, sure we get upset, but we recognize that it's their ignorance, which is normal for that particular stage in their development. As parents, we wait patiently for that stage to pass, because the fact is, we've all gone through the same developmental stages."

"Now we're going from being ignorant to being children," Frank responded sarcastically. "That makes me feel better."

Xavier was evidently really moved by this discussion and its implications and asked Carina, "So why bother trying to change anything? Should we simply allow the corporations and the right-wing agenda to roll over us with a smile and a bow while saying 'namaste'?"

The focus was now back on Carina, who looked at everyone at the table and genuinely appreciated the attention everyone was giving to her point. She took a sip of wine, closed her eyes for a second, and spoke. "First and foremost, I am not proposing a paradigm but rather a vision that is not my own. It is based on the ancient teachings of the Vedas, Hindus, Buddhists, and many sages who have walked the earth. Even Jesus Christ was noted to have said, 'Forgive them, Father, for they know not what they do.' I simply pointed out that whenever I hear people talking about politics, social justice, or human behavior, it is often done outside of the context of human evolution. I simply pointed out that, similar to the way humankind is only capable of visualizing a limited spectrum of light and is only able to hear within a limited decibel range, humankind has inherent limitations that are readily available for our analysis when we look back at our history. One such limitation is the inability to grasp those limitations when looking at contemporaries and ourselves. We are blind to our own limitations, which I would call, not in the least bit pejorative sense, ignorance."

Carina's tone changed now. She had at first given the air that she was simply exploring and sharing ideas without any particular agenda, but it was clear now that she was driving home a point. "Once one is able to grasp the depths of this ignorance and takes into account the larger forces that influence us, like the mighty waves that propel a massive ship in the same way it does flotsam— uncontrollably, in ways that the human intellect cannot even begin to comprehend—then one arrives at the same inevitable truth that all sages, all enlightened beings, and even the more often than not misguided established religions have come to." She again paused to allow everyone to mull over what she was saying, and then, with emphasis, concluded, "And that truth is to surrender to what is."

Both Frank and Xavier exclaimed, "Bullshit! Nonsense! I can't accept that!"

Carina, without any emotion, responded, "The raging ocean doesn't consider what that flotsam or the largest, most sophisticated cruise liner believes or accepts. It simply does what it does."

Xavier responded, "Then answer my question: Why bother doing anything? Why bother? Do we just wait for the corporations to understand that it is not in anyone's best interest, except their own, to rape the earth? Do we wait for the next Martin Luther King, Malcolm X, or Gandhi to take us to the next level?"

Orfeo, who had contributed absolutely nothing to this leg of the conversation, jumped in, saying, "I'm picking up on a disconnect here. I don't think that Carina is advocating for a utopian society but simply asking if we, in the here and now, would expect to find those examples in an evolved society. Correct me if I'm wrong, Carina, but from that perspective, the issue that you're trying to bring to light is that we are presently acting out of limited perspectives, in the same way that our ancestors did before us." He looked at Carina and pointed out that he thought some of the strong reactions that she had precipitated came from her choice of the word *ignorance*. He continued, "The example that comes to mind is how a great mind, such as Galileo, was persecuted for suggesting that the earth revolves around the sun rather than the reverse, which was the ignor—" Orfeo caught himself and redirected himself to say, "The limited perspective and majority belief at that time. I really get it now. What Carina is saying is that we are presently experiencing the actions of the not-as-yet-recognized limited beliefs and actions of those in power." He again looked over at Carina with a big smile and asked if he'd gotten it right. She nodded in the affirmative, told everyone to wait a second, and leaned over and kissed him. Everyone simultaneously cried, "Awwww!"

Carina continued, directing her comments to Xavier. "It is a question of time for this era of ignorance—no, Orfeo, I don't like euphemisms—to come to a close. Revolutionaries, such as Gandhi and Martin Luther King, did not emerge in a vacuum. There were extenuating circumstances that commanded their attention and consequently forged their beliefs and convictions. Those same extenuating circumstances commanded the attention of the masses and consequently cultivated their ears and hearts to prepare them to receive the message of those designated by history to be its messenger. Likewise, Hitler, Mussolini, and Mao Tse Tung could not have captured the hearts and imaginations of the masses outside of a prescribed timeframe that demanded a voice. They simply complied. Either way, it's the same process."

"How do you propose that this should happen?" Emil, who had been rather quiet and pensive, asked.

"I do not believe that it is something that one can 'propose.' That idea comes from the typically arrogant assumption that the piece of flotsam in the ocean has a say in its experience. Rather, it is something that evolves as a natural movement in the evolution of humankind. It cannot be forced, just as the Civil Rights Movement, the fall of the Berlin Wall, the Arab Spring, and countless other examples could not have occurred before they did. Consequently, the next revolution will not be a result of bloodshed but rather of the evolution of human consciousness."

"In my humble opinion ..." Carina started, but then she interrupted herself to say, "For the record, I am not suggesting that I have the answers. I'm only sharing a perspective that I find infinitely more interesting and compelling than pitting Democrats against Republicans, adding a spice of Libertarians, or arguing the benefits of socialism versus capitalism. So, as I was saying, the answer to that question is that we do what we must do. That is the human drama. As Shakespeare said in *Macbeth* 'Tomorrow, and tomorrow, and tomorrow, creeps in this petty pace from day to day, to the last syllable of recorded time; and all our yesterdays have lighted fools the way to dusty death. Out, out, brief candle! Life's but a walking shadow, a poor player that struts and frets his hour upon the stage and then is heard no more. It is a tale told by an idiot, full of sound and fury signifying nothing.'

"And on that note, now that I've strutted and fretted my hour upon the stage, the idiot has told her tale, full of sound and fury, signifying absolutely nothing, I'll say no more except to ask who's up for a kick-ass dessert?"

CHAPTER 5

On the Run

Rude Awakening

On the following morning, Carina and Orfeo fell in and out of sleep wrapped in each other's arms. They enjoyed fragments of many delightful dreams interspersed with brief exchanges of tender, loving pleasantries, never knowing whether these exchanges took place in their dreams or in reality. Their bedroom window, on the fourth floor, was within an alley that created resounding echoes, such that someone on the street whispering in front of the alley would sound as though he or she were in their bedroom. This was annoying most of the time, but every morning, except on the coldest days of winter, the birds would park on the fire escapes, and their melodies would fill the alley, creating the impression that they were in some idyllic countryside. On such mornings, Orfeo would occasionally open his eyes and, looking at this beauty who lay before him in all her splendor, express such gratitude to the Universe for bringing her back into his life and whisper in her sleeping ear, "I love you madly!" Then he would gently hover back into a deep sleep.

On this morning, Carina abruptly awakened Orfeo when she suddenly jumped out of bed and slyly peered out the window. Orfeo was about to speak when she, with all the grace and speed of a tiger pouncing on its prey after patiently stalking it, jumped on the bed and firmly covered his mouth. She gave him a look that was so forceful that he immediately, without understanding, silenced himself. He had never seen her like this.

"They found us," she said ever so matter-of-factly, all the while still covering his mouth. He was about to ask her what was going on, but she again gave him that look and covered his mouth even more forcefully.

"Do you love me?" she asked. Orfeo's mouth was still covered and even hurt a bit from the pressure, so he simply nodded yes.

"I really need you to trust me right now. It's a matter of life and death. Orfeo, can you do that right now, without asking any questions?"

He hesitated, and she pressed on his mouth even harder, insisting. "Orfeo, right now! I need you to do exactly what I say. Right now! There's no time to explain. Okay?"

He had never seen her like this and knew that whatever was happening, it was serious. He nodded yes.

"Without one sound—not one word—get dressed, grab your wallet, passport, car keys, and whatever cash and credit cards you have, and be ready to split in the next ten minutes. Can you do this for me?" It was clearly more of a directive than a question. He again nodded yes, and she put a finger to his mouth, indicating that he had to be silent. "Let's go," she commanded. "We have ten minutes."

Carina again moved to the window and peaked out. While getting up to go to the bathroom to piss, he heard her whisper to herself, "Shit, shit, shit!" By the time he had come out of the bathroom, she was dressed and was pulling a box and two cases out of the closet. She gave him a look that insisted he get his shit together rapidly and stop dillydallying. He had never heard her speak with such authority and intensity. While gathering his stuff, he looked over and noticed that she had emptied one of the cases onto the bed. There were three guns, bullet cartridges, silencers, two knives, documents, several passports, a lot of cash, and a holster that she was putting on very quickly.

Seeing this, he stopped in his tracks. He had a shocked, stupefied, and incredulous look on his face, and his mouth dropped open. He couldn't believe what he was seeing. She looked him deep in the eyes with such an intensity that it made her seem like a completely different person than the woman with whom he had just been lying in bed.

As she stepped away to gather her weapons, she could see that he was distraught and confused, so she walked back to him and gave him a big hug and a long, wet kiss. "Babe, I love you so much ... I promise I'll explain everything later … but we really have to roll right now. Please … trust me." She smiled in that way that always melted him to the core.

He was sitting on the edge of the bed as she loaded the cartridges, rapidly placed the silencers, and holstered the guns in a manner that demonstrated that she certainly was not a novice. She then opened the longer case and unwrapped a cloth, revealing a samurai sword and two medium-sized swords. She put on a utility belt and loaded everything, and then she threw on a long overcoat similar to the one she had worn the night they met. He wondered if she had been as armed to the hilt on that evening as she was now and considered what would have happened if he had been some asshole inappropriately pushing himself on her. What a thought!

She sat next to him and kissed him again. She held out the third gun, suggesting that he should take it. "Have you ever shot a gun before?" she asked. He shook his head no. "No worries. Just do exactly as I say, when I say. If I say shoot, just point and shoot. No second guessing … No thinking!" She paused to make sure he had registered everything. "Orfeo, this is not a game, okay? This is life or death … got it?" Again she paused, waiting for his acknowledgment. "I say shoot, you point and shoot … Okay, let's go!"

She opened the front door, gun in hand, and signaled for him to follow. He was about to head down the stairs, but she grabbed his arm and indicated with hand signals that they were going up to the roof. Orfeo started to say something, but she immediately silenced him, shaking her head in a way that made it clear that he should shut his trap.

She ran up the stairs, looking back every once in a while to make sure that he was close behind. They went up to the roof, crossed over two buildings, climbed down a fire escape in the back alley, and walked through the alleys to exit onto the next block over.

"Where's the car?" she asked.

Orfeo had to think for a moment but then remembered that it was one block away.

"We're going to jump into the first cab we see and circle around to the car."

As luck would have it, there were no cabs in sight, so they finally called an Uber, which arrived in less than three minutes.

Orfeo started to ask a question, but she stopped him with a kiss, saying, "We're almost to the car, my love. I'll explain everything later."

They jumped into the car, and she drove off at high speed. He asked impatiently, almost with the tone of a sulking child told to sit in the corner, "Can I talk now?"

She looked over to him, smiled, and responded. "Of course you can, my love. Sorry I couldn't talk before; it was a little hectic back there." She beamed one of her disarmingly charming smiles and asked in a half-joking tone, "What's on your mind, love?"

"What's on my mind?" Orfeo asked, becoming agitated. "What's on my mind?" He closed his eyes, trying to calm himself, and exhaled deeply. After a minute, he opened his eyes and continued calmly. "What the hell is going on? Who are you?"

She laughed. "What do you mean, who am I?" She looked over to him with a loving smile. "I'm the woman of your dreams who loves you more than anything in this whole wide world. That's who I am. Next question."

Orfeo was not at all amused and again, after a pause, asked, "Carina, what the hell is going on? What happened backed there? Where did the guns come from? Who the hell has silencers ... and a samurai sword ... really?"

They were on the highway now, and she looked straight ahead at the road, weaving in and out of traffic at high speed while thinking about how best to answer his questions.

"Well?" he insisted. "What haven't you been telling me?"

She looked at him with a dead-serious look, returned her gaze to the road, and asked softly, "Orfeo, what haven't you been telling me?" She looked at him again for a brief moment that, for him, seemed like a long time, and it unnerved him.

"What do you mean? I'm not the one with guns and silencers. I'm certainly not an expert, but I've watched a lot of movies. The only people who have silencers are killers, assassins." He paused.

"Is that what you think? That I'm an assassin!" She paused. "If I wasn't driving, I'd ask you to stare into my eyes and tell me whether you truly believed that. Then I'd kick you in the balls!"

"Well, it's obvious that you have a lot of secrets that you haven't shared … some really big ones that have to do with 9mms and samurai swords. What the hell am I supposed to think?"

"Orfeo, are you telling me that you don't have secrets?" She waited. When he didn't answer, she yelled in frustration, "Bullshit! You are so full of shit!"

"Are you trying to turn this around now? You hand me a gun and tell me 'I say shoot, you point and shoot … okay,' and I'm the one who's full of shit?"

There was silence. Carina looked straight ahead and drove. Orfeo thought she was ignoring him to avoid the confrontation, but in fact, she was thinking about which of the exit strategies she had prepared would be best. One plan was to head straight for the airport and fly to India, where they couldn't be traced, but that meant that she would have to leave her guns behind, which would be risky. Plan B was to go to her friend's country home, which her friend had offered to let her use while she was traveling on business to Dubai. This appealed to her, because it would give her time to sort things out. She knew it was inevitable that they would catch up to them, but like a criminal who's planned a heist without considering the possibility of getting caught, she hadn't been expecting this.

She looked over to Orfeo as she would have on any other beautiful day and, in the most loving voice, asked, "So how long were you looking for me, and how long were you stalking me before you had the balls to say hello?" Bam! This floored him. She continued to drive in silence. Her question had not been intended to solicit an answer but was simply a means to cut through the bullshit and change the tack of what she felt to be an inane discussion for which she had no time or patience. Without looking over at all, Carina continued in a matter-of-fact tone. "Sweetie, you don't have to answer that, but let's chill for a while until we get to where we're going. Then we'll put all our cards on the table. Okay?"

Orfeo was completely dumbfounded. He sat back in his chair and looked out the side window. She reached over with her right hand and, holding his chin, turned his head toward her. Looking in his eyes, she said, "Babe, our lives will change completely now. Do you understand? ... There is no going back." She waited for a reaction that didn't happen. He merely looked back into her eyes with a confused, dazed look. "You know what doesn't change, and what will never change?" No answer. "Take a guess. Come on, babe! Take a guess!"

He looked down and then straight ahead, obviously avoiding eye contact.

"What will never change, under any circumstances, is my love for you." She paused. "You sang for me once, 'Ain't no mountain high enough! Ain't no river low enough! Ain't no valley wide enough to keep me from gettin' to you, babe!' Well, multiply that by the power of a million and by all the eternities that we've been separated, and then you'll begin to have an inkling of my love for you."

Orfeo was notably caught off-guard by her words *all the eternities that we've been separated.*

"Welcome home, babe! Now fasten your seatbelt, 'cause it's going to be a bumpy ride … but we're together. I love you!"

It was dark by the time they arrived at her friend's cottage. It was small and cozy. They unpacked the groceries they had picked up on the way, and Orfeo putzed nervously around, making himself seem busy.

Carina sat on the couch and broke the silence. "Come sit with me, love."

He gave her a forced smile, walked over, and sat on the opposite side of the couch.

"Really?" she said, almost laughing as she slid over and pulled his arm around her. She gave him small kisses on his face and lips. "Babe, I know this is a lot to take in, but it's all good. We're together aren't we?"

"When were you going to tell me the truth?" he asked.

Carina responded: "When were you going to tell

me the truth?" She continued to give him soft kisses. "Listen, the fact is that we love each other profoundly, always have, and neither of us wanted to crash this wave that we were riding. *N'est-ce pas?*" She sat up and looked into his eyes. "Correct me if I'm wrong, but you were thinking to yourself, 'To hell with all these past lives, the spiritual mumbo-jumbo, and Consciousness. This is the real deal here and now.'"

He was still silent.

"Am I wrong?" She held his face in her hands, forcing him to look into her eyes.

He looked down and shook his head no.

"Well, I felt the same way. To hell with everything except the here and now. Remember Abbey Lincoln singing 'Live for Life'?"

He didn't respond.

She continued, "Come on, you've sung this to me a million times. 'Yesterday's a mem'ry, gone for good forever, and tomorrow is a guess. What is real is what is here and now, and here and now is all that we possess. So take my hand, and we will take the moment, if for just the moment's happiness.' Well, this is the here and now, and it's all that we possess. It's been amazing, hasn't it? But right now, here and now, we're in deep shit, and I need you to get yourself together. I don't want to lose you again."

"Lose me again!" he said as he pulled her hands

down. "You were the one who was lost, and it took me so many wasted lifetimes to finally find you."

"Babe, I know it seems like that's what happened, but it's not. I'll explain everything, but right now"—she changed her demeanor with a devious, devilish look on her face, now speaking in a sexy, sultry voice—"how about some crazy, passionate, monkey-chandelier sex?"

For the first time since they were forced out of bed earlier that day, Orfeo smiled and allowed himself to be swept away by this woman, whom he'd thought he knew so well but now realized he didn't know at all. The guns, the samurai swords, the confidence and authority—all of this flashed through his mind as she kissed him and, like Beatrice did Dante, led him gently into uncharted territory. She had never seemed sexier to him, and never before, in all his human incarnations, had he experienced such sexual bliss. That night, she transported him to other dimensions that he had never explored.

When he woke up from a deep, refreshing sleep, she was already up and dressed. The guns were disassembled on the kitchen table, and she was cleaning each part meticulously. When she noticed him, she leapt up, gave him a tremendous hug, and sat him at the table. She nonchalantly pushed all the gear to one side and poured him a cup of coffee.

"Babe, I know you stopped drinking coffee, but you wouldn't believe what I found in the cabinet. Did you know, Mr. Know-It-All, that there are only three coffees in the world with the 'super premium' designation? Well, there's Kona, from Hawaii, Blue Mountain, from Jamaica, and low and behold"—she held the package next to her face as though in a TV commercial—*"yo te présento, de Puerto Rico, el café Alto Grande,* the coffee of popes and kings! And you, my love, are my one and only king." She slowly poured him a cup, insisting that he luxuriate in the aroma. "Just take a whiff, love. Isn't that heavenly?"

He brought his head down to the cup, closed one nostril with a finger, and gave an exaggerated inhalation as though he were doing a line of cocaine. Then he threw his head back and, while shaking his head back and forth, let out, "Whoa! Now that's some good shit!" They both laughed their heads off.

Orfeo, taking another sip of the coffee, asked, "Do you remember the scene from *Pulp Fiction* when John Travolta and Samuel Jackson accidentally shoot the kid in the head in the back of the car and go to Quentin Tarantino's place to have the car cleaned? Tarantino gives Jackson a cup of coffee, and while he talks about the mess of blood and brains in the back of the car, Jackson takes a sip of the coffee and exclaims, 'Now that's a damn good cup of coffee!'" They both laughed so hard that they had tears in their eyes.

He got up, gave her a big hug, and said, "I love you madly." Then he reflexively added his usual, "Thank you for being you." After saying this, he caught himself, paused for a second, and followed it, as though amused, with the thought, "But will the real Carina please stand up."

She hugged him so hard that it took his breath away. "I'll tell you what, it's a gorgeous day out. Let's have breakfast first and then take a long walk and have a picnic. Are you in?"

Orfeo nodded yes.

"Great! We'll have plenty of time for me to explain everything. You make breakfast, and I'll prepare the picnic." While they were both preparing, Carina added, "I remember taking a nice hike on a mountain trail not too far from here. The vistas are breathtaking."

"You're breathtaking!" Orfeo interjected.

She responded, "That's so sweet. Thank you. You're not too bad yourself, kid. By the way, you should bring a jacket. I remember it getting pretty windy up there."

They drove the car to the trailhead and followed the trail. Carina led the way, at first walking at a leisurely pace and then gradually increasing to a really brisk walk. The path went deep into the woods, ascending gradually up the mountainside with an occasional steep climb. Orfeo was slightly winded trying to keep pace with Carina, who was obviously in better physical condition. As they proceeded, he began falling way behind and was struggling to breathe. She waited for him on top of one of the steep ascents and gave him some water.

Carina pointed out, seemingly unaffected by the brisk

pace and ascent of their hike, "Isn't the air so refreshing up here? Did you notice how deeply you slept? I always have the best sleep in the country. I'm convinced that it's because of the density of the air."

"Yeah, I completely agree," Orfeo said in between his gasps for air. "The crazy day yesterday also helped. I was exhausted."

"Look over there!" Carina pointed up to sky. "There's a hawk just hovering over the mountain. Don't you wish you could fly?"

"Absolutely!" Orfeo responded, still noticeably out of breath.

"Are you ready to continue?" Carina asked. But she didn't really wait for an answer. "Hang in there, babe. We're almost there."

"*No problema!*" He smiled back.

After another two miles of a relatively steep ascent, Orfeo caught up to where Carina was waiting in a beautiful clearing. There they had a 360-degree view around them.

"Wow! This is amazing!" Orfeo walked up to her, still out of breath, and gave her a hug and a kiss, almost forgetting the purpose of their hike. He breathed deeply while hugging her tight.

Carina laid out a blanket, followed by a veritable feast of fresh bread, cheese, sausage, hummus, fruits, wine, and a thermos filled with the "coffee of popes and kings."

He couldn't believe that she had been carrying all that weight and still managed to dust him on the trail.

"Are you hungry yet?" she asked as she beckoned him to sit.

As Orfeo sat, he noted the butt of her 9mm peeking out of the knapsack. This very quickly brought him back to the purpose of their hike.

"Starving," Orfeo responded.

Carina dipped her finger into the hummus and licked it. "This hummus is so good. You have to try it."

"Can you spread some on a piece of bread for me while I open the wine?" Orfeo asked.

"Sure, but you don't 'spread' hummus, silly. You 'wipe' it," she quipped. "That's what the Israelis say."

"Okay. Can you please wipe some hummus on your ass so I can lick it?" Orfeo joked back.

"You, mister"—she feigned a pimp slap—"have a one-track mind!"

After eating, they lay down perpendicular to each other, completely satiated. She laid her head on Orfeo's stomach and dozed off for a while as a cool breeze offset the heat of the noon sun. They awakened, feeling completely refreshed, with the hawk hovering above them. They just lay silently for a long while, basking in the sun and the blue, cloudless sky.

Orfeo finally broke the silence, saying, "I wish we could spend the rest of our lives like this. Wouldn't that be so wonderful?"

"Hmmm," she purred like a cat. "That would be so nice." There was again a long silence. Neither of them wanted to spoil that glorious moment of bliss.

Finally, Orfeo asked, "So what happened?"

"What do you mean, what happened?"

"Why did you leave Consciousness?"

Carina sat up to face him. "For the same reason we always left Consciousness and got dumped into the earth-realm. I got distracted, and for a long time, I couldn't get back."

"I guess that was the wrong question. We had both been dumped into the earth-realm many times before, but we would eventually return. You were gone for much longer than usual. I waited and waited. I got worried that something had happened and spent lifetimes looking for you. What happened?"

Carina took his hand and responded, "Well, at first, it was the usual. I was lost. I couldn't remember. Then, in one particular lifetime, I met some enlightened beings, who were aligned with the forces of the Light. They turned me onto the truth of what was really going on ..."

"The truth?"

"Yes. They taught me about this battle of Consciousness that's been raging throughout the ages and how the odds were then tipping in the favor of the Dark forces, whose leader was..."

Orfeo, appearing confused, interrupted, "Carina, what are you talking about? Who were these so-called enlightened beings? What is this nonsense about a battle, Light forces versus Dark forces? How come I've never even heard about this?"

Carina put her hand on his chest. "Orfeo, please just listen to me. This is really important."

"I'm sorry. All of this is a bit much. Please go on."

"It'll all make sense soon. Just trust me, okay?" Carina rattled Orfeo's hand she was holding and asked, "You trust me, don't you?"

"Yes."

"Dude, that was not a very convincing response. You really need to work on that!"

"Be patient with me. You've just dumped a truckload of shit on my head, and I'm knee-deep, trying get my bearings."

"Orfeo, I completely understand. Are you ready for the rest?"

He sat up and responded, "Shoot!"

"So, I learned that there was this battle between the Light and Dark forces over the consciousness of humankind, and the leader of the Dark forces is this dude they call the Master."

"The Master? This is beginning to sound like a really bad movie."

"Orfeo, this is important!"

Orfeo lay on his side and said, "Sorry. I promise I won't interrupt again."

"All of a sudden, I had found my purpose. To be on

the side of the Light, to battle against the Dark forces of the Master became my highest calling. Throughout all my lifetimes, it was the central theme that kept me going."

Carina poured a glass of wine, took a sip, and then handed Orfeo the glass. He took the glass but didn't drink. Carina asked with a big grin on her face, "Would you like me to 'wipe' some hummus for you?"

Orfeo finally smiled and shook his head no, saying, "Thanks, but I'm stuffed." And he handed the glass of wine back to her.

"So, I dedicated myself to becoming a warrior of the Light. I spent lifetimes mastering the martial arts, weapons, and meditation and searching for the Resistance."

"Did you find them?"

"No. I've learned that since the Master's forces have become so strong that the Resistance has been in hiding, only revealing themselves when absolutely necessary. In the meantime, I've been preparing myself."

"So, did you ever consider returning to Consciousness?"

"Of course! I spent the vast majority of my lifetimes without any awareness of Consciousness. I was just living out a human existence. When I learned about the war against human consciousness, I found my purpose but still didn't have a clue about where I'd come from, and I had no recollection of you, of us. When I finally remembered—remembered you—my work to make myself into the best possible Light warrior for this battle became even more important, because I felt not only that I had to get back but that I had to protect you, protect Consciousness. Do you understand now?"

"But why didn't you come back to Consciousness, to me?"

"I did, Orfeo" Carina said while caressing his cheek. "I did return, but then you weren't there. You were gone."

"So, we were both on wild-goose chases searching for each other."

"Yup."

Orfeo appeared perplexed, which then suddenly changed to frustration when a light bulb appeared to go off in his head. He removed her hand from his cheek and asked, "So when I found you, you knew who I was? You knew exactly who I was this entire time ever since we found each other. Why the lies? Why the games?"

"Babe, I didn't know if I could trust you."

"What! What are you talking about?"

"I had been following you for a while and wanted so badly to reveal myself, but …"

Orfeo was now becoming irritated. "But what!"

"Whoa! Chill out, brother! You had been following me for a while as well. Why didn't you approach me?" She paused, waiting for him to collect himself and calm down. "Well … I'm still waiting for an answer."

Orfeo hesitated, knowing she had made an excellent point. He started to mumble something when she interrupted.

"Babe, don't worry about it. Let's just agree it was complicated for the both of us. Okay?"

"Yes, it was certainly complicated enough before you added all of this other stuff."

Carina went off into the woods to pee. She returned but remained standing up. She extended her arms to the sky and threw her head back, exclaiming, "What an absolutely perfect day!" Not hearing a response from Orfeo, she turned and looked at him. He looked up at her, one hand blocking the sun from his eyes and the other gesturing "comme ci, comme ça."

She walked over to him and made a ridiculous contorted facial expression while mimicking his "comme ci, comme ça" hand gesture. Then she suddenly dropped her knees into his stomach and tickled him, causing him to double over on his side and laugh uncontrollably. He could barely get out the words "yes, yes, I agree ... I agree." He grabbed her and hugged her tightly in order to stop her from tickling him, and after a bit of struggle, they settled into each other's arms and just lay together. After a while, he said, "Yes, it's a perfect day."

They remained in each other's arms in silence for a long time before she sat up, tapped him on the chest, and indicated that it was time to go. She packed up, threw on the backpack, and started walking down the hill. After a few steps, she stopped, looked back, and said, "This time, keep up!"

Lobotomy and McCallan 25

It was just getting dark when they arrived back at the house. After they both showered, Carina sat directly in front of Orfeo, their knees touching, and held both of his hands. "Are you okay?" she asked. "I know it's a lot to take in, but think about how difficult it would have been for you to explain to me how many lifetimes you spent searching for me. It's mind-blowing, isn't it?"

Orfeo nodded in agreement.

"Babe, if only you could know how difficult it was for me to hold myself back and not run over to you, hug you, and kiss you. I died every day knowing that I had to wait until I could be sure that the Master hadn't compromised you.

"And now … Are you certain now?"

"Yes. I knew that shortly after we hooked up but then just didn't know where to begin. Isn't that the same reason you didn't tell me?"

"Yeah. I was completely swept away with all the crazy emotions I had being with you, the mad love we were sharing. After a while, nothing else mattered except being with you. I even stopped thinking about Consciousness."

She had tears in her eyes now. They embraced each other for a long time, weeping in each other's arms. While still in their deep embrace, Carina, weeping softly, continued, "I wanted to explain everything, share everything I learned, so we could be a team again, but now with a higher purpose. I just didn't know how or where to begin."

Orfeo pulled away just enough to make eye contact. "Honestly, I'm not really sure that I understand what this war is about … but it's all good. Right now, it's all a blur, and I can't quite get my arms around it. Regardless, what's important is that I'm with you, and I trust you implicitly. I'm ready to follow you to the ends of the universe."

"Thanks for saying that. It's really important … not just to me. There's a lot at stake." They both sat down again. "Would you like some tea?"

"Actually, what I need is a shot of something strong. Is there any alcohol here?"

Carina got up, walked over to the cabinet, and returned with a bottle of McCallan 25. With one of her devious smiles, she said in an English accent, "Will this be to your liking, sir?"

"Wow! Your friend has good taste! It's just what the doctor ordered." Carina poured two glasses. Orfeo held his glass, and she did the same. They looked in each other's eyes, each waiting for the other to toast. They both started to speak at the same time, laughed, and then indicated that the other should start.

"After you, love," Carina said.

"No, *amor*, you go first," Orfeo insisted.

She settled it with a firm glare, a tilt of her head, and one raised eyebrow.

Orfeo complied and, looking deeply into her eyes, toasted, "Peace, love, and chocolate." They clinked their glasses, and Orfeo closed his eyes, savoring the taste of the Scotch as it bathed and saturated his palate. A Billy Holiday lyric came to his mind:

You go to my head
Like a sip of sparkling burgundy brew,
and I find the very mention of you
Like the kicker in a julep or two.

What a day! he thought to himself. There were so many thoughts running through his head … so many questions. He accepted that everything would become clearer in its own time. For now, he was content to surrender to the moment and to Carina. He opened his eyes, looked at her, and said in the sincerest way, "Thank you … thank you for everything … thank you for your patience with me …"

"Oh, baby! That's so sweet! You don't have to thank me. That's what love is: being there no matter what …

good times, bad times, hell or high water. Thank you! In your own way, you did the same for me, searching for me all those lifetimes. I can't imagine how distraught you must have been. Thank you!" They embraced each other again even harder, glasses still in hand. Carina felt a drop spill on her shoulder and whispered in his ear, "Careful, love, you just spilled about $100 worth of Scotch on my shoulder." They both giggled.

"Orfeo," she said, changing to a more serious tone of voice, "for the record, this is the last drink we take." Orfeo was never really much of a drinker, but he seemed surprised by the timing and tone of her statement. Carina explained. "Babe, for the rest of our lives, we'll be looking over our shoulders, and we'll have to be ready to fight for our lives at a second's notice. We can't take any chances and put our guards down by being fuzzy with even one drink"

"Really?" Half in jest but mostly serious, he flippantly added, "Why? Are you afraid of dying?"

Carina knew exactly what he was trying to say. They had both evolved sufficiently to know that there was no such thing as dying. The concept of death was nothing more than a construct. Death, in fact, was more like changing your clothes in preparation to go to another event. Orfeo had "committed suicide" innumerable times whenever he believed that a particular lifetime was a dead end in regard to his search for Carina, because he knew without any doubt that he could step into another life at will to continue the search for his love.

Carina took his hand, sat on the edge of her seat, and responded, "No, my love, we both know better than to be afraid of something that doesn't exist. It's not death that I fear. What I fear is losing you forever. What I fear is having either of us stuck, forever, in the endless cycle of illusory death and rebirth without the knowledge that we are Consciousness. Remember your so-called lost lives? At least you had a deep, subconscious awareness, a feeling that there was something more. You desired more. That gap between your human experience and what, at a subconscious level, you desired and even knew was your birthright resulted in a level of suffering that propelled you forward. It was a catalyst."

She paused, allowing him to absorb what she was saying, before continuing. "This is why enlightened individuals who graced the earth-realm knew better than to take away someone's suffering, even when it would have been so easy for them. They must have seemed so cruel, but they knew that people's suffering is the only glimmer of hope to stir them vigorously enough to break them free of the quicksand that condemns them to this existence and to lifetimes of dreaming. The wise ones knew that the more painful the experience, the better the chance to wake up."

"Now imagine being lobotomized and never having the opportunity, the slightest hope of waking up. Just lifetime after lifetime, for all eternity"—Carina gestured at the room as a reflection of the earth-realm—"of this." She paused again, and then added, "Sisyphus without a purpose, condemned to push that rock up the hill only to have it roll down the other side, never realizing the futility of it all, that there was something missing in his life."

Orfeo was deeply affected by what she was saying and was drifting in the ramifications of her words. Carina gently squeezed his hand to get his full attention. "This is what I'm afraid of. Do you understand now?"

"Yes," Orfeo responded. "This is some really deep shit." He stood up and poured the rest of his drink down the sink."

"Orfeo, what the fuck are you doing?" she shouted, half-serious and half-amused.

"Well, the only thing that I can think of worse than what you just described is penile dysfunction," he said with the most serious expression he could muster. He then jumped into a ridiculous karate stance and, in an even more ridiculous, uninterpretable foreign accent, said, "An' no one take ma woman away while have breath in body." They both laughed so hard that their ribs hurt.

"Come here, you silly man ... right now!"

Orfeo slowly walked over and, at the last minute, threw himself on his knees and buried his head in her lap, saying, "I love you so much."

"I love you more," she said without a pause after his last word.

With his head still buried in her lap, he said, almost to himself, "When the student is ready, the teacher appears."

After a long pause, she picked up his head with her hands and brought her glass of Scotch to his lips. After he took a big sip, he again closed his eyes and savored the smooth, woody flavors on his palate. She waited until he opened his eyes, and without any hint of joking around, told him, "Orfeo, I feel I need to clarify. You are not, in fact, ready. I don't want to pop your bubble, but you are not even close to being ready." She allowed that to sink in, still holding his face in her hands.

"What I'm talking about is war, babe," she continued. "It's a war between the Light and the Dark. Imagine the universe without Light, without Consciousness. Imagine a universe without the light of Consciousness to guide us, nourishing the journeys of those, like you, on the return. Imagine never having a 'wise one' suddenly appear at that precise moment in your life, offering that little, seemingly inconsequential piece of the puzzle that allows you to take a step in a direction that averts lifetimes of being lost. Without the Light, we are all lobotomized patients in a psychiatric ward, guarded by other lobotomized individuals. No one knows why they are there or where 'there' actually is. How fucked up is that!"

Orfeo took the glass from her hand and gulped the rest of the McCallan down as though it were a shot of cheap Tequila, grimacing as he felt the burn in his chest. "That's really heavy!"

"Babe, I'm really sorry that I've had to lay all of this on you like this, but the fact is, I really need you. I can't do this on my own. We need each other … and there isn't a lot of time." She paused for a brief moment, looking around the room. She lifted the glass to her lips to take a sip of the McCallan but found the glass empty. "Bastard! You could've saved me a sip! Could you please bring the bottle over? This requires another drink." While he poured the McCallan in both of their glasses, she asked, "Are you in?"

He handed her the glass, clinked it with his own, and asked, "Do I have a choice?"

"The truth?" she asked rhetorically, looking into her glass and admiring how the light reflected against the gold-colored liquid as she swirled it in her glass. "Absolutely not. The difference is whether we go into this side by side as partners or with me having to carry you like a cripple." She finally looked up at Orfeo. "Love, I doubt we'll get very far if I have to carry you."

Orfeo took another gulp and finished his glass but didn't say a word.

Carina got up, took the glass from his hand, and gave him a firm kiss on the lips. "Let's get some rest. You start training first thing in the morning."

Orfeo had a surprised look on his face. "Training? For what?"

As she walked toward the bathroom, with her back turned, she said while waving her finger in the air, "War, love. Training for war. The only war that was ever worth fighting for in the history of humankind: the war for Consciousness." Just before stepping into the bathroom, she half turned. "It's not the most important thing or the least important thing. It's the only thing." She then left Orfeo in the room by himself to ponder the bomb she had just dropped on his lap. But a moment later, she suddenly stuck her head out of the bathroom sideways, catching him by surprise, and with the biggest smile, asked, "Did I mention today how much I love you?"

He could only bring himself to smile, shaking his head from side to side, still in shock over everything that had transpired. He walked over to the counter and poured himself another drink. He realized that he was already quite buzzed. As he cherished the last time he would experience the luscious fragrance and taste of the McCallan making love to his mouth, the voice of Abbey Lincoln came into his mind. *Yes,* he thought to himself, *live for life.*

Orfeo woke up to the sound of Lee Morgan's solo in "Ceora," which they both loved. Carina just loved the recording, but Orfeo, who considered himself to be a "solologist" à la Dean Benedetti, really only listened to

Lee Morgan's solo. Dean Benedetti was so inspired by Charlie Parker that he followed him everywhere and would only record his solos. "Imagine that!" Orfeo would often say. "Here's this guy who is overlooking the 'music' on which the solos are based and the other legendary players who preceded and followed Charlie 'Yardbird' Parker on the stage, such as Miles Davis, Dizzy Gillespie, Thelonious Monk, and Bud Powell. He would hit the record button only when Bird started his solo and the stop button a few seconds after he ended. Bird's solos were obviously genius, but it's incredibly frustrating to hear the start of Miles Davis's or some other legend's solos and then be abruptly cut off. Imagine that! Now that's badass."

Orfeo would take solos that moved him—Dino Saluzzi's solo in "Falling Grace" on Al Di Meola's *World Sinfonia* album, Bobby's McFerrin's scat solo in "Moondance," Lee Morgan's and Clifford Brown's solos in "A Night in Tunisia," Miles Davis's solo in "So What?," and almost every solo performed by Dexter Gordon on the *Ballads* album, especially in "Willow Weep for Me"—listen to them over and over again, isolated from the song itself, and dissect them. He could hum every note of these solos. Interestingly, Orfeo was never interested in being a musician himself; he simply loved the solos.

After taking in Lee Morgan's solo, he was amused as he imagined Carina playing with her guns. This thought was cut short by a throbbing headache that hit him as soon as he sat up. He thought back on the night before and admitted to himself that those last few drinks were a bit excessive, to say the least.

"Mornin', sleeping beauty," Carina beamed as she came into the bright, sunlit room with a hot cup of coffee. "You look like shit, love. This might help." She handed him the cup. "A double-shot cappuccino with a touch of cinnamon. Just the way you like it."

Smiling, Orfeo mumbled under his breath as he took the first sip, "Ah, the coffee of popes and kings." He wondered if the popes or kings were ever as shit-faced as he was now when they enjoyed the 'super premium' Borinquen brew, likely thinking of some young, olive-skinned Puerto Rican boy dancing Salsa to Eddie Palmieri's 'Puerto Rico.'

"Thank you, baby," Orfeo said. He then took another sip, just a little too fast, and burned his tongue. "Thank you for everything."

"Aww! That's so sweet!" She was careful not to spill his coffee as she slipped herself into his arms and gave him a big hug. She got up and signaled for him to get up as well. "I went out to stock up on supplies so we could minimize our exposure. You won't believe what I found in town—a genuine French bakery. They had this gorgeous Senegalese women working there with the most beautiful, charcoal-black skin and lovely lips. I took the opportunity to brush up on my French. It apparently shocked her that someone in this community spoke French. I commented that my speaking French was only as shocking to her as finding a lovely Senegalese woman working in an authentic French bakery in this white-bread, homogeneous community was to me. We had a good laugh. I bought a shit-load of croissants and other goodies."

"Yummy! Let's have breakfast in bed and then cuddle all day."

She grabbed his free hand, gently encouraging him to get up. "Sorry, pasha. Rise and shine ... time to get out of bed. It's your first day of training!"

"Wunderbar!" he muttered with a sarcastic tone as he slowly got up, first pausing until the dizziness subsided. His head was still throbbing. "Babe, I've got a splitting headache. How about the hair of the dog that bit me?"

"Absolutely not!" she snapped in an authoritarian, no-nonsense voice. "That's what you get for drinking so much. And don't even think about whining your way out of the training session. We're going to hit it as soon as we finish our *petit déjeuner*."

"We're going to 'hit it'?" he beamed excitedly, winking at her with one of those off-to-the-side, cocky smiles.

"Wishful thinking, you lush! Let's see if you have that smirk on your face during the work out?"

"Okay, okay. Do you happen to have Tylenol or Motrin?"

"Sure, but what happened to Mr. 'I Don't Believe in Taking Medicine because I'm So Cool'?"

"Oh him? He skipped out of town sometime around when you put on your leather and strap-on. He told me to apologize and said something about preserving his virginity." They both laughed, but he stopped himself because laughing made his head feel like it was going to explode.

Seeing Orfeo so miserable, she put her hand on his shoulder and said, half-mockingly and half-lovingly, "Poor baby. I think I saw some in the bathroom. Go sit down; I'll bring them to you."

After a delightful breakfast of eggs scrambled with onions, peppers, spinach, herbs, and cayenne pepper on a warm croissant, Orfeo felt much better, and after a long shower, he felt like a new man. He put on the sweats, t-shirt, and sneakers she had just bought for him, stepped into the living room, posed, and started singing, "Don't you wish your boyfriend was hot like me. Don't you wish ..."

She giggled, watching his ridiculous performance and, in between giggles, said, "Babe, you look sooooo hot!"

Orfeo suddenly became dead serious and said, "So let's hit it. I'm ready!"

Carina sat at the table across from Orfeo. "Let's start by being as clear as possible. Right now, you're as vulnerable as a hen in a fox's lair. You have a lot to learn, and we don't have much time, so we won't have a minute to waste. The reality is that if they were to find us today and you had to confront them, you would, in no uncertain terms, die immediately ... no contest. Remember that this is not a simple 'death' where you get to return and continue where you left off. As I explained before, it's death death! You get a lobotomy and castration, both for the price of one, and will be lost in the earth-realm, serving the Master for all eternity. *Capisci?*"

"*Capisco!*" he said assuredly.

"If they find us in six months," she continued, "and you've trained diligently every day, balls to the wall ..."

Thinking about how he could have never imagined this side of Carina—so confident, sure of herself, in charge, no-nonsense, simply badass, and now the de facto "boss of him"—he was just about to smile and say something witty, but then caught himself. He recognized the gravity of what was not so much "their" situation as his and put on his game face.

"... you, my love," she continued matter-of-factly, "will still die immediately, without ever having had a chance in hell." Carina paused to let it all sink in. "This means that every minute of every day that you train increases your chances of survival from nil to negligible." She again paused, studying him carefully to ensure that he was on the same page. "Do you think I'm exaggerating?"

"No, I believe that you're giving me an accurate picture of what I'm up against. May I ask you a question?"

She nodded yes.

"Why not end this life and avoid all of this?"

"It would make sense except for the fact that, one, you can't get back to Consciousness until you complete your work in the earth-realm; two, they'd find you just like I did; three, there's the risk that they'd find you at a younger, more vulnerable age, which would put me at a disadvantage; and four, there's also the risk that you would have amnesia until an even later age, and then we'd be really be screwed. Since you're young and strong now and have your wits about you, I believe that this lifetime is the best chance we've got at fighting back."

Orfeo had a perplexed look on his face. "Fight back? I thought we were just hiding."

Carina answered, "Yes, until you're strong enough. Sooner or later, they're going to find us, and we won't have a choice but to fight. Alone, we won't stand a chance, but together, there's a chance."

Orfeo asked in an urgent tone, "Can we get help? There must be others?"

"Let me ask you a question. In all your incarnations, how many awakened humans have you encountered?" She paused waiting for an answer. "I didn't think so. There are only a few awakened beings in the earth-realm at any given time. Most choose to remain in

Consciousness and only return, as I said before, when called upon. That means that we're on our own."

Orfeo remained silent, searching his mind for potential solutions. Carina interrupted his train of thought, saying, "Babe, there's no other way out but to face them."

Orfeo sighed deeply and said, "Well, if that's the case, we better get started. I'm ready."

The Resistance

The training sessions were brutal, but after the first three months, Orfeo felt stronger and no longer dreaded them. He was making slow but steady progress, but he was still aware that confrontation still meant certain death and that he was nowhere near the negligible-chance-of-survival phase of his training.

Carina's training strategy was simple and straightforward: kill as efficiently and rapidly as possible, and then run for cover before reinforcements arrived. This principle was then broken down into endurance training, hand-to-hand combat, and weapons; and for Carina, everything was a potential weapon and had to be mastered as such. Finally, there was the mental preparation required to kill, kill, and then kill again. There was never mention of the word *self-defense*.

Orfeo's routine was consistent. He would go to bed early, rise early, meditate, study martial arts, meditate, do endurance and high-intensity training, lunch, nap, have more combat training, rest, and then study weapons. Despite their rigorous training schedule, Orfeo's mood was upbeat. He had found a new, higher purpose for his life, and he dedicated himself whole-heartedly. More importantly, aside from their love for each other, which was constant and blossoming, they shared a vision of conquering anything that would threaten their love and return to Consciousness.

Even with the intensity of their training, there were equal and perhaps more intense moments of tenderness between them. The clear understanding that at any moment they could be caught, effectively lobotomized into a *"metro, boulot, dodo"* existence like 99.999 percent of humankind without any memory of their true selves or purpose, and worse, without any memory of each other or the eternities through which their love had been sustained. The thought of that bitter, pathetic finale made every moment they shared—whether knocking each other down sparring, enduring the inevitable lacerations sustained while training with samurai swords, or passionately making love, transcending that mind-body in and out and transporting each other to otherworldly dimensions—as precious as the air they breathed.

It was sometime around the fifteenth month of training that Orfeo hit his stride. Everything that Carina was teaching him made sense at every level, and all the facets of his training started to flow. It would have been evident to any onlooker that Carina was the teacher, but Carina was now beginning to see him as a partner.

She began to really enjoy their sparring sessions, because although she could still get the better of him in all areas of combat, he had now started to present challenges to her. Their sessions were not just about teaching or correcting him but were an exploration of his skills. It became more of a *jogo*, a game of capoeira, the Brazilian dance/martial art in which the "players" feigned attacks and defenses in the guise of a dance set to the music of the berimbau, pandeiro, and conga drums. They both looked forward to these sessions.

Since their escape from the apartment in Manhattan, Carina and Orfeo had moved several times, staying in their friends' vacation homes or country houses that were not in use. They had become used to their nomadic way of life and more and more looked upon it as a grand adventure. One day, Carina returned from shopping incredibly excited and interrupted Orfeo's meditation. She was pacing back and forth, beaming, and kept on repeating that she couldn't believe what had happened and that it was the best news ever.

"Babe, will you calm down and tell me what happened."

"I can't believe it!" she said again.

Orfeo waited patiently for her to calm down. "Orfeo … the Resistance just made contact. Do you know what that means? I can't believe it."

"That's amazing!" Orfeo exclaimed. "How did you find them?"

"They found us!" Carina responded. "I'm in line at the grocery store, and this woman comes up to me and offers her hand. She introduces herself as Diedra and says, in the same manner as one would comment about the weather, 'You're not alone.' I, of course, had no idea what she was talking about and just smiled back to humor her. I told her my name and hoped she would walk away, but she didn't. She put her hands on both of my arms in a very gentle way, which really started to creep me out, and said, 'We know about you and Orfeo. We can help. Can we talk?'"

"How did they find us? Can we trust them?" Orfeo asked.

"Well, the fact is that they have apparently been following us since we left the apartment, and if they wanted to do us harm, they could have done so at any time. They waited all this time to make sure we were the real deal. I invited them over for dinner tonight."

"Tonight?" Orfeo exclaimed, obviously disturbed.

"Yes ... tonight. What's the matter?" Carina asked.

Orfeo responded. "I'm just a little upset because you made the decision unilaterally, without asking my opinion. I thought we were"—Orfeo paused and used hand signals to indicate quotation marks—'partners.'"

Carina explained in a soft voice, "Orfeo, we are partners. I'm sorry, but I had to go with my gut and didn't want to lose this opportunity. If this pans out, this is a game changer. It would give us a fighting chance. Do you understand?"

"I do understand," Orfeo said. "I probably would have done the same."

Maya

When Carina opened the door, Diedra was there with another woman, who she introduced as Maya. Maya was perhaps in her late forties and had a very soft, tender face, which was not at all what either Orfeo or Carina imagined when thinking about the leader of the Resistance. After sitting, Orfeo offered them some wine. They politely declined. *Of course not,* Orfeo thought to himself, feeling somewhat foolish for having even offered.

Maya, who was very thin, had grey hair pulled back in a ponytail and very fine, chiseled features. She opened with, "I can't express what a great pleasure it is to finally meet you." She paused. "I'm sure it was as much a surprise to you to hear from us as it was for us to find that there were other awakened beings, and more importantly, beings who were taking part in the struggle."

Orfeo jumped in, "Yes, it was quite a surprise, but the only struggle we've been taking part in up to now is the struggle to survive."

"This is true," Carina added. "We've been aware of

your existence, and I've been searching for you over many lifetimes, but up until now, we believed that we were alone."

"That must have been a terrible feeling," Maya said, "to believe that you were all alone. Those of the Light are never alone, especially during these dark times. There is too much at stake."

"Then where were you during this time?" Orfeo asked in a pressing voice.

Diedra responded very calmly. "We have been aware of Carina for a very long time and became aware of you when you both fled from your apartment in New York City."

Orfeo, in a somewhat hostile tone, asked, "Why didn't you make contact, help us? What were you waiting for?"

Carina, a bit taken aback by Orfeo's harsh tone, exclaimed, "Orfeo!"

Maya interjected, "It's okay, Carina. These are perfectly reasonable questions."

"Well, then, what were you waiting for?" Orfeo asked again and then, as though a light bulb had gone off in his head, added, "You were using us as bait, weren't you?"

Both Diedra and Carina looked at Maya simultaneously. After a pause, Maya responded, "Yes."

Orfeo exclaimed, "I knew it!"

Carina appeared perplexed and asked, "But why? Why would you do that? If you've been watching us, it should have been obvious to you that Orfeo wasn't, and still isn't, ready to take them on; and by myself, we never would have had a chance." Carina was becoming visibly upset as the picture that Orfeo was painting became clearer to her.

Maya sat up at the edge of her seat and said, "Carina, Orfeo, just listen to what I have to say before you jump to any conclusions. Yes, we were using you as bait. We've been trying unsuccessfully to find them, to draw them out, for a long time now, and their attempted attack on you in the city was a marked departure for them. There must be something special about one or both of you that caused them to break their pattern and risk exposure as they did." She now spoke more intensely. "We were caught off guard then, but we've been preparing for months for another such attack. We're ready for them. Somehow or another, you're both very key players in this. Do you have any idea why they're after you?"

Both Carina and Orfeo shook their heads.

Maya continued, "Do you understand now why we couldn't make contact? A victory on this front could have been decisive in our favor."

Carina and Orfeo looked at each other and nodded affirmatively.

"Then why make contact now? Doesn't this risk your entire operation?" Orfeo asked, now without any anger.

"No, it doesn't," Diedra answered. "Carina has done an outstanding job of keeping you off the grid, and at this point, it made sense to introduce ourselves, let you know that you are not alone, and extend an offering to join forces with us." Diedra paused to allow them time to register the offer and consider.

"How would joining you benefit us?" Orfeo asked. "We were doing fine without you."

Maya turned to Carina. "Carina, I believe that you have a better idea of what you both are up against. What are your chances of survival on your own?

Carina, who was intently looking at Maya, moved her eyes over to Orfeo's and then, looking down at the ground, responded almost in a mumble. "Zilch."

Orfeo immediately stood up and, more agitated than ever, flailed his arms, blurting out, "Zilch? What do you mean by 'zilch'? Then what was the purpose of all this training? Why bother? Why waste the time and energy?"

Carina looked up and reached out for his hand. She looked into his eyes and, again almost in a mumble, responded, "Hope. Just hope. That's all I had left—a glimmer of hope ... the foolish belief that we could survive this together."

Orfeo abruptly turned away and walked into the bedroom, slamming the door behind him. Carina buried her head in her hands and began crying. Maya stood, walked over to Carina, pulled her up to her feet, and hugged her with such strength that it took Carina's breath away. Carina lost all the strength in her legs. If it were not for Maya's strength, she would have fallen to the ground. Carina felt like a limp noodle, drained of all her strength and energy. For the first time that she could remember, she did not have to play the role of the badass with all the answers. She did not have to provide the encouragement and motivation to take the next step. She did not have to be the source of hope. Without realizing it, Carina had never been able to allow herself a moment of weakness or vulnerability, and she had exhausted herself. She was running on fumes.

Feeling the strength in Maya's arms, Carina was bawling uncontrollably at this point. She felt the love and security of a mother holding her baby in a moment of need. Maya repeatedly whispered in Carina's ear, while rocking her back and forth, "It's okay, my dear … it's okay. Let it all out. You've been carrying so much weight on your shoulders … so much responsibility. You're not alone now. Let it all out." Carina cried and cried, and just when she thought it was all out, another burst of tears would follow, stronger than the previous wave.

Orfeo walked back into the room at the sound of Carina wailing as he had never before witnessed. Carina's legs were just dangling behind her, and Maya was supporting her entire weight. Orfeo started to approach them, but Diedra stood in his path, her hands in prayer position, silently pleading with him to not interfere. Somehow, Orfeo understood immediately, and he stood back and observed. Carina must have cried uncontrollably for at least half an hour, without ever moving from Maya's embrace. Without consciously realizing it, in those moments in Maya's arms, she was releasing lifetimes' worth of pent-up anxiety and suffering. She felt the void that had been left after being drained of the energy required to mold herself into the savior, their only hope of survival, which she never truly believed she was. It was as though she had finally found someone who could relieve her of that burden, which was like a Boa constrictor around her chest, taking her breath away. In Maya's strong arms and from the motherly energy that she exuded, Carina now felt for the first time in a long time that she could breathe. She could finally let it all go and trust that someone was there for her to support and guide her. Carina felt that she was liberated.

Maya instinctively knew precisely when Carina had released everything that was necessary and gently laid her down on the couch like a baby. Maya put one hand on her head and another on her chest and said, "You are not alone, my child. You are of the Light and as such are protected by the Light." She kissed Carina on her forehead and told her to rest.

Maya stood up and turned to Orfeo, who was just about to apologize for his childish outburst. She opened her arms, inviting him to embrace her. Orfeo awkwardly stepped forward into her arms and felt a surge of energy move through his body, which disarmed him completely. He, too, felt a mother's love in her embrace that no words could ever describe. Maya's only words to him were, "She needs you more than ever now." Then she stepped back, and as Diedra had done before, she held her hands in prayer position and bowed to him. She added as a directive rather than a question, "Let's meet tomorrow afternoon."

Diedra followed suit and bowed to him and to Carina, who was curled up on her side, softly sobbing on the couch. Orfeo let them out and, as soon as they left, ran over to sit by Carina, placing his hand on her shoulder. She didn't move from her position but held his hand tightly. They sat quietly in that position for a long time, and when she finally moved, she did not have the strength to stand steady on her own two feet. Orfeo had never seen her like this.

Orfeo had no idea what had happened while he was in the room, but he understood how significant it must have been for Carina. He placed a glass of water on the side table and went outside to sit on the porch and stare at the night sky full of bright stars. He knew that something monumental had just occurred, and no matter what he himself thought, he was prepared to follow Carina wherever she led him.

When Orfeo went back into the house, he noticed that Carina had fallen asleep. He didn't want to disturb her, so he simply covered her with a blanket. He was still thinking about what had happened and had mixed feelings about a Resistance that would use them as bait. But he had already decided to put his gut feelings aside and defer to Carina's judgment.

It was very late, and despite his habit of going to bed by 9:00 p.m. in order to be well-rested for their 5:00 a.m. meditation, Orfeo was wide awake and quite energized. Nonetheless, he decided to lie down and try to fall asleep. Rather than tossing and turning, he meditated, allowing his mind and body to sink into deeper and deeper levels of stillness. Orfeo was already quite familiar with the numerous levels of consciousness that resided between wakefulness and sleep, each with its distinct attributes. The untrained mind was only familiar with the three pedestrian levels: wakefulness, daydreams, and sleep. Orfeo chose to remain at a particular level of consciousness that could be characterized as "mind alert, body asleep," which Orfeo found to be very soothing. It was here that he could find total and profound relaxation but keep his mind alert enough to analyze a particular issue from many perspectives and receive pertinent insights that he himself would not have considered. It was as though a channel opened while in this state to a higher wisdom that offered him guidance without the distractions of unnecessary and often confounding thoughts and emotions. There was clarity.

When describing this to their very few friends, who believed that this was a rare gift, Orfeo would insist that this was a state to which everyone had access. He described their limitations to be the result of a low signal-to-noise ratio. Orfeo pointed out to them that their lives were lived for the most part in between two stations of a transistor radio and were consequently filled with static. As with a transistor radio, a signal would occasionally come through clearly, even when between stations, and their untrained minds called this clear voice "intuition," implying that it was a rare but valued occurrence akin to a non-reproducible mystical experience. He would insist that with training, they could turn their minds into accurate receivers of a clear signal and could have access to all the wisdom of the Universe. They were usually intrigued but never enough to take him up on his repeated offers to teach them.

All the thoughts that had been whirling around his head again, like the debris captured in a massive tornado, were now laid before him in a straight, coherent line. Orfeo began to visualize and understand the big picture of everything that had transpired between Carina and him and now appreciated the relevance of meeting and becoming part of the Resistance. What still eluded him was why the followers of the Master had, as Maya had explained, broken from their modus operandi in exposing themselves during their attempted attack on them in their apartment in New York City. Orfeo had no recollection of ever having crossed paths with them and consequently could not figure out why they were after him and Carina.

After a while, Orfeo began to doze off into a deep, restful sleep. It had been a long and eventful day, and he welcomed the yawns and the drifting gently into unconsciousness. He thought of Carina and wondered why she had cried so forcefully and then collapsed on the couch. He had never seen her in that state—so vulnerable, almost weak. He then realized that this was the very first time since they had consummated their earthbound relationship that they had not slept in the same bed. Orfeo's last thought before losing consciousness was of how much he missed not having her by his side.

At some point during the night, Orfeo awakened in what he immediately recognized as a nightmare. He was in a dark cave, and there were fires everywhere. There were also legions of soldiers in uniform, arms in hand, marching in formation. Orfeo suddenly realized that he was tied very tightly to a stake and couldn't get loose. He then abruptly awakened in a cold sweat, momentarily disoriented, unsure where he was or what time it was. After a few minutes, the fog lifted, and he recognized that he had just had a nightmare.

Orfeo got up and went to the living room to check on Carina, who was in a deep sleep, snoring loudly, which he had never witnessed before. He adjusted the blanket to cover her properly, got himself some water, and then, without even thinking about the nightmare he had just had, went back to sleep.

When Orfeo woke up, the sun was shining brightly into the room. For months now of consistently getting up at about five o'clock, it had always been still dark when he woke up. He looked over at the clock on the nightstand and was shocked to see that it was 11:00 a.m. He jumped out of bed, expecting Carina to be up and about, and was quite surprised to find her still on the couch sleeping. He considered waking her up but decided against it. The fact that he had gone to bed really late surely accounted for why he overslept, but Carina had fallen asleep much earlier. He knew that if she was still asleep, then it was what she really needed.

Orfeo realized that they had not taken a single day off since his training started. Those sweet mornings of lounging in bed, making love, and drifting back to sleep again were a distant memory. He stared at her sleeping so quietly and felt so much love and gratitude for this woman. He had always loved her simply for who she was, but since she had revealed herself to be such a badass and self-designated bodyguard and trainer, his love for her had grown exponentially, and true gratitude had become an inseparable part of the package. How could he ever repay her?

He was about to make himself some coffee and have a piece of toast and some blackberry jam when the answer to that question presented itself. It certainly was not intended as a quid pro quo, but it dawned on him that, even before her badass-slave-driver, you-must-train-every-waking-moment-or-die-a-horrible-death phase, he had never prepared breakfast for her. Although he was an early riser by nature, she had always managed to be up earlier and have breakfast ready for him. This was his perfect opportunity.

Orfeo closed the kitchen door and quietly prepared a spinach, tomato, and mushroom omelet with a toasted baguette and brewed some coffee just the way she liked it. The timing couldn't have been more perfect. Just as he had prepared the plates and coffee on a tray, he heard her calling his name. He walked out with the tray in hand, beaming as he said, "Mornin', sleeping beauty."

Carina was completely discombobulated and still had not registered his gesture. Still disoriented, she asked, "What time is it? Have I been sleeping long?" Wishing he had a camera to capture this moment, he put the tray down, waved the coffee under her nose, and told her that she had slept for about twelve hours. She was still half asleep and clearly did not completely register what he said. She took the cup from his hands and took her first sip of coffee. Before even swallowing the coffee, her eyes opened wide. She looked straight at him and exclaimed in disbelief, "What? Twelve hours? Really?" She thought about this, took another sip of coffee, and added, "I feel like I was run over by truck." She took another sip of coffee. "And why did I sleep on the couch?"

Orfeo, not used to seeing her like this—confused, out of sorts, and vulnerable—had an amused look on his face.

She quickly added, "And why do you have that shit-eating grin on your face?"

Orfeo didn't answer. He simply picked up the tray and put it on the coffee table in front of her, saying, "Breakfast is served, Your Royal Highness."

Carina's face suddenly changed as it finally clicked that Orfeo had prepared such a beautiful breakfast for her. "This is amazing! Thank you!"

They ate in silence, exchanging awkward glances. What had happened last night had definitely thrown Carina off kilter, and neither of them knew how or where to start. Carina ate very slowly, savoring every bite. When they finished, Carina plopped herself back on the couch under the blanket, and Orfeo brought the plates back into the kitchen and cleaned up.

Returning from the kitchen, he nonchalantly pointed out, "I've never seen you sleep like that. You must have been exhausted."

Carina was very slow to answer but finally said, "I was dead. I don't remember ever feeling so drained."

"By the way," Orfeo said, "I'm really sorry I behaved like a total ass toward Maya. I just couldn't accept the fact that they were using us as bait. I get it now, and I'm fine. But I just had this horrible feeling of being used and couldn't handle it. I'm really sorry."

Carina reached out her hand to hold his, and told him that everything was okay. She said that she completely understood. She had felt the same way at first but wanted to hear what they had to say before passing judgment.

"So what did they have to say?" Orfeo asked.

"Well, we never got to that part," she answered. "I don't know what came over me, but when you stormed out of the room, I was all of a sudden overwhelmed with emotion. At first I just started to cry, not really even knowing why, and then my emotions took me like a tsunami. I started to bawl. Didn't you hear me in the room? Holy shit! A river poured out of me. Then Maya came over and lifted me into her arms like a child. She was so strong. Even if I'd had any strength left in my body, I don't think I could have resisted."

Carina paused for a while, trying to understand herself what had happened, and then she continued. "When she lifted me into her arms, I felt all the strength leave my body ... I couldn't even support my own weight! Just when I thought the crying was over, another wave of emotion came over me, and I started bawling again. There was something about her that was so nurturing and reassuring." She paused again. "It was as though everything that I had been holding back—the fear, the anxiety, all the responsibility that I was carrying—just burst through this dam that I had erected in order to be this strong warrior to get us through this mess. It all came tumbling down ... and somehow, Maya made it all okay. She gave me the strength I needed to completely let go. The energy that moved between us was so overwhelming but at the same time so reassuring ... like being comforted by a mother's love."

Carina looked up at Orfeo, wondering if he could

possibly understand, because even she was unable to fully grasp what had happened. She added in a clearer, sure voice, "I guess the bottom line is that ... and please don't take this the wrong way"—she squeezed his hand—"I felt as though I were carrying the weight of the world on my shoulders. I know you've been making tremendous progress, but I still felt that if we were confronted now, it would basically come down to me." Carina looked down. "And ... I was afraid ... afraid that I wouldn't be strong enough to protect you ... to save you ..." She started to cry. "Orfeo, you're all I have in this universe, and the thought of losing you ... forever ... is a fear that I've been carrying with me every day since they found us in the city. Do you understand?"

Orfeo nodded and knelt down next to the couch to embrace her.

"So after the Resistance made contact with us and I felt that certain something about Maya—that she exuded strength, somehow—I was so relieved that I wasn't alone. There was hope. And I just lost it." Carina was now half-laughing and half-crying. "Boy, did I lose it!"

"Sweetie," Orfeo spoke with his head still buried in her neck, "I love you so much ... and I get it. I completely understand the burden you've been carrying. That's why I've been working so hard. Thank you, thank you, thank you!"

Carina hugged Orfeo harder, and whispered in his

ear, "I think everything is going to be okay now. We're not alone." After resting a long time in each other's arms, she gently pushed him away. "Would you mind if I stayed in bed by myself for a few more hours? My body is just craving to be in bed. Okay?"

"Sure, love. We're meeting Maya and other members of the Resistance later this afternoon. You rest, and I'll wake you up an hour before it's time to leave."

"What will you do?"

"It's a spectacular day. I think I'll take a long walk and clear my head."

"You think that's a good idea?"

"No worries, Ms. Boss-of-Me Carina. I think I can take care of myself for one afternoon."

"Orfeo, please don't go too far. It's still dangerous out there."

"Got it! I'll gear up and stay in the 'hood." He kissed her on the forehead saying, "You rest up. We have an important date with our future this afternoon. Love ya!"

While Orfeo packed the 9mm, two extra clips, and his sword, he thought to himself how there was something gentler, softer about Carina. It was more like the Carina he'd known before they had escaped from New York City and their lives had been thrown into turmoil. As he was walking out, Orfeo reminded himself to apologize to Maya and thank her profusely.

CHAPTER 6

The Master's Lair

The Master's Lair

Orfeo regained consciousness and felt as though every bone in his body was broken. The pain was excruciating. He was gasping for breath because his nose was broken and a mixture of clotted blood, mucus, and fresh blood was pouring out of his nostrils and down the back of his throat. He leaned his head forward to allow the blood to flow out of his nose and onto his face and chest rather than obstruct his breathing. Each breath required a concentrated effort because of the pain from the broken rib fragments.

Orfeo was experiencing unbearable pain, and the ambient heat was stifling. He was sweating profusely from what felt like 110-degree heat with 100 percent humidity. His eyes burned from the sweat pouring into them, and as his hands were tied behind his back, he couldn't wipe them. The heat, the pain, and the deafening drone of what sounded like marching feet and military calls and responses overwhelmed his senses. Orfeo was occasionally able to open his burning eyes and see that he was in a large cave with many levels carved out of the walls. There were large bonfires all over the place that seemed to be forming naturally from the ground and walls, perhaps from underground gas. They were likely the source of the heat.

Orfeo was naked, covered in sweat and blood, and strapped to some contraption that was angled back to about forty degrees. He was able to see his left foot but not his right. From the throbbing, lancinating pain that he was feeling just below his knee and the pool of blood accumulating where his right foot should have been, he surmised that his right leg had been amputated. Orfeo amused himself with the calculation that this would certainly be a limitation in beating the shit out of the eight-hundred-plus soldiers he imagined marching in formation in the dark, dank cave below and escaping on his own. He started to laugh, but the excruciating pain cut the levity of that moment.

This entire scenario seemed familiar to Orfeo. He had been in this very place before but only in fragmented dreams. He wondered if he was in fact dreaming. He comforted himself with the thought that he was still breathing and that he still had his mind. Knowing that this could be the very last time he would be able to remember, he savored the memory of Carina, of all those amazing souls he had met on his journey, of those so-called lost lives that he now cherished, and most of all, of being in Consciousness and having the hope of return.

Orfeo remembered Kostos the Greek, telling him

many lifetimes ago about the five most important things—love, passion, adventure, risk, and most of all, memory. Orfeo had always wondered if Kostos really understood the true significance of what he was saying and now was convinced that he must have been of the Light. Orfeo now understood that it was not an accident that he'd met him precisely at that moment in his development. Kostos was selflessly pointing Orfeo in the right direction. Orfeo recognized that it was not necessary but expressed gratitude to those of the Light, such as Kostos, who had guided him patiently during so many lifetimes. He repeated again and again, "Thank you, thank you, thank you …"

Orfeo spit out a large blood clot and, for a second, was able to take a good breath, now only hampered by the pain of his broken ribs. He was comforted by the realization that he still remembered that he was of the Light, of Spirit, of Consciousness, and that Carina would always exist in his heart as she had during all those lifetimes he'd searched for her. He kept repeating to himself, like a mantra, that he was so much more than this mess of torn flesh, broken bones, and limited thought patterns. He repeated it more and more forcefully, as though to engrain it in every fiber, every cell in his body so that even if he were literally lobotomized or decapitated, the smegma formed on the foreskin of his penis would serve as a glorious stem cell to resurrect that knowledge.

Orfeo recognized that for many earthbound individuals, this was a question of belief, of faith, of hope that there was more to this existence than their earthbound bodies, thoughts, emotions, beliefs, and dramas. For Orfeo, it was a matter of fact, and the thought of having that knowledge taken away, of being condemned to an earthbound existence for all eternity like Sisyphus pushing his rock up the hill without any purpose, was an entire edifice of hell, below the seven rings, that Virgil had not dared reveal to Dante. Aside from the fear of never finding Carina, this was the only fear that Orfeo had ever known in his entire existence.

The pain was steadily increasing, and it was becoming more and more difficult to breathe. Orfeo was praying for death, no matter how painful, which was his only chance of true survival, of having another chance. He saw now that, as Carina had mentioned so matter-of-factly on the first day when he'd learned the truth, this war was not the most important thing or the least important thing; it was the only thing that mattered. He looked back on his life up until that point as such a waste of time. It was exactly because he'd wasted all that precious time when he should have been preparing that he was so easily captured, like a child surrounded by wolves. Although he recognized the futility of the thought, he decided that if he were to have another chance, he would start to train as soon as he could walk. He realized that this would completely freak out his "adoptive" parents, seeing their toddler butchering his GI Joe and coming home to find him studying mixed martial arts footage instead of animations. Orfeo concluded with a chuckle that nearly took his breath away for the pain of it that he would then be ready for this precise moment. The excruciating pain, the heat, the blood loss from his leg, and the struggle to breathe overwhelmed Orfeo, and he again lost consciousness.

Orfeo was abruptly awakened by warm water splashed on his face. The sudden shock caused him to take a deep gasp of air, resulting in the sensation of sharp, serrated knives sawing through both sides of his chest, which again caused him to lose consciousness.

When Orfeo woke up, he was now able to open his eyes easily. There was no sweat and no pain, and he was breathing normally. He still found himself bound to something, which was now leaning him forward at about a fifty-degree angle to the floor. For some reason, there was no blood dripping from his nose. The cave seemed smaller than before, and the fires appeared to be larger and closer together. But there was no heat. Suddenly, Carina appeared from out of nowhere, a machine gun in hand, and while untying his hands, said with pressured speech, "Let's get you out of here, babe. Do you think you can you walk?"

Orfeo looked down at both of his feet and responded yes. Carina untied his hands and feet, handed him a machine gun and an extra clip, and signaled for him to follow her. She said the Resistance was waiting for them not too far from there. In a manner that was now simply a reflex, just as Carina had drilled it into him, Orfeo made sure the gun was loaded and the safety was off. He followed closely behind Carina. They stayed low and close to the walls. Just below, there were battalions of soldiers marching in formation, but the constant drone of their military call and responses was gone. Orfeo thought it strange that it was so quiet. After about five hundred yards, a loud, clear voice—Orfeo's voice, in fact—resounded and echoed throughout the cave.

"Orfeo, you're going the wrong way."

Orfeo paused the first time he heard it, but believing it to be a figment of his imagination, he continued behind Carina. After a while, the voice again resounded throughout the cave, now more insistent and forceful. The echoes, rather than fading, became louder and louder. Orfeo tugged on Carina's belt indicating that she should stop. He asked, "Did you hear that?"

Carina turned to face him and, in that authoritative voice that he hadn't heard for months now, said, "Ignore it, Orfeo. It's a trap. Let's keep moving."

"Orfeo," the voice resumed, "you're going the wrong way, and you know it."

Orfeo stopped in his tracks and sat on the floor, confused. He recognized the voice. It wasn't the first time he'd heard it. He told Carina, "Wait a minute. I know that voice."

Carina abruptly interjected. "Orfeo, there's absolutely no time. We gotta move, now!" She started to walk away, but he just sat there, confused and paralyzed. Carina returned, held his hand, looked into his eyes, and pleaded with him. "Orfeo, we really don't have much time. Please trust me. Please. Let's keep moving."

Orfeo was awakened by a warm, moist cloth gently wiping the blood and sweat from his face. He could again feel the sharp pain that cut through his ribs with every breath he took, and it was a struggle to breathe through his blood-clot-packed nostrils. Although the water on his face was at first cool, within seconds it felt as though it were boiling on his skin from the ambient heat. "Carina ... Carina," he shouted a few times, but he stopped because of the pain it unleashed. He realized that it must have been a dream. The lines between reality and his dream state were now completely blurred.

Orfeo at first could not open his eyes because the sweat had congealed and glued his eyelids shut. After some gentle scrubbing, Orfeo was able to open his eyes to find the incongruity of the delicate scrub he was receiving and the sight of a formidable giant, who must have been at least seven feet tall and was extremely muscular and whose hands appeared to be twice the size of Orfeo's head.

Orfeo remained silent while the giant bathed him. After a while, the giant spoke in a soft, welcoming voice. "Welcome to the Master's home, Orfeo. My name is

Dolton." After bathing him, Dolton looked down at the stump of Orfeo's right leg, which was bleeding, and said, "Well, we certainly can't have you bleeding to death, can we?" He stepped out of the room for a minute and returned with something in his hand. He knelt on one knee. "This'll just take a second … just a twinge of pain. Are you ready? Take a deep breath. And one, two, three …"

Orfeo expected the worst, but as Dolton had said, he only experienced a momentary twinge of sharp pain. He heard a hissing sound, which was immediately followed by the smell of burning flesh as Dolton applied the electrocautery to his stump.

"Now that's better," Dolton said, evidently pleased with himself. "You're all fixed now." Dolton turned away and then returned with a glass of water that he delicately brought to Orfeo's lips.

"Where am I?" Orfeo finally spoke, struggling to get the words out. The giant was just about to answer when another, deeper, more ominous voice responded from the shadows. "You are home, Orfeo. You are finally home." A dark, tall figure wearing a black, hooded cloak stepped out of the shadows and walked over to Orfeo. As he approached Orfeo, he said, "I have been looking forward to meeting you for a very long time."

"Who are you?" Orfeo asked.

"You may call me Master."

"Master?" Orfeo responded sarcastically. "Aren't you a bit full of yourself?"

"It's a nickname that was given to me eternities ago," he said as he removed his hood, revealing a beaming smile and a gentle face. The Master appeared to be in his sixties. He had distinguished creases on his forehead and cheeks, and his hair was white and well-trimmed in the way of a Wall Street executive. "I didn't feel comfortable with it at first, but it stuck. In time, I learned to carry it with pride." The Master paced back and forth in front of Orfeo as though thinking what to say next. Finally, he asked, "Do you know why you are here, Orfeo?"

Orfeo, now distracted from the pain, responded that he had no idea but that he knew that the Master was a bad guy.

"Me, the bad guy?" The Master laughed out loud. "Is that what Carina, Maya, and their so-called Resistance have been telling you?" He paused and then continued to pace back and forth. With his back half-turned to Orfeo, he turned his head and added, "Really?"

"Well, you kill people. You kill innocent people. That makes you a bad guy, doesn't it?" Orfeo exclaimed in an accusatory tone.

The Master replied, "I prefer to think that I liberate them."

Orfeo looked surprised and volleyed, "Well, that's convenient."

"Orfeo," the Master replied in a professorial tone,

"over thousands of years, I've only liberated—or killed, as you prefer—a mere fraction of the lives lost in the senseless wars of humankind or from hunger, which is due solely to human neglect."

"So you want a medal for your restraint?" Orfeo interjected sarcastically.

"Orfeo, you are missing an important point here. Those souls came to me asking for liberation. I performed an in-depth screening to determine if they were worthy of such an honorable death and liberation. There was no coercion on my part. I only accepted those who had achieved the highest levels of consciousness and were fully aware that the body and this life were illusory."

"In other words, you brainwashed them."

"No, Orfeo, no!" The Master was still pacing back and forth. "It isn't me but the world that has brainwashed humankind into herds of sleepwalkers. I have no interest in the world. I am only a facilitator, nothing more than that. I offer assistance to those in need."

"You facilitate death … suicide. This makes you a murderer."

"Orfeo, please," the Master snapped back, still pacing and on the verge of losing his patience. "You know better. You've been around the block a few times. Those poor souls were on the verge of liberation. They felt trapped within their bodies that they knew, at least intellectually, were illusory. They sought release, liberation." The Master stopped and stood directly in front of Orfeo, verifying that he had his attention. "They had all achieved very high levels of consciousness via meditation and esoteric practices and had hit a wall. They could go no further. They came to the conclusion that it was through intense pain and concentration that they could transcend this reality and enter the next phase."

"But it's not necessary" Orfeo stated. "It's not necessary, and you know that."

"Yes, Orfeo, I know that it's completely unnecessary, but it is their path. They can see no other way. I counsel them, offer them alternatives, but they choose this path because they believe not only that it is the right one but also that it is the higher path." The Master paused, sat down, and then added, "Orfeo, I am simply a facilitator. Nothing more."

"Then why is the Resistance after you?"

"Ah, the Resistance. That is a question that you should pose to them. Don't you agree?"

"I'm asking you."

"Okay. It appears that they too have achieved a very high level of consciousness and have hit a wall. Similar to those to whom I offer assistance, the Resistance also seeks liberation."

The Master paused. He poured himself a glass of water and, without asking, poured another glass and held it to Orfeo's lips. Orfeo hesitated.

"Orfeo, please drink. How do you expect to heal if you don't hydrate yourself?" Orfeo at first turned his head away, but then his thirst overwhelmed his better judgment and he gulped the water. The Master nodded in approval and continued. "The Resistance, however"— he paused for emphasis, drank from his glass, and looked directly into Orfeo's eyes—"they are cowards. They fail to see that the wall that they have hit is within themselves. They have somehow come up with the delusion that it is I who keeps them and humankind from liberation, from transcending their very own, meticulously constructed prisons." The Master laughed, almost choking on his water. "As though I had this power. Such foolishness!"

Orfeo was about to object to the Master's words, but the Master continued.

"They are blocked, and they set me up as a scapegoat to blame for it. Over millennia, I have grown in the minds of the Resistance to become this all-powerful representation of evil—evil personified—who attempts to rob humans of their consciousness." The Master stopped, and pointed to himself with both hands, half-jokingly asking, "Orfeo, you're a good judge of character. Do I look like a bad guy to you?"

"It doesn't matter what I think."

"But it does, Orfeo … it does matter what you think. Orfeo, I am a man, like you, who has awakened from one level of the dream. No more. Even if I desired it, I do not have the power to impede anyone else from achieving Consciousness or to steal their Consciousness. This is a fiction created by cowards who can't face the reality that it is they themselves who impede their own progress and maintain their prisons."

"Bullshit!" Orfeo exclaimed.

"All that I ask, Orfeo, is that you keep an open mind."

"You're lying. It's all lies. You're a murderer!" Orfeo screamed out.

"We shall see who is the liar. As I said, all that I ask is for you to keep an open mind." The Master paused to sip his water and again placed a full glass of water to Orfeo's lips. Orfeo now drank without hesitation. The Master continued, "Although misguided, I value and respect those who come to me for liberation, because they recognize the block to be within and have the courage to seek the solution within. They are at least on the right path. They are earnest in their desire for truth and liberation. It is because of this sincerity that I offer my assistance."

"Are you saying that the Resistance is lying?"

"No, Orfeo," the Master responded sympathetically. "The Resistance did not lie to you or their followers. They genuinely believe that there is a force outside of themselves, which they believe I personify, that imprisons them."

"Then why am I a prisoner?"

"You are not a prisoner, Orfeo … You are my guest." The Master then bowed to Orfeo and exited.

Orfeo's mind was reeling after everything the Master had told him, and the pain he was experiencing all over his body felt like a massive toothache. He was confused, but he forced himself to reject any possibility that anything the Master said was true. He convinced himself that it was all part of the brainwashing process and that he had to keep his guard up. Physically and mentally exhausted, Orfeo drifted off into a restful sleep. In what felt to Orfeo to be only a few moments after falling asleep, he was forcefully awakened by Carina tapping on his shoulder and shaking him. She covered his mouth so that he couldn't make a sound and whispered that they had to move fast. She grabbed his hand, pulled him off the cot directly onto the floor, and handed him a machine gun. She pointed with her index and third finger in the direction they would take. As in the prior dream, his legs were intact, he could not appreciate the stifling heat, despite the fires raging around them, and he felt no pain. She indicated that they had to stay low and crawl alongside the wall. She then stopped at a turn, below which were the battalions of soldiers marching in silence, and signaled that he should follow her. They hugged the wall and stayed low. Again, the voice, his voice, now more forceful than ever, exclaimed, "Orfeo, stop! You are going in the wrong direction. You must stop running. Stop fighting."

Orfeo dropped and seated himself on the floor. Carina didn't notice at first that he had stopped and continued moving forward. Upon looking back, she indicated with a look of annoyance that he should catch up. Orfeo was confused, again paralyzed, so Carina returned to him, grabbed him by the shoulder, and attempted to tug him to stimulate him to follow.

The voice insisted, "You must look inside. See through the illusion. That is your only salvation." Orfeo placed his face in both hands and shook his head.

"Orfeo!" she shouted. "We have to move now. Let's go!"

Orfeo then awakened in a cold sweat that caused him to shiver, which in the ambient heat was quite refreshing.

Orfeo was alone for long periods of time. He had no concept of whether it was day or night. He was left alone with his thoughts, the stifling heat, and the deafening drone of the soldiers marching back and forth, chanting their military war cries. What overwhelmed Orfeo now was not the heat or the sweat pouring from his body, to which he had grown accustomed, but rather his thoughts. He was confused by the incongruities that confronted him in that seeming hell.

What was incontrovertible in his mind was the following: He had awakened to find himself captive, bloodied, battered, his leg amputated, in what any witness would agree was hell. He was in such agonizing pain that he, for the first time since discovering the whereabouts of Carina, was calling upon death for her mercy. Beyond these purported facts, everything became fuzzy. First, he had been greeted, bathed, and cared for by a gentle giant. Second, the Master, who the Resistance and Carina had proclaimed in no uncertain terms to be the enemy, evil personified, did not appear as such. Third, the Master had planted the seed in Orfeo's mind that perhaps he was mistaken. Fourth and most disturbing, he was experiencing the recurrent dream fragments in which his love, Carina, miraculously appears, frees him from his bondage, and starts to lead him back to the safety of the Resistance, but a voice, his own, tells him that he is going in the wrong direction. He asked himself over and over again what this could possibly mean.

Dolton returned first and after bathing him again, released him from his bonds. Dolton carried him over to a chair that was in front of a table on which were a glass of water and a bowl. Orfeo, who had not eaten for so long, looked into the bowl with caution and smelled it.

Dolton indicated that he should eat, that it would help him to regain his strength. Orfeo rationalized that if they wanted to kill him, they could have done so at any point. Besides, being poisoned would certainly not be the worst way to die. The broth was repulsive at first, but after a few gulps, its saltiness and the chunks of some unidentifiable meat seemed more like a delicacy prepared by the finest French chef.

Orfeo considered possible escape routes, but the reality was that such an attempt in his weak condition and with only one leg would be futile. He watched as Dolton meticulously washed down the metal table to which Orfeo had been affixed. Since he was still alive,

Orfeo wondered what the Master wanted from him. After Dolton cleaned the table, he walked over to Orfeo, and noticing that Orfeo had eaten all of the soup, he took the bowl away, leaving only the glass of water on the table. Dolton then returned and tapped him on the shoulder. He pointed to a cot that was situated in the corner of the cave. Orfeo stood up on his one leg and started to hop toward the cot, but Dolton stopped him, picked him up as though he were a Chihuahua, and gently placed him on the bed. Dolton said that he should rest and relayed a message from the Master. He apologized for being such a poor host but explained that he had some urgent matters to attend to and would return to see him as soon as possible.

A few days passed, and Orfeo was feeling stronger. The sharp pains in his ribs had now become a dull, persistent ache, and unless he touched it, the pain in his nose was undetectable. More importantly, he was able to breathe normally. His stump was bandaged neatly, and Dolton, without any conversation, changed the dressing, debrided the stump, and generously applied some type of cream to it before meticulously redressing it twice daily. Dolton, sensing that Orfeo was strong enough, brought him crutches and suggested that he begin to exercise, insisting that it would make him feel better. Orfeo wasn't sure if it was just a question of habituation, but the meals he was served now seemed quite delicious, and they were served with wine. All of this made him even more suspicious of what was to come.

After Orfeo ate a delectable meal of succulent lamb over polenta and caramelized onion, carrots, and peppers, Dolton appeared and asked if he wanted another serving. Orfeo was tempted but politely declined. Shortly after Dolton left with the plates and cutlery, the Master appeared and, with a warm smile, beamed, "I'm so happy to see that you are recovering so rapidly."

Despite Orfeo's underlying distrust of the Master, he could not help but respond warmly to the Master's congenial greeting. "Yes, I feel much better, and I'm grateful for your hospitality."

"I trust that Dolton has been taking excellent care of you and attending to your every need."

"Yes, he's been really great. I still can't believe how such a giant can be so gentle and caring."

"As you will learn, Orfeo, appearances can be deceiving."

The Master's response caught Orfeo off guard and left him with a puzzled look on his face.

"Is there something the matter, Orfeo?" the Master asked. "All of a sudden, you look perplexed. Was it something I said?"

Orfeo paused, thinking carefully before he answered. While he was gathering his thoughts, Dolton reappeared with another glass for the Master. He poured the Master some wine and then refilled Orfeo's glass. The

Master lifted his glass as though to make a toast. After hesitating, Orfeo lifted his glass and looked deeply into the Master's eyes, attempting to detect any inkling of a malicious or evil nature, but he could find only warmth and generosity.

"*Salud*! To your health and well-being" the Master toasted. Orfeo started to take a sip but was captivated by the Master as he sipped the wine, closed his eyes, and seemed in rapture, savoring the taste and texture of the wine on his palate. Orfeo was drawn to the Master as a moth to the flame. There was something compelling about the Master, and Orfeo wanted to like him. But he feared that he was being seduced and, like the moth who orbits too close to the fire, would be burned.

Orfeo heard Carina's insistent voice in his head, saying, "Death? Afraid of death? Death would be a gift in this circumstance. What I am afraid of the most, as you should be too, is to forget why we are here and where we are going. What I am afraid of is losing you again, this time without any hope of ever finding you again. What I am afraid of is being condemned to this earth-realm without the slightest possibility of ever returning to Consciousness. We'd be just like the masses of human beings, walking like zombies without a purpose, wondering why we were so miserable inside. You and I know well that there is no heaven or hell, but that to me is the definition of hell! This is what the Master will do to us. It's basically a lobotomy. This is the only thing worth fearing. This is why we run. This is why we train. This is why we will fight until we can't fight anymore."

The Master's voice startled Orfeo out of his reverie. "Do you like the wine, Orfeo?"

"Yes, it's delightful. I hadn't had a taste of wine for over a year, and I missed it."

In a sincere and genuinely curious tone, the Master asked, "Why have you deprived yourself for so long of one of humankind's greatest companions?"

"Well ..." Orfeo started to answer, but then he caught himself.

The Master waited patiently. Then raising his eyebrows, he indicated that he was waiting for Orfeo to continue.

"In order to train," Orfeo finished.

"What on earth were you training for that would make you deprive yourself of the comforts of wine?"

After a long pause, Orfeo looked defiantly into the Master's eyes and said, "For war ... for this."

The Master took another sip, put his glass down, and asked, "And what is 'this'?"

Orfeo looked away, avoiding further eye contact. He was confused. It wasn't that he didn't want to reply, but at that moment, he could not come up with an answer that rang true. He finally replied, still looking away, "This is war."

The Master waited to see if Orfeo had more to say

before asking, "If this is war, Orfeo, whose war is it? Who is the war against? What are you fighting for?"

Orfeo felt as though he were in a high-stakes game of poker, not knowing if he was being bluffed, and he was careful not to divulge anything that would weaken his position. He finally rallied his nerves, looked directly at the Master, and blurted out that he would not allow himself to be brainwashed.

"Ah, I see," the Master responded, and after a pause, he continued, "Unfortunately, my dear guest, if this is what you fear, you are much too late." The Master stood up and bowed to Orfeo. "What if you are mistaken? What if everything you were told and believe is false? Please consider this carefully. I will return tomorrow."

Turtles All the Way Down

Orfeo's head was again spinning. There were so many questions. What if he were in fact mistaken? But how could this be? Carina had in fact saved him from the Master while they were in their New York City apartment. She had warned him about the Master. She had been protecting him all this time ... training him ... preparing him for this war. She had warned him and prepared him for this moment. Yet, he was confused. He wondered if his confusion was because of the wine, but he concentrated and was sure he'd only had two glasses at most. Why the confusion? This was not at all what he had expected. If it weren't for his amputated leg and broken bones, there would not be any evidence of the war she had prepared him for. What if they, Carina and the Resistance, were mistaken? How could he know for sure?

Deep in his heart, he was certain of only one truth— that he loved Carina and that she loved him. Other than this, everything was circling in his brain like a twister, leveling everything in its path. Their love was the only constant. He trusted her more than anything in the universe. But what if she was mistaken? Could this be possible? Why was the Master treating him so well, nursing him back to health, feeding him with such delightful meals and wine? Was this part of the brainwashing? Yes, Orfeo thought, that must be it. That was the Master's method. He realized then that he had to be more careful. He could not let his guard down.

Orfeo was exhausted from all of the mental acrobatics and without even realizing it, dozed off into a deep sleep. He was suddenly awakened by Carina. She pulled him to standing position and hugged him as though she were seeing him for the first time in eternities.

"Thank goodness you're okay. I was so worried about you. I thought I was too late." She separated herself from him but still held his two arms firmly, looking at him up and down. "Did they hurt you?"

"Not at all," Orfeo answered.

Carina again pressed herself against him for a long while, squeezing him in her arms. She separated herself from him again, and said, "Let's get you out of here." She took his hand and started to lead him away, but he pulled her back. "What's the matter, Orfeo? Let's go. The Resistance is waiting not too far from here with a helicopter to get us to safety."

"Carina, what if you are mistaken?"

"Mistaken about what? What's there to be mistaken about? The Master and his army? They're evil, and they want to destroy us … well, worse than destroy us … they want to imprison us in this earth-realm for all eternity. What are you asking?"

"I'm asking you if there is the smallest possibility that you and the Resistance could be wrong. What if there is no war? What if there are no evil forces out to get us? What if—"

"Are you out of your mind?" Carina embraced him tenderly, saying, "They've already started to brainwash you, but it's okay. The Resistance can help you. Let's just get out of here to safety. We can talk about this later, okay?"

Orfeo unconvincingly nodded yes. Carina held his face in her hands, forcing him to look at her, and asked, "Orfeo, who loves you more than anyone in this entire universe?"

Without any hesitation, he replied, "You do."

"Who knows you better than anyone in this entire universe?"

"You do."

"Who would happily sacrifice her life for you without a second thought?"

"You would, without any hesitation, as I would do for you."

"Then please trust me. Just follow me, and we can sort all of this out later. Okay?"

Orfeo paused, his face still cradled in her hands, and then said, "Okay. Let's go."

As Orfeo walked behind her, his hand in hers, he heard a booming voice that stopped him in his tracks. "Orfeo, wake up!" Orfeo's body went into a spasm, causing him to jump up and fall onto the floor. He landed squarely on his bandaged stump, which caused him to scream in agony. Dolton rushed in, picked him up as though he were a toddler, and gently rested him on the bed.

"Are you okay?" Dolton asked with a sincere, concerned voice. "What happened?"

Orfeo was still crying in pain, hyperventilating, sweating profusely, and rocking himself back and forth while holding his leg. The bandage was now infused with blood. Dolton carefully removed the bandages and, shaking his head, said, "Bummer!" He hastily wrapped the stump with the bloodied bandage, and ran off, stating that he would be right back.

In a few minutes, he rushed back in with fresh gauze, bandages, a bucket, and what Orfeo now recognized to be the electrocautery device. Dolton told Orfeo to sit tight for a moment, and just as he was about to complete the sentence, Orfeo interjected, "I know. It'll just sting for a second." Dolton smiled and applied the electrocautery to the sites of bleeding. Then he nodded to himself, approving his handiwork. He brought the bucket closer to the bed and washed off the blood. He applied the cream, which was incredibly soothing, and then redressed the stump.

The pain had mostly subsided now, and Orfeo, remembering Dolton's question, responded that he must have had a bad dream that jolted him out of bed. Orfeo thanked him for his care. Dolton left, stating that he would be back to check on him shortly. Orfeo, still feeling that his head was spinning from the confusion, which was now even worse after his dream, accepted the pain in his leg as a welcome distraction.

Had the voice commanding him to wake up signified that he should wake up from his actual sleep? This seemed an oversimplification, and Orfeo knew that there was a deeper meaning. His thoughts, now in the rhythm of the pulsating pain in his stump, turned to the idea that he was perhaps asleep in a metaphorical sense and needed to wake up from his waking dream into what was real. But how?

Orfeo's head was pounding to one rhythm, his stump to another. Together they resembled the polyrhythmic Afro-Cuban *guaguancó* conga beat. This was accompanied by the spinning in his brain, driven faster and faster by the rhythm of the guiro, like one of those playground roundabouts.

Orfeo's thoughts were all over the place. There were so many unanswered questions. What did the Master mean when he said that if Orfeo was concerned about being brainwashed, it was already too late? Did it mean that Orfeo had already lost the battle of all battles, the war of Consciousness, before he was aware that it had even begun? Is this what Carina meant when she'd stated that if he came face to face with the Master, even after years of training and preparation, his chances of survival were somewhere between zilch and negligible? Orfeo understood clearly now, despite his growing suspicion that he was going mad, losing his mind, going bonkers, that this was never intended to be a physical battle but rather a mental one, which he perhaps had already lost. This was Orfeo's last thought before dozing back to sleep.

Orfeo awakened spontaneously from a deep, uneventful sleep. He felt completed rested, and he noted that the *guaguancó* rhythm that had been pounding in his leg and head and the spinning sensation driven by the guiro had subsided. There were no dreams, no distractions. It was simply a profound, restorative sleep. His eyes were open, but he just laid in bed, stretching in different directions. He recalled the wonderful feeling of waking up after such rejuvenating sleep to the sound of birds on his fire escape in New York City and, upon stretching to one side, finding Carina's eyes staring at him, already saying *"Yo te quiero màs que muchissimo"* before a single word was uttered. He often thought to himself how words were somehow redundant and could never capture the essence and depth of that emotion. He missed Carina terribly and started to sob. He tucked himself into a ball on his side, and for the first time in a long time, just bawled and bawled, releasing pent-up emotions he had been carrying for so very long. Orfeo could sense that these tears had a density to them and were washing away the waste of so many lifetimes, the false beliefs about his purpose and about who he was. The tears fell like bricks with the density of black holes onto the bed and through the cave floor, penetrating through to the other side of the earth and then breaking through the pull of earth's gravity and cascading toward other false planets and galaxies that would soon be devoured mercilessly. But within these tears, there was a hint of amusement at the realization of how supremely pathetic he was to have believed that he had "chosen" to enter the earth-realm to "save" Carina. All these beliefs and the surrounding layers of bullshit that were necessary to maintain the central foci of what he now recognized to be absurdity were washing away in the tsunami of Orfeo's tears. The tears flowed for what seemed to Orfeo like hours. When the tsunami passed, Orfeo felt lighter, relieved, and somewhat purified.

Even if Orfeo were to go truly mad or be completely brainwashed into that horrific image he had of the majority of lobotomized human beings, living their *"metro, boulot, dodo"* lives without purpose and completely oblivious to what was real, he was comforted by a single hope: He imagined that he would at least be elevated to the level of the so-called idiot, confined to a mental institution, who never speaks or relates to the outside world but has a perpetual smile on his face indicating that he knows a truth so beautiful, powerful, and liberating. Yes, Orfeo thought to himself, even in that lobotomized state, he hoped that he would find his salvation in the memory of Carina and the idea of Consciousness indelibly imprinted on his Being. This radical image of himself as lobotomized idiot rendered him fully fearless to face whatever would come to pass.

Dolton prepared the most spectacular breakfast for Orfeo. There were pancakes filled with ripe banana, strawberries, and blueberries and drizzled with some type of fruit purée and poached eggs covered in herbs and spices on top of a grain that Orfeo couldn't identify. It was a veritable feast. Orfeo ate very slowly, extracting every flavor from each morsel, as though it would perhaps be his last. He washed each mouthful with what appeared to be some plant- or root-based ambrosia steeped in honey. Despite having had the best sleep he'd had in a very long time, the tears, which he'd felt were purging the weight of accumulated lifetimes, had exhausted him. Orfeo wondered if the Master could read his mind and this feast was sort of a celebration for his achievement or if it was completely unrelated and was in fact his last meal before the lobotomy that Carina had described. Regardless, Orfeo surprisingly felt himself to be at peace.

"How was breakfast?" Dolton asked in a tone belying the fact that he already knew the answer.

"Amazing! Simply amazing!" Orfeo replied. "It

appears that you may have missed your true calling in life."

"What would that calling be, Orfeo?"

"A chef, of course. You are an incredibly talented chef, and I've thoroughly enjoyed every meal that you've prepared. Thank you."

"No. I thank you. It is my pleasure to serve you. This, in fact, is my calling: simply to serve. It is not limited to preparing meals but includes providing service in every regard and doing so selflessly. Would you like more?"

"Thank you for everything, Dolton, but no. I'm completely satisfied. Will the Master visit today? I'm looking forward to seeing him."

"Yes. The Master will join you for lunch today. He, too, is looking forward to meeting with you."

Orfeo was truly looking forward to meeting with the Master, and this enthusiasm made him wonder if he was beginning to suffer from the Stockholm syndrome. What really concerned Orfeo was the fact that he was not at all bothered by the idea that he could be suffering from this syndrome. He wondered if this could have been a consequence of the brainwashing procedure. Orfeo imagined the image of "turtles all the way down," reflecting his predicament of puzzles within larger puzzles ad infinitum.

The Art of Brainwashing

The Master and Orfeo were seated at a medium-sized table draped with a white table cloth. Orfeo's crutches were on the floor next to him. Dolton had just ladled a stew into their large bowls, and the cave was suffused with its rich aroma. Orfeo almost stuck his head into the bowl to fully absorb its bouquet and to more closely appreciate the art-like composition of colors and textures of the vegetables, onions, potatoes, and rabbit. Orfeo was again reminded of the incongruity of it all—of Dolton, as giant and culinary artist; of the bleak, dark, damp walls of his new home being inhabited by the rich fragrance of a meal one could only imagine in the best of five-star Parisian restaurants; and of the fact that, despite being a prisoner, he was treated as royalty. As he closed his eyes, allowing the plumes of delight to enter his nostrils and bathe his senses, Orfeo uttered in amusement, "Turtles all the way down."

"Excuse me? I didn't catch that," the Master said as he was pouring the wine.

Orfeo opened his eyes, taking his face out of the

bowl, and replied, "It was just a random thought. Never mind."

"I'm happy to see that you are regaining your strength. You seem to be much better."

"I feel better. I finally had a good night's sleep."

"I heard about your little nocturnal adventure. Have you been having nightmares?"

"Not so much nightmares but these recurrent, vivid dreams that seem so real. If it weren't for the fact that my leg was intact in the dreams, I'd have difficulty discerning my dream state from reality."

"What's the message?" the Master asked.

"What do you mean?"

"What do you think the dreams are trying tell you?"

Orfeo paused, deciding on how much he should reveal. "I'm not sure yet. I feel that sometimes they raise more questions than they provide answers."

"Sometimes the right question is actually much more valuable than the answer to that question. The question guides you to an inquiry that leads you to novel and unconsidered terrain. Dreams are often the subconscious trying to provide portals to new vistas, new paradigms that the conscious mind has either been incapable of acknowledging or has refused to do so." The Master raised his glass and toasted, "Here's to dreaming!"

They both took a sip, and the complexity of the wine overwhelmed Orfeo's palate to a state of ecstasy. "This wine is fantastic! How do you manage to maintain such a collection?"

"As you well know, my friend, there are advantages to immortality. With time, it is easier to separate the proverbial wheat from the chaff, the sublime from the pedestrian, and to discriminate between fine gradations of beauty at the narrowest margins of the asymptote."

Orfeo now raised his glass and toasted, "Here's to the beauty at the margins of the asymptote."

They both ate in silence for a while, thoroughly enjoying the meal that Dolton had so lavishly prepared. Halfway through their culinary adventure, the Master made a gesture to Orfeo and asked, "May I?"

Orfeo correctly interpreted this as a request for permission to speak, and with his mouth still full and palate exploding from the assault of flavors and scents from his last bite, he nodded yes.

"Your comment the other day about being brainwashed has remained at the forefront of my mind. Aside from its pertinence to your situation here and now, it is a subject that fascinates me."

"How so? Why?" Orfeo asked, still chewing very slowly and consciously.

"What fascinates me is the question of why people adopt certain ideas and behave in certain ways and how individuals and masses are influenced. I'm intrigued by how a certain idea is implanted in the collective consciousness of the masses and blossoms into mythic proportions, and more so, how others plant those seeds to suit their own purposes. Don't you find this subject fascinating?"

"Absolutely! It ultimately begs the question of free will, doesn't it?"

"Ultimately, yes," the Master replied, "but it is not this overriding question that intrigues me. Rather it is the application of influence that captures my interest. For instance, how does one family influence their child to practice the piano or study five hours a day rather than spend the afternoon goofing around with his or her friends, or how does one convince someone to kill another in the name of some cause?"

"Aren't those completely separate issues?" Orfeo asked.

"Are they? On the surface, they appear to be, but ultimately, they are both the result of what may be lumped under the umbrella of brainwashing. There are clearly positive forms, such as having children adopt the practice of discipline or delayed gratification, as well as negative ones, such as a Hitler, Mao Tse Tung, or Stalin capturing the imaginations of their subjects and influencing them to commit unimaginable atrocities. Do you see my point?"

"Yes," Orfeo conceded.

"The real question, at least for me, is how, in either the positive or negative cases, this is accomplished. It is not only a question of persuading an individual or a nation to believe something, but also how to actually entice them to put those ideas into action. I find this fascinating."

The Master paused to take a sip of wine, take a bite of food, and noting that Orfeo's glass was almost empty, refill both of their glasses. While he physically chewed the succulent rabbit, Orfeo's furrowed brow indicated that he was mentally chewing on the subject of brainwashing. The subject was already unavoidably at the forefront of his mind because of his own predicament. Consequently, the words were not merely relegated to intellectual wrangling; they managed to weigh on his own existence.

Orfeo offered, "This point makes me think about the Chinese communists during the Korean War, who were apparently experts in the art of brainwashing. Are you familiar with their tactics?"

The Master shook his head no.

"Well, there are many examples throughout history of prisoners of war being brutalized and tortured in attempts to secure valuable information or coerce them into coming over to the other side. While these tactics were occasionally successful, the Chinese had an entirely different approach that was brilliant and quite successful."

"This sounds interesting," the Master said. "Please continue."

"Rather than use force to coerce the American

POWs, they reportedly utilized what turned out to be more compelling and successful methods. For instance, the Chinese treated the American POWs with kindness and treated them well. They would host essay-writing contests on the subject of problems with Western capitalism. What was interesting was that the Chinese never asked the POWs to state that communism was better but simply to delineate some of the weaknesses of America that they perceived. The winners of the essay contests would receive a nominal prize, such as a few cigarettes, and have their names posted as the winners. What was most interesting, and almost inconceivable to the Western mind, was that little by little, these methods managed to convert many of these POWs to communism, or at least cause them to become sufficiently critical of America to offer secrets and become traitors."

"That was brilliant!" the Master blurted out. "However, I will counter that it is the Americans who are the true experts in brainwashing the masses."

"I think I see where this is going, but I'd like to hear your point of view."

The Master seemed about to start saying something but then recoiled, as though reconsidering his thesis. "There are so many examples that I'm not sure where to start." After a considerable pause, he began, "Don't you find it incredible that Americans file into work every day, slaving away and wasting the only commodity that truly has any value—their time—while pursuing the 'American dream' that so few of them ever realize? What is even more clever is how they are duped into confusing the idea of the 'American dream' with being good consumers. Now that is brilliant!" The Master was notably excited.

"Do you believe that this is all willfully orchestrated?" Orfeo asked.

"Without question ... and you, my friend, are being provocative. We have both been around long enough to see through the deception? Am I correct?"

"Yes. I was just looking for clarity ... to ensure, if you will, that we were on the same page."

"Orfeo, as you will come to learn, we are more on the same page than you can possibly imagine."

"Is that before or after I am brainwashed?" Orfeo uttered, half in jest.

"As I stated before, Orfeo, you have already been brainwashed, and it is my hope that you will see this with your own mind." The Master paused, raised his wine glass to Orfeo's, and toasted, "Here's to clarity."

After they sipped their wine, the Master asked, "May I continue with my example? It is so rare that I have the opportunity to express these observations."

"It is rare for me to have the opportunity to sit with someone with your experience, and I'm enjoying your perspective. Please continue."

"Consider the American educational system, which is in large part an indoctrination process, gentler, prolonged, but certainly no less insidious than the boot camp imposed by the military. Both the education process and boot camp teach unsuspecting dupes that they are doing something for a higher, noble cause. The student is taught to believe that he or she must do really well in school so that he or she can then secure a great job to become a productive member of society. Are you following me?"

Orfeo nodded yes.

"What they are not told, and the ruse is almost never realized, is that the vast majority of what they learn in school is false. The things that they spent so many long, arduous hours memorizing are useless and will never be utilized. Furthermore, the most important skill that an educational system should provide is the ability to be an effective, independent, and critical thinker. With the exception of elite schools, this is rarely offered. Rather, students are taught to be obedient servants of the system who 'contribute' to society by being good consumers to feed the state apparatus and contain themselves within the mental shackles of a two-party political system and of beliefs, such as that the United States is the greatest country in the world with the best healthcare system, et cetera, et cetera. This is brainwashing in its highest form."

Dolton returned to clear the table and asked if they needed anything else before he left to attend to some errands. They both expressed that they were fully satiated, and Orfeo thanked Dolton profusely for his exquisite lunch, care, and attention. Dolton was very pleased with the adulation Orfeo offered, and he bowed to the both of them and took leave.

The Master continued, "Similarly, the soldier is brainwashed into believing that he is fighting and dying for God and country. Is it a surprise that the military recruits eighteen-year-olds? What is even more interesting is that the powers that be are losing out on great numbers of recruits who could 'fight the good fight' because, for the most part, they ignore older, more mature citizens, who hold on to this same cockamamie belief rather than seeing the obvious—that they are being exploited for the benefit of corporate profit." The Master paused to let his point sink in and perhaps to take a breath. "Do you think that the Chinese could hold a candle to the Americans when it comes to manipulating the masses?"

"That's a pretty compelling argument," Orfeo responded. "I've always wondered how such a system of manipulation came about. Was it planned out ahead of time, step by step, and set into motion as planned, or did it evolve spontaneously to a point where the potential to capitalize on what already existed was recognized by a group, which then simply ensured that there would not be any further evolution out of that system? In the latter case, it would simply be a case of maintaining the system as it was recognized to derive maximum benefit, which would not be as exciting as a Machiavellian plot to create from scratch and, moreover, to implement and maintain it."

"Yes. That is a great point. I hadn't considered that."

Orfeo asked if he could share an idea, which a colleague in the Resistance, Marcus, had recounted, that was completely in line with what they were just discussing. Immediately after he said the word *Resistance*, there was a more than subtle change in Orfeo's demeanor. The word had reminded him that there was in fact a struggle, a war, and that although he was confused, the Master was still the enemy. Furthermore, it reminded him that the discussion of brainwashing was not one of an abstract notion but of an issue highly relevant to his present predicament. Orfeo wondered who the Master represented in relation to their discussion. Was he operating at the level of, or superior to, the American masters of deception?

The Master noted the change and also recognized the trigger. He asked Orfeo if he would prefer to continue their discussion another time. Orfeo was ambivalent, but he insisted on continuing what he was now beginning to consider their game of chess. As he had previously surmised, this war would not be fought on a physical battleground but on a mental plane. He was beginning to understand that these early sessions were merely occasions for them to assess each other's strengths and weaknesses and establish their positions.

Orfeo started paraphrasing what Marcus had told

him, but he did so in an energetic manner altogether different from his manner just prior to having been snapped back into the reality of his situation. "Most indoctrinatory processes—or stated bluntly, methods of brainwashing—as we were discussing, are able to convince the herd that a particular cause is a noble one. Marcus, however, pointed out that this works best in groups. The hapless fool who finds himself alone in a trench hole can suddenly have major doubts that make him question why the hell he is there to begin with. In other words, the brainwashing mechanism in these circumstances requires a herd mentality to maintain itself. Does this make sense?"

"Yes. It makes complete sense," the Master replied cheerfully, but in his mind, he wished that he would have insisted that they postpone the discussion, which for him was truly a pleasure. As he had stated, it was extremely rare for him to have such intellectually stimulating discussions with someone of Orfeo's state of evolution. He considered Orfeo, in many ways, to be a peer, a collaborator, and now, after Orfeo's shift to a more defensive, distrustful posture, their latitude for exploration was limited.

Orfeo continued. "Even more profound is the soldier who finds himself face to face with his opponent. Suppose there is a split second before one kills the other, and in that split second, they make eye contact. Perhaps each begins to ponder that the other bloke is just like him—has a family and a sucky life, doesn't know what the hell he's doing there either, and just wants to be home with the boys smoking a spliff or throwing back some brewskies ..."

The Master's befuddled look caused Orfeo to pause, and the Master, almost embarrassed, asked, "Spliff? Brewskies?"

Orfeo smiled and explained that *spliff* was street jargon for a marijuana cigarette and a *brewsky* was an alcoholic beverage, typically beer. He continued, "So this kid, who would obviously rather be home with the boys smoking a spliff or throwing back some brewskies, knows deeply that it is simply a matter of luck who gets the bullet in his head. Unfortunately, that split second is rarely long enough for this poor bloke to question this tragicomic play within which he finds himself— this fool's errand—and realize that there is an alternate ending he can choose. At this moment, he may realize that they both, the hunter and the hunted, are merely pawns in this game and that with a slight shift in reality, they'd be in a bar arguing about whether soccer or baseball was truly the best sport and turn their heads simultaneously as the hot babe passes by. With this realization, this now enlightened bloke may, as some have done in times of war, put down his weapon, make his way back to the trench hole, and then be sent to a medical facility because he's 'lost his nerve.'"

The Master gestured to ask permission to interrupt,

and Orfeo gestured back in the affirmative. The Master said that he wasn't sure if it was because of Orfeo's use of rich street jargon, but he couldn't find the relation between what Orfeo was recounting and their prior discussion on brainwashing.

Orfeo responded with a smile. "You must have patience, Master. All will be revealed in due course."

The Master beamed back and nodded in agreement. "Please continue."

Orfeo pressed on. "Marcus pointed out that, although the methods of brainwashing the youth into going to war for God and country were the same today as in the past, the response to these methods, perhaps due to the internet and more access to information, has not been as robust as it once was. In wars of the future, boot camp will be the first round of indoctrination, but another tier will arrive to separate the proverbial wheat from the chaff, the true believers. The second round will be as follows: A new recruit will be directed into a stark-white room that is completely empty, save for a chair in which another young man is bound and a small table in the corner of the room on which there is a telephone and a black box. On the floor behind the chair will be a large piece of plastic. The young man that is bound will have the same racial profile as the recruit. Are you following?"

The Master, whose interest was now piqued, responded affirmatively. Orfeo told the Master to interrupt if he didn't understand something, because this was the crux of the entire discussion, the thing that linked back to their prior discussion on brainwashing. Again, the Master nodded in affirmation.

Orfeo had set the stage, and he could feel the tension that he had created. He continued. "The recruit's instructions will be to ask the young man who is bound to the chair a series of questions. Question one: Who are you? The young man will respond that he's from some small town, likely similar to where the recruit is from. Question two: Why are you here? The young man will respond that he doesn't know. Question three: How did you get here? The young man will say that he was at a party with some friends, was drugged and abducted, and woke up in this chair and in this room. Question four: What did you do? The young man will "Nothin'. I didn't do nothin'!"

By the look on the Master's face, Orfeo knew that he had the Master's undivided attention. He continued. "At this point, the telephone will ring. The recruit will walk to the desk and pick up the phone. The voice on the other end will say, without emotion, 'The man in the chair is a terrorist responsible for the deaths of many Americans and must be executed immediately. We already have the information we need; just ask him for the names of his colleagues. In the box, you will find a gun and bullets. Execute him. This is a matter of national security.'"

The Master was now on the edge of his seat. Orfeo,

for dramatic effect, allowed some time to idle away before he continued.

"The recruit, with little hesitation, will open the box and load the gun. Just as he is done, the phone will ring again. He'll pick it up. The same voice, now in a softer, more human tone, will say, "By the way, I forgot to mention that the agents that brought the terrorist here were utterly incompetent, and rather than placing the chair in the center of the plastic cover on the floor, they placed him on the far edge. The cleaning division has been complaining a lot lately about the mess that we've been leaving all over the floor. Apparently, brain material, when mixed with blood, is quite difficult to clean up. Just so I don't get shit from that division, can you please execute him with a bullet in the forehead so that the mess lands on the plastic? We'd really appreciate this. Thanks."

The Master's eyebrows were raised in apprehension. Orfeo asked the Master if he was following. The Master eagerly answered yes and indicated that Orfeo should continue.

"The recruit will now walk over to the other young man, face him, raise the gun to his forehead, right between his eyes, and tell him that he is only going to ask once: 'What are the names of your colleagues?' The young man, seeing the gun, will start screaming, crying, and pleading for his life. He'll say that he doesn't have any colleagues. He'll repeat imploringly that he is innocent and hasn't done anything. He'll desperately explain that he has a wife, a kid, a mom, and a dad. He'll beg for mercy, and his crying will turn more and more into soft whimpers. There will be a moment of silence when they'll both know what will inevitably happen. Their eyes will meet."

Orfeo again paused for effect. The Master sat at the edge of his seat, which was almost about to tip over. Orfeo changed his tone and asked, "Will the recruit pull the trigger?" Orfeo hesitated, waiting for the Master to respond, and when the Master didn't say anything, he continued. "If the recruit pulls the trigger and shoots the young man point blank in the head while looking him straight in the eyes, then he is clearly one who is worthy to join the ranks of true believers willing to fight for God and country. Those who cannot pull the trigger, perhaps because they question whether or not the young man is guilty, consider the issue of due process, or are able to see humanity is his eyes, are sent to clean latrines or perform some other function that doesn't jeopardize the cause, infiltrating the rank and file like a virus."

"Whoa! That's powerful! I definitely see the connection now," the Master exclaimed. "But why go to such extremes? The military has no shortage of mindless automatons programmed to do their bidding, and they have the brainwashed masses to support their cause, all while they pound their breasts in the name of the cause du jour. Doesn't your colleague … did you say his name was Marcus? Isn't Marcus's vision too drastic?"

"I really don't think so," Orfeo responded. "In this day and age of ready access to information on the internet, where everyone can openly question the government, not only with just cause but also with rabid fervor when they learn that there is actually a movement, a larger group, that shares their same anti-government ideas, the methods of brainwashing the masses will have an increasingly diminishing effect. The question is, how else will the military of the future know for sure that soldiers won't defect to ISIS—the Islamic State in Iraq and Syria—or our enemies du jour who are holding democracy and its gold under their oil wells? The military of the future cannot risk deserters or those who will suddenly find God in the eyes of the enemy. The risk of inoculating others would be too great."

"Touché!" the Master admitted.

"This strategy tests the mettle of the soldiers, as well as that of the leaders. It requires a lot of chutzpah to put a recruit in a position to shoot someone between the eyes at point blank while making eye contact. What better test is there? After this, the leaders know exactly who their soldiers are and what can be expected of them in dire circumstances. Furthermore, the soldiers know exactly who their leaders are. There is no confusion, as they are cut from the same mold."

They both sat back in their chairs and luxuriated

in the wine, which seemed a perfect match for their conversation. The Master closed his eyes, and Orfeo wondered if he was savoring the wine or thinking about what Orfeo has just recounted. After a while, the Master asked, "So, what would you do in that situation?"

"What do you mean?"

"Would you pull the trigger?"

Orfeo wasn't expecting that question and was clearly uncomfortable. "I'm really not sure."

"You mean that since you've heard Marcus's anecdote, you've never asked yourself this question?"

Orfeo was silently thinking, feeling somewhat trapped. He wondered if this was part of the game of cat and mouse between them. For a moment, he'd felt that he had gained the advantage in the discussion by one-upping the Master with his story of the recruit, but the Master very quickly escaped his arm-bar and again took control of the match.

"Ultimately, isn't the most important question that this story begs: What would you do?"

Orfeo hesitated. Like a chess player, he considered the ramifications of what he was about to say, the possible responses and alternative advances. Then he said, "I don't think I could ever be in this situation."

"You mean to say that you cannot envision yourself having to shoot someone point-blank in the head or that you cannot envision yourself brainwashed?"

Check, Orfeo thought to himself. He had

underestimated the Master and was cornered. Orfeo knew that, from the very beginning, their discussion about brainwashing had never been an abstract or intellectual one but rather a challenge, a battle, and as Carina and the Resistance had warned him, the prize was his very own consciousness.

Orfeo, feeling pressured, responded that he could not envision himself brainwashed to the point where he would do something contrary to his core beliefs, without being able to think independently.

"But isn't that the very definition of *brainwashing*, to coerce one into not be able to think independently and doing things that one normally would not do. Do you believe that you are immune to such coercion?"

"I believe that I would be aware of it taking place and would guard myself against it."

"If this is the case, Orfeo, this places you in the ninety-ninth percentile of humankind, because the remainder of those mere mortals are oblivious to such brainwashing. You must have seen this in your everyday experience, no?"

Orfeo, feeling even more cornered now and playing from a defensive posture, responded, "Yes, I agree that most humans are blind to what motivates them and consequently makes them more susceptible to manipulation, but I also believe that it is a question of evolution. It's not that I am arrogant, but the fact is, I am more evolved than most of humankind."

"Ah, I see. So you believe that being more evolved makes you immune to brainwashing. Is that the case?"

Orfeo could no longer see where the attack was coming from but felt that the Master was very close to a checkmate. He answered with a feigned air of confidence, "Yes."

The Master simply smiled and nodded. After a long pause, he said, "I'm sure you are familiar with the popular adage 'the bigger they are, the harder they fall.'"

Orfeo nodded affirmatively.

The Master stood up and said, "I unfortunately have some duties to attend to, but I would encourage you to give this idea some thought, specifically as it pertains to you."

Orfeo jumped to his one foot, using the table to balance himself, and boldly asked, "When will I be released?"

"Released?" the Master asked with a surprised tone. "You ask this as though you are being held captive. As I told you before, you are here as my guest and are welcome to leave as you wish."

"You mean I can leave right now?"

"Yes, Orfeo, of course. At this point, however, I would ask you, as a favor, to stay for just awhile longer. I am truly enjoying your company and sincerely believe that you will find it to your benefit. Is that okay with you?"

Orfeo was confused, but he answered, "Yes, of course." He'd believed all this time that he was the

Master's prisoner and that he was being treated well for the purposes of being brainwashed. After the Master left, Orfeo again considered what the Master had asked him when they first met: "What if you are mistaken? What if everything you were told was false?" He also considered the Master's suggestion that he give thought to the adage, "the bigger they are, the harder they fall." Especially in light of the revelation that he was never a prisoner, this was a game changer. Orfeo realized that perhaps he was mistakenly playing chess while the Master was playing the board game *Go*.

On the following day, the Master visited without being announced. Orfeo was now accustomed to his beaming smile and welcoming demeanor. After a brief exchange of pleasantries, they sat in silence. The Master could sense that Orfeo had a lot to get off his chest, so he waited patiently. After a while, Orfeo broke the silence.

"I'm lost."

"Yes, I know. Doesn't it feel better to know that you are lost than to be lost and not know?"

"I'm not so sure about this. I'm feeling rather lame now, knowing that almost everything I believed is false."

"The bigger they are …"

Orfeo smiled, shaking his head at the irony of his predicament. "May I ask you some questions?"

"Of course. I am at your service."

"If I was never a prisoner, why was I so brutally

beaten? Do you typically cut your guest's legs off and break their ribs before inviting them to dinner?"

The Master looked at Orfeo with an expression of bewilderment. "Do you recall the circumstances that brought you here?"

"Not completely. I recall Carina being completely spent after we met Maya and deciding to take a walk to give her some space."

"And then what happened?"

"I remember that it was a beautiful day and that it felt really great to be outside and walking. At one point, I had a sense that something was wrong … as though I was being watched. I started to head back and, although I was nervous, I was somewhat comforted by the fact that I had brought my gun and sword. I was completely pumped, because I had been preparing for an entire year for that moment.

"So, did anyone attack you?"

"No. There were a few men, and one of them called out my name. I responded and asked what they wanted."

"And what did they want?"

"They said that they just wanted to talk. They said that they had a message for me. I thought of making a run for it but realized that there might have been more of them than I could account for, so I agreed to talk."

"Did they surround you or behave in a menacing manner?

"No. There were four of them. They approached me

calmly, and when they saw that I had a gun in my belt, they stayed back."

"Then what happened?"

"Well, one of them said that you wanted to speak with me about an urgent matter and invited me to accompany them to meet you. Carina and the Resistance had filled my head with so much stuff about you that I interpreted what they said as a command rather than a request. I guess I was already jumpy, expecting the worse, and had my hand on the gun. So, when I heard some noise behind me, I automatically assumed that there were more of them and drew my gun. There wasn't anyone else that I could see, but there was no turning back. I had my gun in hand and was pointing it at them. They had their hands up and promised me that they meant me no harm. They reiterated that you only wanted to speak with me. I remembered that my heart was pounding out of my head, and based on everything I had heard about you, I felt as though I was being tricked."

"Did any of them exhibit any aggressive behavior?"

Orfeo did not meet the Master's eyes and looked at the ground, responding, "No. I was just really afraid … I heard the rustling of twigs behind me, and I turned suddenly and fired into a bush. When I turned back to your men, I thought that one of them was reaching for a weapon, so I shot him. The other men quickly dispersed as I tried to shoot them as well."

"So, you took the first shot and killed one of my men."

"Yes. I see now that this was a mistake."

"What happened afterward?"

"Your men moved like ninjas. I tried, but I couldn't nail them. The next thing I knew, there was a sharp blow to my wrist, and I dropped the gun. It was all a blur after that. I remember they kept on shouting for me to calm down and saying that they didn't want to fight, but I kept on fighting. They tried to restrain me, but I fought even harder."

"My men told me that you were very well trained."

"Bullshit! I felt like an amateur in a professional mixed martial arts fight. They were so fast. They could have stopped or killed me at any point. In retrospect, I see now that they were holding back."

"Yes. I gave them strict orders not to harm you."

"I quickly recognized that I couldn't match their skills, so I managed to get my sword, and was able to get them to back off. They kept on saying that they didn't want to fight and were actually backing away. I don't know what came over me, but rather than allowing them to walk away, I impulsively attacked. I never had a chance. They quickly got the sword away from me and again started to back away, but when I went for the gun that was on the floor, your guy, who now had the sword, did some kind of crazy summersault. The next thing I knew, I was on the floor, and my leg was on the floor in front of me. I then passed out."

"I can assure you that my men showed the greatest

restraint. They were specifically instructed to back down and walk away from the situation if your reaction was, let's say, unwelcoming. It was a calculated decision on their part to neutralize you by amputating your leg before you forced their hand and caused them to really harm you. For this, I apologize, but you really didn't give them any options."

"What was the message you wanted to give me?"

"It was an invitation to the truth. By the way, the men that Carina saw who prompted your swift departure from your apartment were carrying the same invitation."

"And what truth would that be?"

"Simply that there was no war of Consciousness, no 'Dark' or 'Light' forces, no—"

Orfeo interrupted, "Are you suggesting that Carina lied to me? That just isn't possible."

"No, Orfeo. I am not saying that she lied to you. She was simply telling you what she sincerely believed, just like the Resistance was telling you what they sincerely believed. They were simply operating from a wrong set of assumptions, which have inevitably led them to the wrong conclusions." The Master paused to let the message sink in, and then continued. "Isn't this the case with the vast majority of humankind? Hasn't this been your experience? You, from your 'evolved' perspective, can certainly appreciate how those most human behaviors that appear to be undeniably ridiculous are usually the result of a lack of perspective and only rarely the result of malicious intentions. Don't you agree?"

"Yes, clearly."

"Then, this leads us back to the question I posed to you earlier: Does the fact that you are more evolved, actually quite highly evolved, render you immune to brainwashing, coercion, and consequently, these lapses in perspective?"

Orfeo looked directly into the Master's eyes but could not respond.

"Perhaps to make my point more forcefully and illustrate it more concretely, are you any different than the recruit you described?"

Orfeo could no longer maintain eye contact. He looked at the ground and, almost mumbling, said, "I guess not. I never realized this, but I see it now."

"Do you believe that anyone brainwashed into doing anything, from the average person pursuing the American dream to a prisoner of war revealing classified information to a suicide bomber, ever 'realized' what they were doing? Orfeo, this is, by definition, what it means to be brainwashed. You are manipulated into seeing reality a certain way, and then you naturally fit everything into that vision without ever realizing it. Once you've created that vision, anything that is not congruent with that vision is invisible to your eye, even if it's as big as a gorilla standing right in front of you, trying to shove a banana in your mouth. This new illusion now becomes your reality, which is reinforced by those around you who share the illusion. Those who simply provide an alternative vision are invisible or ignored, and those whose arguments are strong enough to get your attention and challenge that illusion are defined as enemies. Do you see now, first hand, the power of brainwashing?"

"So much so that I find it hard to believe." Orfeo paused as though deep in thought and then asked, "But who is responsible for this? Who is doing the brainwashing?"

"Ah! Now that is a great question? But I have a better one: Why did you leave Consciousness?"

Orfeo smirked to indicate to the Master that it was unfair to answer a question with a question, but he answered. "To find Carina. I believed that she was lost, and I came back into so many lifetimes to find and bring her back to Consciousness so that we could remain merged as we had been."

"Do you still believe this?"

"No, not really. I learned from Carina that, in fact, she had found her way, and I was the one who was lost."

"Let's ignore for the moment the reasons for which she returned to the earth-realm and focus on you. Can you think of any other reasons why you may have returned?"

Orfeo was thinking but couldn't come up with anything.

"Would you like to hear my thoughts on this?"

"Absolutely."

"Before I do, let's eat and discuss this over a great bottle of wine. I feel that this will be a rather big pill to swallow on an empty stomach. Get some rest, and we'll meet for dinner."

The Game

Dolton again outdid himself and prepared another outstanding feast. Orfeo was careful not to overeat or drink too much so that he could remain fully alert for what the Master would share. At this point, his head was already spinning from learning that almost everything on which he'd based his reality was false, and he wanted to be as clear-headed as possible. The Master had warned that what Orfeo was about to learn would be a tough pill to swallow, so Orfeo prepared himself for this pill. But he was still having trouble accepting the fact that he had already been brainwashed, which now seemed like a euphemism for *duped, suckered,* or *hoodwinked,* which all seemed rather sugar-coated ways of describing the way he really felt. If it were just one "misunderstanding," that would be bad enough for someone like himself who had been around the block so many times, but being susceptible to such chicanery so many times left Orfeo feeling like the class dunce. *Yes,* he thought to himself, *just as the Master said, the bigger you are, the harder you fall!*

Orfeo began to see the depth of the deception. There were layers and layers of misunderstandings and likely many more that had not as yet risen to the surface. He already considered himself to be a compassionate person, but now he developed even more compassion for humankind. If he, Carina, and the Resistance, who were indisputably so evolved and conscious of the continuity between past lives and their relationship to Consciousness, could be so deceived, what chance would the average Joe have in sorting all of this out? It suddenly occurred to him that it was no surprise at all that humans were condemned to living out their *"metro, boulot, dodo"* lives, again and again, without a clue as to what was going on, and why waking up to their true purpose, realizing that they were one with Consciousness and always have been, was close to impossible.

"You appear to be lost in your thoughts?"

"No, just lost in general."

The Master raised his glass and toasted, "Here's to being lost and found!"

As Orfeo raised his glass and clinked it with the Master's, he felt a wave of emotion and gratitude for how much the Master had helped him and proposed another toast. "To your generosity and beneficence. Thank you."

"It has been my pleasure to serve you. Should we continue our conversation that we started earlier? I believe it will clarify many questions that you may have."

"Yes, please."

The Master started by saying, "Imagine the earth-realm to be a game."

"A game in the sense of a sporting competition?"

"No. It's more like a high-stakes poker game."

"Does one choose to play of one's own volition?"

"Of course. There is no one, no 'other,' in Consciousness to force another to do anything. One enters the game to test oneself, to assess where one is in actuality and what one needs to learn. You may think of the earth-realm as a training ground, a simulation that provides such a self-assessment, and ultimately the experience necessary to navigate and sustain the higher levels of Consciousness."

"I see. But why is it a high-stakes game? What is there to lose?"

"Ah, what is there to lose?" the Master repeated with a wry smile. "Everything, Orfeo … absolutely everything." Orfeo was about to interrupt with a question, but the Master pressed on. "Let me explain. What makes the game even more interesting is that no one choosing to play the game ever has the slightest doubt that they are ready and will have a simple, beautiful, earthly, human experience, as though going on an adventure vacation, and return unscathed.

"What do you mean? They must have some idea since they are entering the game to assess themselves … in order to get to the next level."

"One would think so, but it is easy to delude oneself,

as many do. This is the beauty of the game. It's a self-check to examine deep-rooted beliefs that cannot be readily appreciated. This is why the amnesia is such a necessary part of the game. It forces one to operate on the truth of one's being, not on one's beliefs. It allows you to root out the bullshit and truly see what's under the hood so that you can figure out which pistons are malfunctioning. This couldn't be done with the memory of pure Being, pure Consciousness."

Orfeo's brow was deeply furrowed as though he were frustrated by trying to put the pieces of a complex puzzle together. Finally, he said, "What I don't understand is how someone, after achieving such a high level of evolution, of mastering and being able to maintain the state of Consciousness, could in fact be, as you are suggesting, so thoroughly deluded. It just doesn't make sense to me."

"I see," the Master responded. He crossed his arms and massaged his chin in that universal professorial manner, indicating that he was deep in thought and in the process of composing a brilliant response. "Let's use your case as an example, which may clarify matters. Why did you come to the earth-realm?"

"As I told you before, I believed that Carina was lost and couldn't find her way back."

"So, in other words, both of you had 'arrived' at Consciousness, Carina somehow lost her way in the earth-realm, and you put on your white, shining armor to rescue your great love."

Orfeo smiled at the Master's humor and said, "Yes, but without the white, shining armor. But I still don't understand why this makes me or anyone else deluded."

"This will become clear as we go on. But as I was saying, it is very easy to delude oneself. The words or beliefs are irrelevant because the mind, especially when higher levels of consciousness are achieved, becomes more deluded, more deceitful, and more cunning. Thus, the adage 'the bigger you are, the harder you fall' is easily applied here. There are many levels of ignorance."

"Can you give me some specific examples?"

"Sure. For instance, consider the most pious believers who perpetrate great crimes in the name of their own version of 'God.' Holier-than-thou 'spiritual' beings who would never think about harming a fly but deep down inside, even if they don't recognize it, believe that they are better than everyone else and, moreover, that they are the sole bearers of the truth. These are just other forms of duality."

"How so?" Orfeo interrupted.

"I promise that I'll come back to this, but allow me to finish my thought."

Orfeo interjected, "I really hope you're keeping track of all my questions that you're putting off for later."

"Patience, little grasshopper. I assure you that all your questions will be answered."

Orfeo chuckled.

The Master continued, "Some of the most prolific ignoramuses that you've ever encountered in the earth-realm actually considered themselves to be the most highly evolved beings in Consciousness. They thought the earth-realm would be a cakewalk, that their return would be for the sole purpose of helping others, to assist others in their journeys, similar to the Buddha or Jesus Christ. Once in the earth-realm, however, their deep-rooted tendencies emerge, and they, having made the commitment to remain in this realm until they finished their work, indeed remain for many lifetimes, many eternities."

"Damn!"

"Damn!" the Master repeated, laughing out loud. "Now do you understand why this is a high-stakes game? You are betting against the depth of your own delusion."

"Damn!" Orfeo repeated. "Why would anyone want to play?"

"Why? Isn't the answer obvious?" The Master paused and then added, "Because everyone loves a challenge … especially when one is sure that one can win."

"But it's not fair."

"What's not fair?"

"The game. It's like a casino where all the games are rigged."

"Yes, but in this case, the player and the casino are one."

"You've lost me again."

"As I stated before, the game is not imposed on the player. The player and the game are one, and the game cannot exist without the player."

"Can the player exist without the game?" Orfeo interrupted.

"Yes, of course, but in a different way."

"Now I'm completely lost."

"Let me clarify. The game, and even the earth-realm, is born out of the thought that duality can exist, that there can actually be 'other,' that there can actually be two and not one. From that thought, the cosmos and the earth-realm is created."

"What is there without the thought of duality?"

"What always was, is, and always will be: Consciousness. What else?"

"Then the whole world, the universe, is a creation of the mind?"

"Of course it is. But you know this, don't you? Is it a surprise?"

"Yes, I've known this on an intellectual level, but I've never understood it at this all-encompassing level."

"And hence, my dear friend," the Master declared with a smile, "why you are having this all-encompassing experience."

Orfeo leaned, placed his head in both of his hands, and whispered to himself, "Fuck me … fuck me."

"Dolton," the Master called out, "please open another bottle of wine. Orfeo is in need of a refreshment."

"No, please" Orfeo said. "I already can't think straight."

"No, please" the Master insisted. "I assure you that this is not a thinking matter. Are you familiar with the expression *in vino veritas?*"

"Yes, it means 'in wine there is truth.'" Dolton arrived with a decanter and poured them both a glass of wine.

The Master raised his glass and toasted. "Well then, let us continue on our journey to truth."

Orfeo clinked the Master's glass and, in a less than enthusiastic tone, toasted, "To truth."

"Orfeo, it is the very belief that duality exists that creates the self—if such a thing could exist—the universe, and hence, the game. It is the mind that creates everything, including the game that you believe is completely rigged and unfair. Is it a surprise that the deluded mind creates a deluded game?"

Orfeo remained silent, but nodded his head to express understanding.

"Rather than being unfair, the game is exactly what the doctor ordered, isn't it? The mind sets up the game in order to create a simulation wherein the mind, through experience, can clear itself, as you clear your sinuses with a hefty dose of wasabi, of all its accumulated nonsense."

"So, all those lost lives, Carina and I on this wild-goose

chase searching for each other over so many lifetimes, weren't ever necessary. It was all a—"

"No, Orfeo, every bit of it was necessary, because it was all part of the game that you both created for the purpose of each other's development, your journey toward realizing the truth. Do you understand now?"

"I get it. But all of this—the fact that it took me so long to get it—just makes me feel like such a loser ... deficient. In fact, I understand your words intellectually ... words that I've read in many books by Adyashanti, Ramana Maharsi, Jed McKenna, and so many others but could never internalize. I feel like a student who keeps failing the class and is made to repeat it, over and over again ... as though I have a learning disability. You know what I mean?"

The Master placed a reassuring hand on Orfeo's shoulder and said, "The notions of time, repeated lifetimes, failure, success—they're all in your mind, an illusion. None of it really exists. It's just your process, your game, that you yourself designed so you could have this experience to bring you back to the truth."

Disillusioned, Orfeo asked, "But why did we have to leave Consciousness to learn this? Why not remain in Consciousness?"

"My dear friend, your very question implies duality. It was because of this very belief that Consciousness is a place where you could leave, return, and sometimes not find again that the mind created the game. At some very subconscious level, the mind knew the truth and left breadcrumbs for you to find your way back to the truth. Even in its deluded state, it knew in its depths that to be in any other state than truth-aware was deficient, and—"

Orfeo interrupted, "And the game, through simulated human experiences, offers the opportunity to return to Consciousness."

"Close, but no cigar. Can you rephrase what you just said to make it true?"

Orfeo thought for a long time, and then, as though hit by a revelation, he said, "The game offers the opportunity to understand the truth that there is only Consciousness, that it is here and everywhere … that there is no need to go to or back to anywhere. Consciousness is here now, and we are Consciousness."

"Bingo!"

"Damn!"

"So do you still think the game to be unfair?"

"No. It's definitely rigged but ultimately to win."

"Bingo!"

"Damn!"

The Master raised his glass and toasted, "Welcome home!"

Orfeo raised his glass, still shaking his head, and the only thing he could think to say was, "Damn!"

The Master, quite amused at Orfeo's reaction, raised his glass to toast again. "To damn!"

After a long pause, the Master added, "So, looking

at your own situation, you must certainly admit that it is more than a tad bit amusing, no?"

"Sure," Orfeo responded sarcastically, "it's a pathetic comedy."

"You are mistaken, my friend. It's the most beautiful story ever told—the story of the return to Consciousness. What's amusing are the plot twists and turns. First you believed that you were returning to save your love Carina. Then you learned that it was not her but you who was lost. You must admit that the game has a penchant for the theatrical, in that it wasn't that you were lost in your belief that you were here to save Carina but that you were lost in a larger sense. You were then recycled through all these lifetimes because of your arrogance— your arrogant beliefs that there could be 'other,' that you could actually save anyone, and finally, that you were so evolved that it was solely for Carina's benefit that you had returned. Now that's grand opera!

Orfeo, now seeing the humor in his story, toasted, "Here's to damn!"

The Master clinked glasses with him and continued. "Along the way, you learned, of course, simply to make the story more interesting, that there are 'Dark' and 'Light' forces at play, that there is a war, and that you are in the thick of it. So far, that's already a compelling story, right?"

"I guess so," Orfeo responded, not sure of where the Master was going with this.

"Then, your story gets even more interesting. You finally had this battle that you'd been preparing for—although for the record you were the only one fighting—and managed to get beat up pretty badly and get your leg chopped off." The Master was speaking in somewhat of a humorous tone, but then he caught himself, pointed at Orfeo's leg, and said, "I'm sorry, dear friend, I realize that it's not a joke."

"No worries. Please continue."

"And then you ended up face to face"—the Master adopted an ominous tone and placed both hands above his head, wiggling his fingers in that universal gesture indicating the presence of evil—"with the 'Dark One' himself in his lair. However, to your surprise, you were wined and dined like a prince, and it turned out"—the Master held both hands out and pointed back at himself—"that I'm not such a bad fellow."

Orfeo was clearly amused by this.

The Master paused, picked up his glass, took a sip, and asked, "Orfeo, you know when you are at a great movie and, having payed the ridiculous amount of money they're asking for at the movies these days, you've suspended all notions of disbelief, and you're completely engaged in the story line?"

"Absolutely. Isn't that why we so willingly pay that ridiculous amount of money? It's for the opportunity to suspend disbelief and enter into that other reality, perhaps to escape from our own if only for the two to three hours the movie lasts."

"Well, I've always wondered if I was the only one who, right in the middle of being fully engaged in the drama, sometimes stops and wonders if the main character has the slightest clue that this story is just a wee bit too over the top to be realistic and wonders if he or she is just a character in a movie. Have you ever had this experience?"

Orfeo adopted a very serious tone and responded, "No, I can't say that I have. It must be just you." They looked at each other and burst out laughing.

The Master suddenly became very serious and asked, "Well, I've always wanted to ask you this: While this incredible story—your story, your life—was going on, did you ever suspect that it was just a tad over the top and perhaps just a movie or theater?"

Orfeo was silent for a long time and finally just shook his head, indicating that he had never considered this.

The Master twisted his head to the side in the same way that a dog does when it doesn't understand something, and with one raised eyebrow, he said, "Interesting."

At that moment, Dolton barged in, out of breath and out of sorts. When he caught his breath, he said with a tone of great urgency, "Master, please forgive me for disturbing you, but there is something that requires your immediate attention."

"Are you sure that it can't wait?"

The look in Dolton's eyes conveyed his response to the Master's question long before the words were uttered to confirm it. "This cannot wait, Master."

"My sincere apologies, Orfeo, but duty calls. I look forward to continuing our conversation." The Master and Dolton left the room in quite a hurry. Once they were far enough away from Orfeo's dwelling space, the Master asked, "Dolton, what's going on? I haven't seen you in a tizzy like this in ages."

"Master, the Resistance is here!"

"Here! What do you mean here?"

"No exactly here yet, Master."

"Then where?"

"About one day away."

"How did they find us?" the Master asked. Dolton was about to respond when the Master cut him off with a wave of his hand. "It doesn't matter. The Resistance is clearly more sophisticated and perspicacious than ever."

"Persp ... a ... cious?" Dolton asked.

"Perceptive. They can no longer be underestimated."

"Should we engage them before they arrive? We could certainly catch them off guard and destroy them once and for all"

"No. Absolutely not!" the Master insisted. "I do not wish to lower myself to their level. They believe that finding Orfeo will lead them to us and allow them to mount a decisive offensive. Our work with Orfeo is basically done. We have led him out of the cave and allowed him to see the light. It is solely up to him now to choose his path. After breakfast tomorrow morning, we will bid our dear friend farewell and drop him off on their path. They'll never find us."

The Price of Truth

Orfeo was more confused than ever, which he recognized to be his typical modus operandi since meeting the Master. Although he did not understand everything the Master had explained, it made sense to him at a primal level. It resonated with him at his core, but he could not reconcile what he was learning with its greater implications. Hoping to take a nap and clear his head, Orfeo left the crutches near the table, hopped over to the bed, and plopped himself down. He closed his eyes and immediately started to drift off into sleep, but he remained in a semi-alert state where his mind reeled with all the information he had just received.

Everything that his great love Carina had prepared him for and that Maya and the Resistance had reinforced—that there was a war for Consciousness, that Carina, the Resistance, and he were of the Light and the Master, the personification of evil, was of the Dark—was now cast in an inescapable shadow.

Orfeo had feared the threat of being lobotomized into forgetting that Consciousness existed, leaving him akin to the victim of a massive brain stroke resulting in hemineglect, losing all awareness that one side of his body existed. He had more reason than anyone else to fear being trapped in the earth-realm, because he "knew" that there was much more, because he had experienced firsthand what it was like to be in Consciousness. Even with the ignorance, the amnesia he had experienced in so many lifetimes, believing that there was nothing else except the earth-realm, there was still an infinitesimally small nidus of hope that there was something else, something more than the reality that presented itself.

These beliefs had provided Orfeo a clear reason for living and struggling, a raison d'être. But now, he was confronted with the idea that the war was a fiction and that, in fact, there was no 'Light,' no 'Dark,' and on a broader scale, no duality. The trap was set in the very belief that duality could exist. Moreover, it was this very belief in duality that not only kept him imprisoned in the earth-realm but that created it. He himself was the sole creator and proprietor of the very game that imprisoned him. What a mind-fuck!

Orfeo desperately tried to quiet his mind and dozed off to sleep, but he was stuck in that state where his body was dead asleep but his mind was alert. He thought of getting up, but for what purpose? His mind would relentlessly take on each of these premises and make futile attempts to dissect each of them, but he knew in his heart that these premises were the closest thing to the truth that he had ever encountered.

One thing that was incontrovertible in Orfeo's mind, despite his confusion over everything else, was that the Master was not evil. After spending so much time with him engaged in lengthy conversations, experiencing first hand his generosity, care, attention, and most importantly, the life-altering insights he provided, Orfeo had no doubt that the Master was a good man. He at first questioned himself as to whether his feelings about the Master were the result of being brainwashed, exactly what Carina and Maya had warned him about, but his conclusion was always the same: gratitude and appreciation for everything the Master had shared with him.

As the Master had pointed out, he had never asserted any position and certainly had never taken an offensive against anyone. Orfeo remembered the genuine look of surprise and ensuing laughter that had followed when the Master had learned that Carina and the Resistance had labeled him as 'evil.' He had often reminded Orfeo that it was the Resistance who had, on many occasions, imposed their will, propagating the absurd belief that there was a war, and that struggle was necessary. "Fight who? Fight what?" the Master had asked. The truth that the Master had shared with Orfeo was that there was only Consciousness. Orfeo remembered vividly how the Master would pace back and forth, a wine glass in one hand and the other hand gesticulating wildly, as though he were conducting an orchestra and had arrived at the allegro section of the opus, asking intensely, "Struggle against whom? Fight with yourself? At war with yourself? This is silliness. You certainly must be able to see this." Yes, Orfeo now saw this clearly. According to the Master, all he offered was the truth, and then it was only to those who asked and were deemed sincere. He provided assistance to those who were so close to the threshold of liberation but were stuck. He offered what was deemed necessary for each individual to arrive at the truth. The Master had admitted that he often considered a particular individual's path circuitous and sometimes even unnecessary, but said it was not for him to judge. He considered his role to be simply that of a facilitator who made himself available throughout the ages to aid those in search of the truth. Consequently, he never imposed his will or forced anyone to do anything, because he knew that only those who were truly ready could make the transition. No one could be coerced, cajoled, or pressed through the portal of liberation. The key was surrender.

The Master had been emphatic that surrender was the final frontier in accessing liberation, and he'd said that very few ever made it this far and that even fewer still ever went beyond. The Master had pointed out to him that this was exactly the point where Orfeo had arrived on his journey. The Master had made it clear that it was now Orfeo's choice to open that portal or to perpetuate the cycle of incarnations and struggle like a mouse on a treadmill for all eternity. But this time, if he chose the latter, he would bear the curse of the knowing that he was not, in fact, going anywhere.

Orfeo finally dozed off into a void without any thoughts or images. There was only darkness. This was exactly what he'd longed for: a profound silence. After what seemed like hours, Orfeo was jostled violently, causing him to abruptly sit bolt upright and gasp for breath. It was Carina. He embraced her so strongly, so lovingly.

She caressed his face with her hand. "I've missed you so much, babe." They embraced again. She then pulled away suddenly and said, "We really have to go. We can catch up later. The Resistance is waiting for us with transport." Carina stood up, walked to the entrance, and peered around the corner. "The coast is clear. Let's go while we have the chance."

Orfeo stood up, walked over to Carina, and put his hand on her shoulder. She turned, grabbed his hand, and started to lead him out. He pulled her back into the room, held her by both of her shoulders, and looked deeply into her eyes.

"What's the matter, babe?" she asked.

"Do you love me?"

"Of course I do! This isn't the time for this. We really have to go!"

"Please give me a minute. Do you believe that I love you more than anything else in this world?"

"Without a doubt."

"Do you trust me?"

"Of course I do. What's this about?"

"Carina, what if I told you that everything you believed was a lie? That we are creating the very trap that keeps us imprisoned? What if …"

"Orfeo …" Carina burst into tears. Through her sobs, she implored him, "Orfeo, how about we get out of here, and we can sort all this out later. Okay? We can help you, but we first need to get out of here."

"Help me with what, Carina? I see now that I'm not the one who needs help. I've learned so much while I've been here, and I can help you and the Resistance." Carina nestled her head deep in Orfeo's chest, and he could feel her tears flowing.

"Carina, there's no danger here. The Master is a really great man who's shown me the truth. I'd like for you to stay and meet him."

Carina recoiled from Orfeo, wiped away her tears with a swipe of her sleeve, and in a clear but forceful tone said, "Orfeo, my love … you need help. You're not thinking clearly now. Please take my hand and follow me. We've been together for eternities … that means something. It means a lot. Please come with me. We can sort all of this out when we get home." She reached out her hand to him. "Orfeo, please. I love you. Please come with me."

Orfeo reached out and embraced her, holding her tightly as she sobbed uncontrollably. It was as though they both already knew that this was the last time they would see each other. Orfeo awakened to find himself laying in a pillow drenched with tears, and he had a heaviness in his heart. He just lay there, immobile and still crying. The thought of the game came to mind. The Master had said that it was a high-stakes game in which one could lose everything. Orfeo now began to understand what he meant. He rolled over on his side and wept quietly.

When they met later that day, the Master could sense that Orfeo was burdened with a heavy weight on his chest. The Master asked in the concerned tone of good friend, "How do you feel?"

"I'm okay, I guess."

"You look like you were run over by truck and then dragged a few blocks."

"Yeah. Actually, that's exactly how I feel."

"Dolton," the Master called out, and he immediately appeared. "Our guest is a bit under the weather. Can you whip up one of your rejuvenating concoctions? I'll take one too." Dolton bowed to the both of them and exited.

"May I ask you a question?" Orfeo asked softly.

"Of course. I'm sure our last conversation left you with a lot of unanswered questions."

"Surprisingly, no. I got it. Everything you said made complete sense and resonated within me as though it were something I already knew."

"I'm extremely happy for you. As I had said before, none of this can be apprehended by the mind. It's much deeper than this."

"I remember my head whirling like a top when I was trying to understand what you were saying intellectually. It was like the frustration you have when there's a word that's on the tip of your tongue that you just can't find, but as soon as you let go and stop trying, the word pops into your head as though it were always there. At that moment, everything you said just made perfect sense." Orfeo then looked down at the ground and was silent for a long time.

"After everything that you've been through, Orfeo, I thought that with the realization of liberation, you'd be dancing and jumping for joy. What's the matter?"

Orfeo remained silent and didn't look up. Dolton walked in with a tray, two glasses, and a large glass pitcher. He placed the glasses in front of them and filled them with a thick, green liquid. Orfeo almost gagged as Dolton poured, because it reminded him of drinking ayahuasca in the Amazon, which had a similar thick consistency and tasted horrible. He remembered how "Mother Ayahuasca" was so sly and infinitely wise. Almost universally, those unsuspecting fools, including himself, would drink the "medicine" the first time and, after having heard from those who were more seasoned how horrible it tasted, would arrogantly remark that it tasted good. Moreover, again almost universally, the first-timer's experience with Mother Ayahuasca was typically described with terms such as *blissful, healing, filled with love, in God's embrace, one with everything,* and so on. It was truly remarkable how rarely one heard of the first-timer who was devastated or had a very difficult first ceremony. It was the classic bait and switch that Mother Ayahuasca used so skillfully to lure individuals who sought self-improvement, seeking to heal themselves from x, y, and z and to connect more deeply with themselves or God, and who ultimately had the audacity to believe they had an inkling of what they needed.

After the first few experiences, which were always just positive enough to bring them back, the bait was taken away and switched for something that the seeker had not bargained for. They were often dropped, although gradually, deeper and deeper into the land-mine-infested fields of their unconscious minds, and if they were fortunate, they would be blown to smithereens without a trace of who they believed they were when they'd first taken the bait. After being annihilated again and again, those who surrendered began to understand the unfathomable depths of the madness of their minds, which in fact created whatever they believed needed to be healed, the nearly impenetrable walls obstructing them from the truth that was always just under their noses.

Mother Ayahuasca's methods were ingenious. Orfeo recalled that while the newbies were basking in the light of the divine and asking when the next ceremony would take place so they could already sign up, the seasoned practitioners would always say at the end of every ceremony, "Never again! This is my last ceremony. I'm done." But they always came back.

As he was drinking what the Master called Dolton's "Green Goddess," which actually tasted pretty good and was quite refreshing, Orfeo thought of a ridiculously easy ploy for the authorities to capture and imprison those seeking liberation through ayahuasca, which was illegal in many countries. All they had to do was place Dolton's "Green Goddess" in a clear glass in front of a bunch of people and look to see who gagged. This wouldn't help with the newbies, but it would certainly allow them to roundup the hardcore practitioners.

After gulping down a second glass, Orfeo already felt better. "Thank you, Dolton," he said. "This was just what the doctor ordered. Have you ever thought of marketing it for hangovers?" Dolton and the Master laughed.

"So what's going on, Orfeo? Why so gloomy on the day of your release from prison?"

"Carina … I'm afraid I'm going to lose her."

"Ah, I understand now."

"How can I get her to see the truth? How can I save her?"

The Master did not respond but looked compassionately into Orfeo's eyes.

Impatient, Orfeo then asked, "Can I save her?"

The Master stood up and started pacing back and forth, as though thinking carefully about how to respond. Measuring each word, each sentence precisely, the Master said, "Orfeo, you can never play someone else's game for them. Just as no one else could play yours for you."

Orfeo slammed his fist against the table, and responded, "But I didn't play by myself. You helped me. Why can't I help her? Why?"

"Orfeo, my dear friend, stop and think for a moment. You said you understood the game, and I know that you do." The Master continued pacing back and forth with his hands held behind his back. "Would you like to engage in an exercise that will shed some light on this matter, which is evidently very near and dear to you?"

Orfeo was clearly exasperated, but he felt that he didn't have a choice. He let out a big sigh and said, "Let's go for it."

The Master stopped pacing, pulled his chair so that it was directly in front of Orfeo, and sat down with his knees abutting against Orfeo's. He opened with, "Who created the game?"

"I did," Orfeo responded.

"Why did you create the game?"

"In order to test myself, to uncover my deep-rooted beliefs and work through them. Because subconsciously, I knew that my beliefs were false."

"So why didn't you just work out those false beliefs in your highly evolved mind while still in Consciousness without all this mess?"

"Because those false beliefs were so deeply rooted that they could not be uprooted with the very same mind that created them."

"Excellent," the Master exclaimed. "So you created this reality as an exploration?"

"Yes."

"So every experience that you've ever had in your countless incarnations was created expressly by you to allow you to see and understand things that you could not see or understand before."

Orfeo, as he so often did when having these types of discussions with the Master, felt as though he were playing a game of *Go* and more and more of his territories were being usurped. He nodded yes.

The Master hesitated, again measuring each word precisely, before asking, "Then who created me?"

Orfeo was obviously flustered by the question. "What do you mean?"

The Master again stood up and started pacing, now with his arms crossed in front of his chest, and asked more intensely, "Who created me? Why am I here? More importantly, why am I here now rather than in any one of your previous incarnations?"

At this point, Orfeo understood where he was being led and responded, "I created you in order to help myself understand what I needed to understand, and I could not have created you at any other time because I would not have been ready yet to see. I understand that if I would have brought you into my story before this, I would not have been able to see beyond my story that you were evil, and anything you said would have been perceived as a lie for the explicit purpose of brainwashing me."

Orfeo again looked at the ground, the tears welling in his eyes, and lowered his head into both of his hands. He now understood clearly what he'd already suspected but was too afraid to acknowledge as truth.

The Master pulled his chair next to Orfeo's and placed his arm around his shoulder. Like a mother who found her child crying in corner, the Master knew that there was no need for words, so he offered the only thing that was of any value during such moments: his presence and a shoulder to cry on. Orfeo wept like a baby. If he hadn't understood before what the Master meant by the game being a high-stakes game where one ultimately loses everything, he understood now.

In between his sobs, Orfeo asked, "What can I do to save Carina?"

The Master hesitated before offering, "Everything that you possibly can, but ultimately, it's her game … just as this is yours. If she is ready, then she will understand everything. If not, she must continue her game until that time when she is ready."

Orfeo did not find the Master's words at all comforting, but they rang true. He also already understood what the Master did not, or perhaps that he would not state: It was never possible to save another because there was no "other." As the Master had pointed out on so many occasions, in Consciousness, there is only one, not two. Therefore, the entire world is a construct of one's imagination. Consequently, in this construct, where there is the simulation of duality, it is the very belief in this illusion that makes it real, that fills its sails with wind and ultimately maintains it. This is the trap. What a game!

Orfeo sat up and thanked the Master. Then, as though he had wiped all his concerns away with the tears from his eyes, he asked matter-of-factly, "So what now?"

"So what now?" the Master repeated. "Now we share our last meal together, embrace each other, and say farewell."

"But why?" Orfeo asked in a surprised and sad tone.

"The Resistance has caught up with us."

Orfeo was stunned by this news, opening his eyes wide in surprise and confusion, but he could not think of anything to say.

The Master stood up in front of Orfeo, took his hands, and lifted him up onto his one leg. He then embraced him firmly. After their long embrace, the Master held both of Orfeo's shoulders in his hands. He looked into Orfeo's eye's and, in the affectionate tone of two dear friends parting, knowing that they would likely never see each other again, said, "You've been an excellent student, Orfeo. There is so much more I wanted to share with you, and I feel that we've only skimmed the surface. But alas, our time together must come to an end."

Orfeo, holding firmly onto both of the Master's arms, pleaded, "But why? I can talk to the Resistance and sort everything out. I can explain that you are not evil, that they've made a mistake. I know they'll understand …"

"Orfeo!" the Master interrupted firmly, shaking Orfeo's shoulders as though trying to wake him up from sleepwalking. "Religious zealots have burned innocents at the stake for much less."

Orfeo immediately understood what the Master meant and looked down at the ground in the manner of a child who has realized that his parents are standing firm and will not yield to his all-important desire to have a sleepover on a school night. They again embraced, and Orfeo held the Master tight for a long time. As they embraced each other, Orfeo was filled with so much love and gratitude for this man who had once been his sworn mortal enemy, the face of evil itself. Now he regarded the Master as his savior. No further words were necessary to convey these feelings. The words and emotions were in the air that they breathed.

Of all the spectacular meals Dolton had prepared for them, this last one was the best. Orfeo asked if Dolton could join them for their last meal together, and the Master complied, inviting Dolton to join them at the table. Dolton poured each of them a glass of wine. They raised their glasses, waiting for someone to toast. Finally, Orfeo toasted with a simple thanks for everything they had done for him. They relished their meal in complete silence.

After they were done, the Master explained that the Resistance was not too far away and that Dolton would take him on horseback to a location where they would find him. He added that by the time the Resistance arrived at the cave, he and his army would be far gone. Orfeo had so many questions for the Master but knew that there was no time. He simply embraced the Master again and thanked him profusely.

Dolton lifted Orfeo onto the horse and they went off at a gallop. After a few hours, Dolton helped Orfeo down, handed him a backpack full of provisions and his crutches, and pointed him in the direction of the place where he would meet up with the Resistance.

Before leaving, Orfeo gave Dolton, his gentle caregiver on his journey to the truth, a big hug. Orfeo had many things he wanted to say to Dolton, but he simply put a hand to his chest and, on his one leg and crutch, awkwardly bowed to him with the utmost reverence.

Dolton bowed his head, smiled, and said, "Farewell,

Orfeo. It has been my pleasure to serve you." Then he turned the horse around and galloped off.

Orfeo was now alone in the forest. He slowly made his way in the direction Dolton had indicated. It was the first time in months that he'd walked any distance at all, and with only one leg and on crutches, he was winded after only a short while. He didn't know if his heart was racing because he was out of shape or because of the anxiety that was building, knowing that he would see Carina again very soon. His love for her was a constant, but he knew that everything else had changed.

CHAPTER 7

Reunion, Part Two

The Debriefing

Orfeo walked slowly through the forest, stopping every once in a while to catch his breath and rest his arms. He could feel that he was developing abrasions in his armpits from the friction of the crutches. He would occasionally hear the abnormal rustling of branches and leaves and could sense that he was being followed, but every time he turned to look, no one was there. Orfeo had no worries now, because his supposed worst nightmare, the Master, had turned out to be his savior. So what was there to fear? he thought to himself. After about an hour, a voice commanded him to stop, put his hands up, and stand still. He held the crutches out by his sides. Then he was commanded to drop the crutches. Orfeo immediately complied, but standing on uneven terrain on one foot proved to be a challenge, and he started to take small hops in order to maintain his balance. The voice firmly told him to stop moving. Orfeo was really making a concerted effort to keep his balance, but the ground was very uneven and on a slight grade. After doing his one-legged dance for a while, he fell to ground. He somehow found great humor in the fact that he could not even stand up on his own and was now on the ground, and this lead to a spontaneous fit of laughter. He saw many men surrounding him, but he couldn't contain himself and continued to laugh hysterically. After a while, he was able to control himself. He sat up and said, "Hi, my name is Orfeo. Could you please take me to Maya?"

The men who were surrounding him stepped aside to make a path, and Maya stepped forward. She looked at him closely, as though studying him, and without any greeting and exhibiting no warmth, she bluntly asked, "Where are they?"

Orfeo pointed in the direction from where he came and responded, "That way. Where's Carina?"

"You will see her soon enough, Orfeo." Maya turned around abruptly and told the men to give Orfeo his crutches and get him onto the back of one of their horses.

"Maya!" Orfeo called out as she started to mount her horse. When she turned around, he asked, "Where's Carina?"

"You will see her soon enough. Right now we need to find the Master and crush him once and for all." She mounted her horse and started to ride in the direction of the Master's camp. Some men helped Orfeo on the back of one of the horses and they took off in a gallop. Orfeo could only think of how badly his inner thighs were chafed and sore after the long ride with Dolton and now back on a horse. His only saving grace was the thought that he would soon be reunited with Carina.

When they arrived at the cave, it was completely abandoned without any signs that anyone had ever been there. The Resistance diligently scoured the area for clues but found none. They couldn't even find tracks indicating the direction the Master fled, which even baffled Orfeo. Maya had a look of exasperation on her face. "Orfeo, this is the closest we've ever been to the Master, and you're our only link. Was there anything you can remember that could give us a clue about where they headed?"

"I wish I could help," Orfeo offered sincerely, "but I have no idea."

It was almost nightfall, and Maya ordered everyone to mount their horses and head back to camp. Orfeo's heart was pounding with the anxiety of knowing that he would soon be in Carina's arms. They rode their horses for about two to three hours to a small road where many cars were parked. Orfeo was packed into one of the cars with many men. There was no conversation during the long drive back. Orfeo noted the signs on the road and realized that they were going in a completely different direction from where he and Carina had been living. They escorted him into a big house and directed him to a dining area with a large table. There were several people around the table who he did not recognize, and Maya was at the head. There was an empty seat for him.

"Good evening, Orfeo," Maya opened. "My apologies for my behavior toward you earlier. It's just that we've never been so close to finding the Master, and I was on edge. Let me assure you that we are extremely pleased that you are back safe and sound."

"Thank you." He wanted to ask again when he would see Carina, but he already knew what the answer would be.

"I know that you are eager to see Carina, and she is just as eager to see you as well, but I implore you to be patient. You will be reunited as soon as we debrief you."

"Debrief me?"

"Yes, of course," Maya said. "You are the only one in the history of the Resistance to have seen the Master, and hence, you are our only link to finding him and winning this war."

"I understand. Where would you like to begin?"

"From the beginning, Orfeo. Tell us everything."

Orfeo spent the next two hours explaining how the Master's men had approached him while he was walking in the woods and describing the fight that ensued and how he'd lost his leg. Orfeo could sense an air of distrust in the room. It was clear that they suspected him, at the very least, of being brainwashed but were also considering the possibility that he had defected to the Master's side and had now returned as a spy. Although everyone was very polite, Orfeo felt as though they considered him to be the enemy and felt that he was being interrogated. He provided them with a large amount of detail but was careful to omit any description of how wonderful the Master and Dolton had cared for him, the friendship that had been forged between them, and most importantly, the life-altering lessons he had learned. He concluded with, "And then yesterday, the Master told me that I would be released. He put me on the back of a horse with Dolton and left me where you found me."

There was a long silence in the room. Maya's question cut through it like a knife. "Is there anything that you are not telling us, Orfeo?"

"I've told you absolutely everything."

"I see," Maya responded. "What I still don't understand is why he didn't kill you? Why did he keep you for so long and then suddenly decide to release you?"

"I wish I had the answers for you, Maya, but I don't." Before Maya had the opportunity to respond, he continued, "I'm really exhausted and would like to see Carina now. I'd be happy to continue this discussion with you tomorrow after I've had some rest."

Everyone looked over to Maya, who said, "Yes, of course. Let's continue tomorrow. Someone will take you to Carina now." Then, almost as an afterthought, she added, "Welcome home, Orfeo. We are very happy to have you back." This rang hollow to Orfeo's ears.

The Reunion

It was dark now except for the moonlight that allowed Orfeo to see that they were in some sort of compound with many small cabins scattered throughout the property. It reminded him of the camping trips he had taken with his Boy Scout troop as a child. The people escorting him pointed him to a cabin and said goodnight. Orfeo's heart was racing with the anticipation of seeing Carina but also with the fear that she, as the Master had warned him, would not be able to see what he now saw. He made his way to the cabin, took a deep breath, and knocked on the door.

Carina opened the door and, upon seeing him, was so excited that she practically threw herself onto him, almost knocking him down. They hugged for a really long time, savoring the moment, both having so much to say but saying nothing. They would separate for a few seconds, look at each other, and immediately fall back into a deep embrace, again and again. He could feel her sobbing against his chest. She nestled her head firmly against his chest, and holding him tight, whispered, "I missed you so much. I thought I would never see you again."

"I missed you terribly," he responded. They hugged again and held each other tightly. After a while, Orfeo whispered in her ear, "Carina, I'm not as good a dancer as I used to be"—he pointed to his one leg—"and as much as I would love to stay in this precious moment, I really need to sit down."

"Oh no! What happened to you? Come inside … let me help you."

"It's okay," he said in a joking manner, plopping himself down on the couch, "I was never really that good of a dancer anyway." Carina stood paralyzed, just staring at his stump, until he snapped her out of her reverie. "Come'ere, you!" He grabbed her hand and pulled her down onto his lap. He kissed her hard on the lips. He then asked her in the most serious tone he could muster, "Babe, this leg thing isn't going to get in the way of our relationship, is it?"

"Not at all, silly. Now you won't be able to run away when I want to make love for the third time in a row." They laughed, kissed, cried, and hugged late into the evening, until neither of them could wait any longer to merge again in their lovemaking. Orfeo could not remember a time in any of his lifetimes, or even in Consciousness, when he had been happier.

They awakened intertwined in each other's beings. There were no words between them. There was, rather, a deep feeling of love and gratitude that did not require expression. They just lay in each other's arms until their bodies were sore and their extremities numb from their coiling. The call to move to a more comfortable position seemed to be synonymous with the invitation to make love again. After more lovemaking, they dozed off in each other's arms again. Orfeo again dreamed of Carina waking him up, but this time she was jumping into bed with him to cuddle, just as they were now.

He asked her in his dream, "Will you stay with me no matter what happens?"

"Yes," she said, "I will stay with you no matter what happens."

"Cross your heart and hope to die?"

"Yes, I cross my heart and hope to die."

Orfeo awakened to find Carina deep in sleep. He looked at her and saw pure beauty, pure love. He had so much to tell her but didn't know where to start, how to start. Fear came into his body at that moment and overwhelmed him.

Carina woke up just in time to catch that look of dread on his face and felt it oozing from his body. "Orfeo ... Orfeo ..." Carina shook him. "What's the matter?"

Startled, he looked at her and forced a smile.

"You were as pale as a ghost. You had a horrible expression on your face, and your body was cold. What happened?"

"Nothing. I was having a bad daydream."

"Can you talk about it?"

"Later. I promise I'll tell you everything later." Orfeo really wanted to tell her everything right at that moment, but he didn't feel secure in Maya's compound. He suddenly wanted to get out of there with Carina. "Are you hungry? I'm famished."

"Sure. There's a mess hall in the compound. We can eat there."

"Not interested. Remember that cute café where we used to have brunch. Let's go there."

"We'll have to ask Maya. Sit tight and I'll—"

Orfeo abruptly interrupted, "Ask Maya? Why?"

Carina was noticeably flustered by Orfeo's aggressiveness. "Babe, Maya's in charge here, and we have to ask her permission before leaving the compound." She noted that he was not very happy with what she'd just said. She waited for him to respond and, when he didn't, continued, "When you were gone, I didn't know what to do, and Maya took me in. I can obviously take care of myself, but it felt good to be around like-minded people fighting for the same cause. Doesn't that make sense?"

Orfeo didn't want to understand, but he realized that this was not the time to have this conversation. He completely changed his demeanor and said, "Yes, absolutely. I get it. You go and ask Maya. I'll get ready."

After about twenty minutes, Carina returned with a big smile, and said, "You see, no big deal. She said it would be a great idea for us to spend some time together away from this place."

Orfeo beamed and said, "Great!" He outwardly projected a big warm smile, but another wave of apprehension enveloped him. There was no question in his mind about their love for each other, but Orfeo wondered if, like Maya, Carina now questioned his loyalty or even his sanity. Even worse, he feared now that Carina could be serving as a spy for Maya. What an interesting turn of events, Orfeo thought to himself. Carina and Maya's fear was that the Master had brainwashed Orfeo into some sort of "Manchurian candidate," sent back to infiltrate and destroy the Resistance, while Orfeo knew for sure that they had all been brainwashed into believing that there was a war and that the Master was evil personified. He could see the layers of subterfuge at play. There had to be a way out of this predicament, he thought to himself. He had to save Carina!

The Café

Orfeo and Carina arrived after the breakfast rush, so the café wasn't busy. They were seated in a large, oval booth with really comfortable oval sofas. They both loved cafés, and this was one of their favorites in the area. As soon as they entered the café, his senses were overwhelmed with the aroma of the coffee beans, fresh breads, and pastries, and he remembered a thought that had almost been forgotten. Before their lives had been turned upside down on that morning in New York City when Carina came out of the closet, they'd often discussed opening a café together. They had even already picked out a few potential locations.

The idea was based on the Parisian cafés, such as Le Select, Les Deux Magots, Café de Flore, and Café de la Paix, where artists such as Hemingway, Gertrude Stein, Jean Cocteau, Henry Miller, Pablo Picasso, Cole Porter, and many others would gather to spend time together and exchange ideas. Orfeo was always fascinated by the idea that so many brilliant minds, many of whom were not even recognized as such at the time, would gather.

What an amazing coincidence, he would always think to himself, that so many of the artists that shaped that era managed to come together in a handful of places, during such a precise moment in history. This had always puzzled Orfeo. What was the attraction of those particular places in that particular city? He never considered himself to be brilliant in any particular way, but he loved the idea of creating an environment that would attract such people before they became such people and of simply being party to their discussions, interactions, and energy.

Orfeo had this grand notion of a space that would be large enough to serve many functions, including café, gallery, performance space, club, lounge, and community center. He already had a clear idea of what the central space would look like. There would be plush, burgundy, leather oval booths asymmetrically dispersed throughout the room, and interspersed among the booths would be sets of three art deco couches arranged as three sides of a square around a low coffee table in the middle. Then there would be smaller tables with two or three huge, high-backed, cushioned chairs for more intimate exchanges. All the furniture would be set on wheels to facilitate moving them about so that every day, the configuration would be completely different. The various areas of the space would be sectioned off with moveable walls, some just high enough to seclude the area when seated, others higher, to provide a sense of intimacy. He envisioned full-size statues of male and female nudes in interesting postures scattered throughout the space, also on wheels so that they could be easily moved.

On one side of the large room, there would be a gorgeous, art deco bar, and the liquor on the wall behind the bar would be set up like works of art against beautiful lighting. The centerpiece of the bar would be a vintage silver-and-gold espresso machine with a very large, bronze statue of a voluptuous, nude woman with wings, whose arms were raised to sky as if communicating with the gods.

On the opposite side of the bar, there would be a stage for musicians, readings, or theatrical performances. The stage would only be elevated about one to two feet from the floor so that a certain intimacy would always be maintained between the audience and the performers. In addition to performances on the stage, the floors could be cleared for dance performances and more interactive theatrical performances. On the third wall, he planned to have a large movie screen that would be hidden during the day by the same thick, burgundy curtains used in movie theaters. Orfeo was somewhat of a film buff and wanted to be able to screen his favorite films and others that friends suggested.

Orfeo envisioned his café, for which he had not yet come up with a name, as serving many purposes and accommodating many spiritual, psychological, culinary, and physical needs. First and foremost, it would be a café that would attract really interesting, intelligent, and creative people to gather, share, and present their ideas and work. Second, the walls, including the moveable partitions and the curtain on the wall covering the movie screen, would be used as an art gallery where artists could show and sell their work. The glue, in Orfeo's mind, that would keep all of this together, and keep the crowds coming back, was the food, coffee, and teas offered, as well as the ambient music, which he would carefully select. His intention was to have everything made fresh on the premises from organic produce from local farmers and merchants. Whenever Orfeo traveled, he kept a diary of wonderful meals and drinks he had encountered himself, as well as those suggested by friends, with the intention of recreating them in his café. These would be the foundation around which all the other ideas would circulate.

As his ideas for his café became more and more grandiose, he recognized how impossible it would be to actually give birth to his vision, but he humored himself and, over the years, continued to build on the idea. From what started in his mind as a café that would nourish the mind as well as spirit, his idea evolved into a sort of community center. He wanted to offer baking and cooking workshops, taught either by chefs he would convince to volunteer their time or by locals, which Orfeo preferred. People would bring in a particular dish they loved and made very well. If Orfeo and others liked it, then that person would be invited to teach those interested how to make and prepare that dish, which would then be served for dinner. Those who had paid a community membership fee would eat for free, while others would be charged a reasonable fee for a fabulous communal meal.

Orfeo also remembered how often he'd heard friends who had children complain of the quality of food served in the schools and the hassle of preparing healthy, wholesome meals for their kids during the morning rush of getting them to school and then getting to work. This led him to the idea of preparing bagged lunches of tasty, healthy meals and treats for kids that were prepaid so that parents could pick them up on their way to school.

Orfeo had two additional ideas for his multifunctional café and community center. First, he wanted a space that was large enough to have rooms separate from the central area where a wide variety of classes for children and adults could be offered: music, tutoring, yoga, and movement. Second, he wanted to convert the cafe at night into a lounge or club with great DJs, live performances, and dancing.

He recalled the wonderful nights he'd spent at the Salsa Meets Jazz series at the Village Gate in New York City, where a salsa orchestra would be joined by a jazz soloist. What a fabulous scene, he recalled, and it wasn't simply because the music was so engaging but more so because of the people it attracted. Unlike in so many of the other clubs in New York City, the people here were open, friendly, and willing to meet and readily embrace others. He had a fond memory of one evening when he met this delightful, gregarious Englishman, who was in his late forties and was quite a storyteller. The man worked in the oil industry and had lived in many countries. Orfeo had asked him which were his favorite places. Without even taking a moment to think, the man had blurted out, in his charming English accent, Brazil, Southern Italy, and Southeast Asia. When Orfeo asked him why, his response had a profound effect on Orfeo that had remained with him to this day. He remembered sharing that response with Carina when he had first met her in this lifetime: These were the few places in the world where people were not afraid to embrace you. They were not afraid that you would somehow take a piece of their souls away and consequently had no fear of being completely open and giving.

Orfeo often wondered what the formula was for attracting such people and cultivating such a scene. This was what he wanted more than anything else: an environment where angels could meet other angels. He remembered his excitement when he'd first presented this idea to Carina and seen her glow, indicating that she was completely on board with being part of creating such an impossible vision. He'd ended by saying, "It's grandiose and insane, *n'est-ce pas?*" He remembered her giggle and respond, "I love grandiose and insane." This idea of opening such a café seemed so distant now, as though it belonged to a different lifetime or perhaps to an altogether different person with whom, for a brief moment, Orfeo had shared a dream of such a delightful place.

Carina was driving the car, and Orfeo was deep in thought, looking for a way to lead her to the truth. He realized that he might appear suspicious by remaining so distant, so he decided to strike up a conversation. "What happened to the house?"

"It's still there. I miss it there. I have fond memories of us in that house."

"I'm sure you do, Ms. Dominatrix. What I remember was you whipping me every day until I dropped from exhaustion, and then you'd manage to squeeze out a little more from me."

"Ha ha! You should be thanking me, Booboo. If it weren't for that intense training, you may have lost both legs. In that light, I regret not pushing you harder."

"In retrospect, it wouldn't have made a damn bit of difference."

"What do you mean?"

"It's a bigger game than you could ever imagine—one that goes beyond the physical. In fact, what I've learned is that the physical preparation wasn't necessary at all." Carina was about to ask another question, but Orfeo cut her off. "Is your intention for us to remain in the compound?"

"I hadn't really thought about it, but yes. Is that okay with you?"

"Babe, I'll stay wherever you are, but if you ask me, I'd rather go back to the house and get our lives back." He waited for a while, but she continued to drive in silence. He asked, "What do you think?"

"Can we make that decision later? I don't want to rush into making any decisions right now. Okay?"

"Sure." Orfeo realized at that moment that this was going to be much more challenging than he could have possibly imagined. He could already visualize the layers of deception piling up like the bodies and amputated parts in the movie *Kill Bill Vol. 2*. He had a mental picture of Uma Thurman, "Black Mamba," in Lucy Liu's palace. There were dead bodies and amputated parts all over the place, and a hundred samurai surrounded Uma. Lucy Liu was at the top of the stairs, and she asked Uma, "Did you really think that it was going to be that easy, little Caucasian girl?" Uma, still in fighting stance, replies, "Yup," and the action starts again. Brilliant, he thought to himself.

Orfeo ordered a double-shot latte and an almond croissant, his favorite; Carina had her usual, an espresso with a toasted demi-baguette, on which she smeared butter with religious zeal, ensuring that every millimeter of the baguette was covered, and then a thin, precise layer of jam. There was an uncomfortable silence while they ate, punctuated by occasional eye contact. Carina broke the ice by asking, "So, are you going to tell me what happened?"

"Sure," he said as he continued to eat his croissant.

Carina was becoming slightly impatient, "I can't wait to hear it." He finally finished eating, pushed his plate to the side, and took the final few drops of coffee. Then he just stared into her eyes, as though trying to figure something out.

"What's the matter?" she asked uncomfortably.

"I'm scared."

"Scared of what? You're safe now."

He hesitated, still making eye contact. "I have the feeling that what happens here this morning is going to determine our fate. That scares me."

"That sounds a little heavy after only one latte. What do you mean?"

"What happened to me is unbelievable enough, but what I learned is so far out there that before I start, I need to know if you're with me ... 100 percent ... do or die, like its always been?"

There was a fraction of a second of hesitation that Carina knew he would not overlook. "Of course I'm with you 100 percent. Why would you ask such a silly question?"

"Well, I saw the way Maya treated me. It was as though she didn't trust me ... as though I were a spy. Then I find you living in the compound, which I understand, but ..." Orfeo stopped, searching for the right words.

"I frankly don't care what Maya thinks about me, but I have an intuition that you don't trust me either … and that hurts more than anything in this world."

"Sweetie, I do trust you. It's just that you've been gone for a long time, and Maya … and I don't have a clue where you've been or what happened to you. We're concerned about the state of your mind …"

"Is that a euphemism for being brainwashed?"

"Yes. It's not just a question of trusting you. We're concerned about you. That's all. You can understand this, can't you?"

"I do understand, but Carina, can I trust you?"

She was somewhat taken aback by this question, but responded, "Unconditionally."

"Okay, then. What I'm about to tell you is a complete mind-fuck, and it's really important that you keep an open mind."

Carina nodded yes.

"So what if everything you believed was false?"

Carina blurted back, "That's not possible."

"Just humor me for a second. What if everything you believed was false?"

"Can you be a little more specific? That's really too vague for me to grasp."

"Okay. What do you think of the average person who's living out his or her life in the earth-realm?"

"I think people like that are doing the best they can with the resources they have. They're misguided."

"What can you say about their resources?"

"They're limited."

"And isn't it because of those limited resources that they are misguided?"

"Yes, of course. Orfeo, we've had this discussion so many times. It's the same old issue of Plato's allegory of the cave or *The Matrix*. What's your point?"

"Carina, this is exactly my point! If you went to any of those people in the cave or in the Matrix and told them that their so-called reality, their beliefs that they were holding on to so dearly, were false, they would at first think that you were trying to pull their leg or had lost your marbles, and if you persisted, they'd try to lynch you."

She looked at him with a look of disbelief and said, "Orfeo, are you saying what I think you're saying?"

Orfeo didn't move his eyes from hers, attempting to gauge her reaction to this violent truth. "Yes."

"But how could that be?" she asked incredulously. "It's impossible."

"Isn't that the same thing that someone in the cave or Matrix would ask? Isn't that the response you'd expect? Isn't that the reason why we don't involve ourselves in their affairs?"

There was a moment of silence. Carina was obviously frustrated by his insinuation that she was as blind as the rest of humankind they encountered.

Orfeo added, "I know this is hard to believe, but

for now, I'm only asking you to at least accept it as a possibility."

She hesitated, still thinking of the implications of what he'd just said and then, hoping to change the subject, asked, "Orfeo, what happened to you while you were imprisoned?"

"First of all, I was never a prisoner."

She looked quite surprised. "What do you mean? What happened to you then? Where were you all this time?"

"When I went for the walk that day, a few men approached me. I don't know how, but I immediately knew who they were. One of them said that the Master wanted to meet with me and had some information that could help me. Based on everything that you and Maya had told me, I thought the worse and attacked. Carina, it was worse than you can possibly imagine. Do you remember what you told me about training for a year, that my chances of survival in a fight with these guys would still be negligible to zilch? The fact is that even after a lifetime of training, I would have never come close to standing up to one of those guys with a hand tied behind his back. They were so fast, so strong, and extremely well trained. I never had a chance, and I was fortunate that they weren't fighting back."

"What do you mean? They chopped your leg off! That's not the sort of thing that happens while shaving your legs."

"Yes, they did do that, but I later learned it was their last resort to neutralize me. They first tried to reason with me, but when they saw my hostility and aggressive behavior, they then tried on several occasions to just back off and walk away. I was so pumped with adrenaline that I just continued to attack. Every time I attacked, they would evade me for as long as possible, but when they couldn't avoid it, they would hit me just hard enough to drop me. In retrospect, I realize they weren't trying to harm me at all, and they showed tremendous restraint, even after I shot one of them. I didn't leave them much choice. I was a complete idiot and was very lucky to get out of that situation alive. It was all my fault. They were just trying to relay a message."

"Are you sure?"

"Absolutely sure. I've run through that scene a hundred times, and they could have killed me at any moment of their choosing. That clearly wasn't their intention."

"Then what happened?"

"I lost consciousness and woke up in this cave, tied to a table."

"Wait a minute. I thought you weren't a prisoner. Why were you tied up?"

"I actually never asked, but I think it was to make sure that I wouldn't go berserk again and suffer any further injury. As soon as they saw that I was calm and cooperative, they untied me."

"Why didn't you get the hell out of there."

"Well, I was beat up pretty badly and had only one leg, so I definitely wasn't going anywhere in a hurry."

"Then what happened."

"The first few days were a complete blur. I was going in and out of consciousness, and Dolton, this seven-foot giant, took care of me and nursed me back to health."

"He was really seven feet tall?"

"Yes, a true 'gentle giant.'"

"Did you meet the Master face to face? What was he like?"

"This is the part that you're going to find very hard to believe. He was actually a really nice guy. Super intelligent with the wisdom of the ages up his sleeve."

Carina looked at Orfeo as though he had lost his marbles.

"I know what you're thinking, but it's true. Dolton cooked the most amazing meals, and the wine was spectacular—"

"Stop! Just stop!" Carina interrupted. "So you're in this cave, your leg is chopped off, there's a seven-foot manservant, and you're being fed caviar and champagne? Am I hearing this correctly?"

"Like I said, this is all very hard to believe. If it hadn't happened to me, I'm not sure I would believe it either."

"But why? Why did they treat you so well? What did the Master want?"

"Nothing really. He somehow sensed that I was at a

fork in the road of my evolution and simply provided me with an alternative to what we viewed as reality, which I now recognize as the truth. I remembered what you'd told me about being brainwashed and lobotomized, and I thought that was what was going on, but it wasn't. The Master and I would have these really powerful conversations about so many different subjects. He was absolutely brilliant."

"Orfeo, you're describing him as though he's your buddy. He's the bad guy. He's the sole reason that the Resistance exists." She paused and then said, "Babe, I think the Master got to you. You need help."

"When I first met the Master, he asked me two questions: 'What if you are mistaken? What if everything you were told was false?' At first I thought they were completely preposterous questions, part of his brainwashing scheme, but the more he explained, the more I began to understand."

Slightly more aggressive now, Carina asked, "And what makes you so sure he didn't, in fact, brainwash you?"

"Well, for one thing, he never asked for anything at all. He never spoke ill of the Resistance except to say that Maya and the Resistance were misguided, in the same way that you agreed that the vast majority of people are misguided about the truth of this reality. Carina, what makes you so sure that *you* have not been brainwashed?"

"Brainwashed by whom? I'm not the one who was captured and imprisoned behind enemy lines, and I'm not the one who was wandering through so many lifetimes, looking for me in order to 'save me,' when it was you who was completely lost and needed saving." Carina blurted this out without thinking and immediately regretted the words and the tone in which they'd come out. There was an awkward silence that filled the space between them and seemed to spread to the area beyond their booth.

Carina reached out to touch Orfeo's hand. "Orfeo … I'm really sorry. That sounded so wrong."

"It's okay … really. What you said was completely reasonable and completely true. I was lost. I see that now. Carina, going back to our metaphor, I know this is difficult to swallow, but swap roles with me for a minute. What would you do if you learned something that was completely life-altering, a game changer, a paradigm shift? Wouldn't you try to get me to see it? Would you give up on me because I couldn't see it?" He paused. "Babe, I couldn't care less if Maya and the Resistance believe me or not. It's irrelevant. The only thing that matters to me is you. That's it!"

Carina looked down, confused. She was becoming more convinced that Orfeo had in fact been brainwashed and was trying to decide whether to turn him over to Maya, who would surely know how to help him.

"Will you give me a chance?" Orfeo asked.

Carina hesitated, looked up, and unconvincingly said, "Sure."

Orfeo really didn't how to proceed. He felt as though

he were in a box with nowhere to go. He looked into Carina's eyes and did not see the same person he had been with for so many eternities, but he quickly realized that it was he who had changed. The eyes through which he now perceived her had been scrubbed of all the accumulated debris, and he was now able to see her and the world's delusions clearly. How could he make her see the truth? He remembered the Master warning him that it was not a reasonable expectation to believe that Carina or anyone else could be *made* to see the truth, because people have to play their own game, as they designed it. Orfeo knew that this was the price of return, that he would have to leave everything behind, including Carina, but he couldn't face this truth. He recognized that this was just another belief, and as the Master had stated so clearly, there wasn't enough room in Consciousness for him and his beliefs. He could feel the tears welling in his eyes.

Orfeo remembered the Master's parting words. The Master embraced him firmly in his arms as a father would hold his son who was going on a journey that the father knew he had to undertake on his own, one for which the father had no doubt his son was ready. The Master had told him, "Consider the teachings of your earthly sages. The message has been consistent from time immemorial, and that message is simply to surrender. You must surrender your will, beliefs, everything. This is the price of return. Orfeo, everything that has ever filled your head … everything … you have to leave it behind. Once you recognize that it, they, everything, is an illusion, then you will understand that there is nothing to leave and nowhere to go."

Orfeo continued, "I really don't know how best to explain all of this, so let me just lay it all out as it comes to mind. All I ask is that you suspend judgment and take it all in, and we'll sort it all out later." Carina nodded yes. Orfeo took a deep breath and started. "There is no war. There never was. There is no Light and no Dark. The Master is not evil. There is no such thing as duality, and that is why we are here in this earth-realm to explore, to learn. It's all part of this game we're playing—"

Carina interrupted, now clearly frustrated. "Orfeo, how can you call this a game? Well, whose game is it, and what if I don't want to play?" Orfeo could see, just as the Master had warned him, that this was going to be extremely difficult and perhaps impossible.

"Carina, it's your game. You designed it in order to—"

"Orfeo, please stop! Please. I just can't." Her eyes were now tearful. "I'm really worried about you, and I don't know what to do. How can I help you?" There was a long period of silence. It was a stalemate, and neither of them could think of anything else to say. They asked for the check, paid, and started the drive back to the compound in silence.

It was during this drive, which seemed to last longer than all of his lifetimes put together, that something clicked in Orfeo's mind. He realized that there was absolutely nothing he could say or do to open Carina's eyes to the truth, to convince her that she, like everyone else in the "cave," like himself before meeting the Master, was on the wrong path. He then corrected himself: there wasn't a wrong path. It's just that they were walking in circles, believing that they were going somewhere. The image of a mouse on a treadmill came to mind again.

Orfeo also realized that the "cave," like Dante Alighieri's hell, had many, many levels—levels of misperception. At each level, as the Master pointed out, were ignoramuses patting themselves on their backs, believing themselves superior to those at lower levels. Having just made the journey to a higher level, Orfeo wondered how many more he would have to negotiate. All of a sudden, he had the disturbing thought that perhaps this was only the beginning of his journey. All these lifetimes were perhaps just to get him to the trailhead. He didn't know whether to laugh or cry at that thought. What a game! At that moment, he was filled with an overwhelming emotion that could only be described as compassion—compassion for himself, for his great love and life-partner Carina, and for all humanity.

Orfeo turned his gaze toward her. He sensed an irreconcilable distance between them that spanned the expanse of the entire universe. It was as though the core of their love had been scooped out and replaced by a black hole, devouring everything in its vicinity. The love was still there, but something was missing. His eyes saw her as they always had, but everything seemed different.

The confusion was now gone and had been replaced with crystal clarity. The path before him was lit as brightly as the lights lining the landing strip for an incoming airplane. At this point, Orfeo asked her to pull over to the side of the road. When she did, without waiting for Carina to look at him, he stated matter-of-factly that he wanted to go back to their house and asked if she would come with him. She was still looking down, eyes tearing. She told him that she wasn't ready yet, that she couldn't. There was another long moment of silence, and he told her that he understood. He asked her to drop him off there and that he would wait for her for as long as it was necessary.

When she dropped him off, she got out of the car, gave him a hug, and said, "I love you!"

Orfeo replied reflexively, as he always did, "I love you more! I'll always love you."

At dawn on the following day, the Resistance surrounded the house where Carina had left Orfeo. They forced entry into the house and searched everywhere, but Orfeo was nowhere to be found. The bed looked as though it had never been slept in, and in fact, there was no sign that he had ever entered the house. There was absolutely no trace of him or tracks indicating even the direction in which he may have headed.

Maya was furious when she heard the news. She brought Carina into a room in the compound that contained only a table, two chairs, and a lamp. It was obviously an interrogation room, and Carina wondered if this was where they would have brought Orfeo and if they would have tortured him. The thought then crossed her mind that perhaps she would be tortured. She prepared herself for the worst.

Carina sat in one chair facing the table, while Maya paced the room. After pacing back and forth for a long time, Maya asked, "Why didn't you immediately inform me that Orfeo requested to stay in your former home?"

"Because I really didn't think it was important. There was some tension between us, and I felt that we needed some space to get our bearings."

"You didn't think it was important? Carina, do you realize that Orfeo was our only link to the Master? Our only chance to locate and crush him? And you didn't think it was important that he just left the compound?"

"No. I thought that this was a personal matter between Orfeo and me and didn't realize that I needed to inform you of our every move."

Maya sighed and continued to pace. "Did he give any hint that he was going to run away?"

"No. Not at all. I'm really surprised … and quite hurt that he would run off like that. It's not like him."

"Well, maybe the Orfeo who came back to us was not the Orfeo you knew." Carina was looking at the desk,

311

overwhelmed with emotions. First, she was in such pain that Orfeo would just leave her. She then felt terrible about the way she had treated him the day before. She understood now that she had betrayed him at a very deep level. Second, she was becoming more and more angry at Maya because she was being treated like a traitor.

"What did you talk about at the café?"

Carina looked up when she heard the question and suddenly realized that they had been followed yesterday and that Maya obviously must have known that she dropped Orfeo off at the house. This infuriated her, but she thought it best to maintain her composure. "We talked about many things."

"Can you be more specific?" Maya asked impatiently.

"Orfeo said a lot of crazy things. He said that he was never a prisoner, that the Master was a good guy, that there was no war, that there never was, and that the Master got him to see the truth. He asked me to consider that everything I believed was false."

Maya interrupted and said, "Sounds like the ravings of a lunatic." She carefully studied Carina's reaction.

Carina understood the game that was being played and replied dispassionately, "Orfeo's certainly been under tremendous stress, and I'm sure he just needs time to heal."

Maya again paced back and forth like a tiger about to pounce on its injured prey. She continued, "Is there anything else Orfeo said that could help us track his or the Master's whereabouts?"

"The only other thing that he started to talk about was something about a game we're playing, but I cut him off."

"A game?"

"Yes, a game that I somehow designed. That's as far as we got." Carina took a deep breath and asked if she could leave.

"One more question, Carina. Do you believe Orfeo?"

Carina did not hesitate. "No. Not at all. I think he was completely brainwashed and needs help. I hope we can find him to give him the help that he needs."

Maya stopped pacing, stood on the other side of the table facing Carina, and looked at her carefully, trying to find a crack to suggest whether or not she was being sincere. "You go ahead. We'll talk later."

EPILOGUE

Many years had passed, and Orfeo had finally realized his dream of opening his café. It was located on a small hill overlooking the Mediterranean Sea. He named it DeVine Pleasures. It was almost exactly as he had envisioned it, and although he would never be able to verbalize the formula if asked, the fact was that the café attracted really interesting, intelligent, and inspired people happy to share their insights, inspirations, and passions. There was a buzz in the place, an energetic flare that was palpable. It was a great place to work, ruminate, find inspiration, meet new friends, have a great meal, or simply observe the beauty of how wonderful life could be.

The café became quite famous for many reasons but most of all for what Orfeo called "nights of sharing." He would pick a theme for an evening, such as word, music, or film. On a word evening everyone would bring a poem or piece of prose, selected or written, and present it to the group. On a music night, attendees would bring a piece of music that was special in some way to them and, before playing it, would explain why that selection was important in their lives. Orfeo found that something about expressing why a particular selection was important to one person, or hearing the story attached to the selection, somehow enhanced everyone else's perception of that selection. A selection that they may have nonchalantly heard many times in the past was now given wings. On film nights, everyone would bring a favorite clip and, again, discuss its relevance to his or her life. Sometimes the clip was so compelling to the group that they voted to include it in the café's film series.

The greatest gift of all for Orfeo, however, was the growing community. Everyone was welcome, but Orfeo asked everyone to offer, as a gift, someone who was special to them and introduce them to the community. This type of offering was quite different than someone just showing up, as different as an individual showing up at a club as opposed to being brought as a special guest to a friend's dinner. In this case, the connection was already established and now only required nourishment in order to blossom. This facilitated a growing community where everyone knew each other and had a context, a frame of reference. This allowed for communication without fear of rejection, as well as respect for personal space. This was a beautiful space for sharing ideas, communicating, and flirting but also a great place to find inspiration to work and create.

Orfeo was quite happy in his new life. If there was one word to describe it, that word would be simplicity. There was no longer a search for meaning, there was no purpose, and he was no longer seeking anything. There was just life that presented itself like the undulations of a wave, in and out, sometimes high and other times low, and Orfeo felt a part of that pulsation and undulation.

It was a glorious morning that promised to be a

delicious day. The sun was brilliant and, along with the cool breeze from the ocean, the sound of the birds blended seamlessly with Sibelius's Opus 47, lusciously filling the cafe.

Orfeo was in the back doing some chores. There was only one customer, a regular, who was settled into his newspaper, and Orfeo wanted to take care of a few things before the morning rush. After a while, he stepped out to check on his customer and caught a glimpse of a woman sitting at a table outside on the deck, looking out to the ocean with her back to the restaurant. He refilled his first customer's coffee and then walked out to the deck to serve the woman. It wasn't until he was just a few feet away from her that he realized it was Carina. He froze and felt his heart palpitating. It seemed to him that he had been there for a while before she turned and noticed him. Their eyes locked onto each other for a moment, and her smile beamed brightly while she stood up to face him. They stared into each other's eyes for a long time without words, but everything that needed to be said was exchanged and understood. They then fell into each other's arms in a deep embrace so tight that only the earth's gravitational pull, or perhaps some undiscovered law of physics, prevented them from collapsing into their very own black hole.

That embrace seemed to encompass all the eternities that they had been separated and the relief of finding each other again. Tears flowed down both of their cheeks and turned into sobs of joy. There was a deafening silence surrounding them, the silence from which all of creation had emerged, the silence that is found in the deepest ocean, in the furthest reaches of the physical universe, and in the foundation of all Consciousness.

They were immersed in this silence, as they had always been when not in body, forgetting for that moment in illusory time that they were in fact in body, in physical space in time, until a voice clamored, in a deep American southern accent, "Excuse me ... excuse me ... Can we have some service please?"

They snapped out of their embrace of infinity, and without missing a beat, Carina wiped the tears from her face, stepped forward, and said, "Absolutely! We're so sorry to keep you waiting. Would you prefer a table inside or outside?" The guests looked at each other, trying to find consensus, and Carina interjected, "It's really too beautiful a day to sit inside. I think you really should sit outside while it's still cool and there's a breeze. You can always come back inside if it gets too hot." Without even waiting for their response, she ushered the group to the outdoor patio facing the gorgeous Mediterranean Sea. "I'll bring menus out in a second. Make yourselves at home."

Carina brought out the menus, and as she was handing them out, she asked where they were from. They proudly responded that they were from Texas. Carina beamed brightly. "Texas! No way! You came all the way from Texas? How wonderful!" Looking over to Orfeo, she said, "I don't think we've ever had visitors from Texas, have we, *chéri*?"

Orfeo was completely dumbfounded by what was going on and by the ease with which Carina was able to adopt this new role, but he responded in character. "No, *chérie*, I don't think so."

"Well," Carina said, turning to the group, "we'll have to celebrate this event. How about mimosas for everyone?"

Some of the Texans seemed perplexed about what a mimosa was, and the others hesitated, with that look that said, "Champagne at this time in the morning?"

Carina, understanding immediately, said, "What's the problem? Do you have to go to work? Aren't you on vacation?"

They were amused but looked at each other not sure how to respond.

"Come on," Carina exclaimed. "Live a little! When in Rome, do as the Romans!" They laughed and nodded in agreement. "And by the way"—Carina turned to look at Orfeo—"it's on the house."

Orfeo had a big grin during this entire spectacle, and he winked at her in approval while on his way to prepare the drinks. Carina imitated their southern accents, telling them, "Y'all look over the menus, and I'll be back to take your orders real soon."

The bright sunlight, the sound of seagulls and the

waves hitting the rocks permeated the café. Customers flowed in, and there was a buzz in the café. Orfeo and Carina glanced at each other, and they were happy. There were few words between them throughout the busy day. Carina helped him and fit in as thought she had been a permanent fixture. He watched the customers respond with such glee to her performance, to how she engaged them with such care, joy, and hospitality. Aside from a few practical exchanges regarding where this or that was located and whether he accepted this or that credit card, their communication took place in their glances, in the brushing of their shoulders while bustling from table to table, and in the energies passing between them as their backs were turned to each other while taking care of customers. All the meaning and intent that they wished to convey was transmitted to the bright-blue sky, the seagulls, and the waves and echoed back to one other with the soft sea breeze gently flowing through the café. Yes, there was so much to talk about, there were details that required clarification, but what was clearly understood was that their love for each other had weathered the storm.

It was a great day at the café. It was busy as always, but Orfeo really enjoyed the connections he made with the customers and the regulars who frequented the place. Orfeo recognized that his café, DeVine Pleasures, was not quite at the level of La Coupole, where Picasso, Hemingway, Jean Cocteau, Gertrude Stein, and Jean-Paul Sartre would mingle and discuss their latest ideas. But then again, he wondered if they, these geniuses who made history and defined their arts, had recognized each other for who they would become at that time or if they were simply struggling artists sharing a cappuccino among friends while taking a break from the masterpieces that had yet to be created. If the latter were the case, Orfeo was pleased to know that perhaps there were budding, as yet unrecognized geniuses sitting in his café on a daily basis, and he treated his customers as such.

They cleaned up and closed the café. It was a gorgeous evening with the almost full moon reflecting on the still sea and the sound of the waves breaking on the soft sand of the beach. Orfeo led Carina to the beach, where they walked at the edge of the water. Carina walked in her bare feet, and Orfeo had his one foot bare and a shoe on the prosthesis. This was his path to the café and back home every day. The walk home on the beach helped him to clear his head and center himself after a long day at the café, and sometimes, he would sit on the sand and meditate for long periods before going home.

They were holding hands and intermittently bumping shoulders because of shifts in the sand and water. "You're walking pretty well on that leg. How does it feel?" Carina asked.

"It feels fine. I sometimes even forget that it's a prosthesis. Modern technology is pretty amazing." They continued to walk in an awkward silence, looking for the words to express the profundity of the feelings that were spinning in their hearts.

Carina broke the silence. "I loved your café. It's exactly the way you described it, and you couldn't have picked a better location."

Orfeo almost slipped in a big wave that came up to his knees, but she caught him. Then he responded, "Yeah, it's a wonderful spot and a great hang."

"Where did you get the name DeVine Pleasures? Carina asked.

He hesitated and smiled, indicating that there was something amusing on his mind.

"What's so funny?" she prodded.

"I named it for you, love. It's a reminder of our time together."

She stopped, pulled him into her arms, and kissed him softly. "Aww! That's so sweet!" They looked into each other's eyes and then continued to walk in silence.

"So how did you find me?" Orfeo asked.

"Now that's a silly question! The same way we've always found each other throughout these lifetimes."

"Right," he chuckled, "silly question." After a few meters, Orfeo asked, "So why did you bother to find me? Are you here to bring me back to the Resistance?"

"That's a more reasonable question ... but no. I left the Resistance."

Orfeo stopped suddenly and faced her. The moonlight

was illuminating half of her face with a sublime light. "Why? What happened?"

"Nothing happened. It just didn't feel right. I didn't see the purpose anymore, and—"

"You missed me terribly and couldn't stand the idea of being without me for another second," Orfeo interrupted, completing her sentence.

Smiling, she said, "You bastard!" She pushed him gently with both hands, forgetting about his prosthetic leg and causing him to lose his balance and fall into the water. She covered her mouth with both hands, embarrassed, and exclaimed, "I'm so sorry!" She extended her hands to help him up, and he quickly yanked her down into the water next to him. Orfeo pulled her into his arms, and they both rolled into the water, kissing passionately.

Carina rolled on top of him and said, "Yes, I missed you terribly and couldn't live another moment without you." They both broke out laughing. They rolled onto their backs looking at moon, which they felt at that moment was present for the sole purpose of their delight. After a long pause, Carina propped herself up on her elbow, her other hand caressing his chest, exploring the curves of his torso as though reacquainting herself with a landscape. "Why did you leave me like that?"

Her voice was soft, but he immediately recognized the intensity from which the question had arisen. He looked into her eyes, thinking of how best to respond, when she asked again.

"How could you just leave me like that?" She sat up, and in the moonlight, he noticed tears rolling down her cheeks. Orfeo tried to sit up to comfort her and reply, but in a flash, she had forced him back onto the sand and straddled him. She started to pound on his chest, again and again, asking, "How could you?" Orfeo pulled her down onto his chest, and she continued to sob softly, repeating, "How could you? You bastard, how could you?"

Orfeo rolled her onto her side, caressing her cheek and pulling her wet, sandy hair from her face. "Babe … leaving you was the most difficult thing I've ever done in all my lifetimes. It was the worst death I had ever experienced, and if I'd had the choice, I would have ended it all." He paused. The sound of her sobbing filled the air. "But it was the only way."

Carina moved out from his arms and sat with her feet meeting the tide, saying, "Leaving me was the only way? Bullshit! What bullshit!" Orfeo was about to respond, but she continued. "After everything we went through together … we were together … and together, we could have figured it all out." Again, he was about to respond, but she cut him off. "But you punked out and left me behind." She threw a handful of mud at him. "You fucker!"

Orfeo saw the opportunity to interject and said

enthusiastically, "Carina … look … you're here, aren't you? You're here. We're together."

"Yeah, I'm here, and I don't even know why. You abandoned me. Even the most unconscious human beings living in the cave, embroiled in all their illusions wouldn't do that. And you, with lifetimes under your belt, the wisdom of the ages tucked in your back pocket, abandon me after everything we'd been through together … and all you have to say is that it was the only way?" She paused and got up. The only sound was that of the waves crashing on the shore. She started to walk away, leaving him seated on the sand, and muttered, "The Master must have really done a number on you."

Orfeo stood up and caught up to her. He tried to take her hand, but she pulled away and continued to walk with some separation from him. The silence between them now stifled the sound of the waves.

Orfeo was at first surprised that she came home with him, but then he understood that it was completely natural. The anger she was feeling and expressing was exactly what he would have felt and expressed. He wanted to explain but knew that it wasn't an intellectual misunderstanding that could be explained away. Rather, it was an emotional one that simply required time. They slept in the same bed as though the Berlin Wall separated them. Orfeo heard her sobbing until she fell asleep. He wanted to embrace her but understood that she needed space for those pent-up emotions to vent. He understood that words would serve no other purpose than to allow those emotions to circulate and collide with the speed of a particle accelerator, creating other unintended collisions and potential damage. Not a word was said.

Carina awakened to the sound of Ahmad Jamal playing "Tranquility." Orfeo loved the young Ahmad Jamal and had always reminded her that in Jamal's early years, he was one of the very few jazz pianists who really had a left hand. The music filled the air along with the fragrance of a wide variety of herbs, onions, and eggs. What was most striking, however, was the unmistakable aroma of El Cafe Alto Grande, "the coffee of popes and kings" from Puerto Rico, which like Proust's madeleine brought back vivid memories of their time together at the cottage. She stretched like a cat and sighed joyfully that her anger had slipped away and lost its way in her dreams.

She sat up. He was already by the side of her bed with a tray that looked like a banquet table. "Yum!" Carina exclaimed, "I can see that your culinary skills have improved!"

"Are you saying that they didn't meet your standards before?"

"No, darling. I've always loved your cooking. It's just been a really long time, and this is completely over the top. Thank you!" She leaned over to give him a hug, and the entire container of coffee spilled on the bed. "Argh! I can't believe I did that!"

"No worries. You didn't burn yourself, did you?"

"No. I'm fine. Please give me a hug." Orfeo got on his knees between her legs and embraced her firmly. With her head buried deep in his shoulder, she said softly, "I'm really sorry about last night. I just needed to get that out."

Orfeo separated himself enough to lock eyes with her. He was going to say something but decided that the words weren't necessary. He simply put his hand on her heart and, never taking his eyes away from hers, said, "*Yo te quiero más que muchíssimo!*"

Carina, smiling, put her hand on his heart as though carrying out a ritual concocted by kids and replied, "*Yo te quiero más que más que muchíssimo!*" They looked into each other's eyes without any words, their hands still over each other's hearts, and simply nodded.

"*Basta!*" Orfeo exclaimed while jumping onto his feet. "Let's eat before my soufflé deflates." He served her and got up to make another pot of coffee.

Another amazing jazz piano song that she didn't recognize filled the room. He was in the kitchen, and she had to scream for him to hear her. "Is that Ahmad Jamal?"

Orfeo started to scream back but realized how ridiculous it was to try to have a conversation from two separate rooms while music was playing. He walked back and, just sticking his head over the doorframe, answered, "No, it's Monty Alexander. I just recently discovered him. He's a total badass, isn't he? Sounds as though he's playing with four hands." He paused for a second to see if she had anything to add and then excused himself, saying that he'd be back in a few minutes. Carina didn't want to start eating without him, so she got up and started exploring the apartment.

The light filled the spacious apartment and brought life to the beautiful pastel and bold colors of the walls. There were plants everywhere, and in the spaces between the notes of Monty's solo, she could hear the sound of the waves crashing on the beach. She opened up some doors that led to a beautiful outdoor veranda that faced the beach. Rather than being a shade structure, it was covered with beautiful silk scarves in colors she associated with Buddhists: orange, burgundy, and yellow. The breeze coming in from the ocean was delightful.

Orfeo was bringing the coffee back to the bedroom when he saw her on the veranda, naked, looking out to the ocean. He just froze in place, admiring her beauty. Carina felt his presence and caught him staring.

"What? You're staring as though you've never seen a woman's body before. Put your tongue back in your mouth!"

Orfeo replied, "If only I had a mirror large enough to show you your wings. Your reaction would delight the gods."

Delighted, she asked, "So you're a poet now? That was lovely."

"Not at all" he replied. "I recently came across that line in a book of poetry, and I immediately thought of you. Would you like to eat out here?"

"Absolutely! By the way, I love your space. Isn't it a little big for one person?"

"I didn't buy it for myself, silly. I spent a lot of time looking for a place that I thought you would like. As soon as I saw this, I knew this would be perfect for us." He waited to see her reaction and continued, "And I was right on the money!"

"Yup." She leaned over and kissed him. "Right on the money!"

Orfeo went inside and brought out the tray. He sadly remarked that his soufflé was flat and cold. Carina had taken one of the orange silk scarves and used it as a sarong. She responded, "No worries, love. I'm sure it's just as delicious. I'm dying for some coffee."

He poured her a cup, and the ocean breeze blew the aroma directly into her face. She took a sip, closed her eyes, and savored the flavor. Then she pulled out one of their old routines, imitating Samuel Jackson in the scene from *Pulp Fiction*. "Now that's a damn good cup of coffee!"

Carina devoured the soufflé and asked for a second portion. "Wow! That was amazing. The chef at the café is training you well."

"Actually," Orfeo started and then paused for a second. "Dolton taught me how to make this."

"Who's Dolton?"

Almost embarrassed to broach the subject, Orfeo answered, "He was the Master's assistant. The seven-foot gentle giant I had mentioned to you. He was an amazing cook, and in fact, many of the dishes I serve at the café are based on his recipes."

"This is unbelievable," Carina said sarcastically. "Enlightenment, the truth, and cooking lessons, all for the price of one leg!"

Orfeo wasn't sure if she was joking or not, but he smiled. "Yeah, it sounded like a good deal at the time."

An awkward silence followed until she broke the ice. "How come you didn't have to work in the café today?"

"I actually don't consider it work, but I'm at the café every day. I called a friend this morning to cover me." They sat in silence for a while and just absorbed the sun's rays, the cool breeze, and the sound of sea gulls scatting over sounds of Art Blakey and the Jazz Messengers.

"So are you going to tell me what happened?"

"Sure." Orfeo took her hand and sat in silence for another long moment before saying, "You asked me last night how I could leave you like that."

"Orfeo," she interrupted, "I was really emotional last night. You really don't have to answer that."

"No, I feel that I do have to explain. But first let me ask you a question. How come you never made contact with me during those years when I was lost?"

Carina immediately understood where he was going

with this. "Because I knew that you had to go through your process and felt that my presence could have gotten in the way."

"Well," Orfeo said, "it's not exactly the same, but I believed with all my heart that the only way we could ever be together again was by leaving."

"How so? I don't get it."

"In the same way that you knew that I had to go through my journey alone, I knew that at that juncture, with all the questions raised by the Resistance about my mental state and where you fit into all of this, you had to be on your own. It was your personal journey to negotiate those minefields and find your way back to me. I knew that all the explanations about what I had learned about the Master, the Resistance, and reality couldn't have convinced you or brought you over to the truth."

"But how could you be so sure that I would come back?"

"That, my love, was the only thing I was absolutely certain about. I had no doubt that you would come back to me. What I didn't know was whether or not you'd bring the Resistance with you. In fact, I'm still expecting Maya to show up with her men any minute now."

"Stop being silly, dumbass. How could you be so sure that I would come back?"

"It was simple. I knew that you knew that I loved you

more than anything in the entire universe. I knew that you've never had one iota of doubt about this. Correct?"

Carina nodded, taking another sip of coffee.

Orfeo continued, "Well, I figured that it would dawn on you that if I left you, despite the immensity of my love for you and the Gordian knot that binds us, then there had to be something in my madness. I was counting on the fact that you would realize this simple truth, the certainty of my crazy love for you, as reproducible and constant as the formula for pi or $e = mc^2$, and that that would make you realize there had to be more to it than was obvious."

"How did you know I'd figure this all out, about the Master, the Resistance?

"I didn't think you would."

Carina looked at him with a look of surprise. "Thanks for the vote of confidence!" The breeze was now a little stronger, and the colorful scarves appeared to be dancing to the Latin jazz montunos filling the space around them. "That was a huge gamble. After all our eternities together, I never knew you were a gambling man."

"No, love, not at all. You know me better than you admit. I'm not a gambling man. Gambling involves chance. This was a sure bet. I knew that our love for each other was the one thing we both could count on, and even without understanding anything else, I was certain that the fact that I left you would make you question everything and that you'd eventually come find me."

Orfeo squeezed her hand. "Wasn't this what prompted you to leave the Resistance and come find me?"

Carina nodded yes.

Orfeo concluded by saying, "So that's why I left you." He bent over, kissing her hand. "Wouldn't you have done the same for me?"

Carina leaned over and kissed his hand and then his forehead, eyes, and lips. Then she nodded yes.

Orfeo suddenly leapt up to his feet and with the excitement of a child, asked, "So do you want to know about the game and the Master? I have so much to tell you. It's going to blow your mind!"

Carina smiled at his youthful exuberance and said, "Orfeo, I don't want to burst your bubble, but for now, I couldn't care less about the game, the Master, or the truth about this or any other reality. For now, there's this moment with you, the sun, the ocean breeze, and beautiful music. *Ça suffit!* Do you mind if we save the secrets of the universe for another time?"

Orfeo was obviously disappointed. He sat down and tried to make it seem as though it were okay.

She then asked, "Would you like to know what I want to do right now, more than anything else in the whole wide world?"

"Pray tell," Orfeo responded.

"I want you to make love to me as though it were our very last lifetime together. I want every moment we have together to be as though it were out last. For now, to hell with the Resistance, the Master, and this so-called game. Let's live this life."

After their passionate, chandelier-monkey sex, they lay in each other's arms. Orfeo understood what Carina already seemed to have gotten without the benefit of the Master's intervention: All the stories they had amassed were nothing more than stories. It was fiction for the purpose of entertainment to pass the time called human existence.

About the Author

The author was born in Haiti and immigrated at the age of six to New York City, where he has lived for the past 50 years. He is a practicing emergency physician who has worked on the frontlines in high volume and high acuity inner city hospitals such as Lincoln Medical Center in the South Bronx and St. Luke's-Roosevelt in Manhattan. These were formative experiences in his life where he learned about humanity and developed a strong sense of service and compassion. He considers the exploration of Consciousness and creativity to be the most important thing in his life, and he has dedicated his life to this endeavor. "The Twin Flames, the Master, and the Game," his first novel, is a monument to this endeavor.

CPSIA information can be obtained
at www.ICGtesting.com
Printed in the USA
BVHW030346170420
577799BV00001B/62